JAN ROMES

Cover Design: Tugboat Design
Formatting: Tugboat Design
www.tugboatdesign.net

Married to Maggie
Texas Boys Falling Fast Series - Book One: Tysen
Copyright 2013 Janice Romes
All Rights Reserved

This book is licensed for your personal enjoyment only. This book may not be resold or given away to other people. If you would like to share this book with another person, please purchase an additional copy for each recipient. If you're reading this book and did not purchase it, or it is not purchased for your use only, then please return to Amazon.com and purchase your own copy. Thank you for respecting the hard work of this author.

This is a work of fiction. Names, characters, places and incidents are the product of the author's imagination or are used fictitiously, and any resemblance to any actual persons, living or dead, events, or locales is entirely coincidental.

Dedicated with love to my husband for believing in me. I also dedicate this to Nancy Ricker, dear friend and nurse for over 38 years. And to Sue Bush Apple, sweet friend and proofreader.

TEXAS BOYS FALLING FAST SERIES · BOOK ONE: TYSEN

Chapter One

Tysen Loy Vincent, III, pulled a pair of black-framed, non-prescription glasses from his pocket, slid them on and ducked into the nearest airport gift shop where he worked his way through the tight aisles until he reached the racks of magazines in the back. From behind the latest issue of Sports Illustrated, he kept a sharp eye on the camera wielding weasel across the wide aisle of Concourse B.

A trickle of sweat rolled down the length of his neck and he muffled a low, throaty curse into the magazine. Someone had to be tipping off the press. How else would Chaz Rosston find him in Nevada?

Ty adjusted the hot, ill-fitting hairpiece setting on top of his head. He was tired of disguises; tired of bobbing and weaving in and out of places to keep from having a camera and microphone shoved in his face. The urge to fling both the glasses and ridiculous wig into the busy corridor for an electric transportation cart to smash was heightened when two teenage girls clad in skimpy tops and low-slung jeans gave him the once-over. One girl nudged the other with her elbow. Their amused expressions said 'nice rug'.

Sweet. The sarcasm was aimed more at him than the girls. Since he'd ditched the environmental conference in Atlanta to play in Reno, he had to suck up the discomfort of the rug and continue to engage in a game of hide and seek. If his grandfather caught wind that he wasn't in Atlanta, there would be hell to pay. T. Loy Vincent, I, had issued a clear warning to Ty before he left for the conference – 'straighten up and play by the rules or clean out your office'. Those words were still embedded in Ty's brain.

Behind the goofy glasses, he narrowed his eyes. Life was too short to play by someone else's rules. His father, T. Loy Vincent II, had played by the rules for fifty-five years. Where had it gotten him? Six feet under and pushing up daisies, that's where. Ty wasn't ready to follow the same life-sucking path and he sure as hell wasn't fond of daisies. He also wasn't ready for the razor-sharp pain that sliced across his chest every time he thought of his dad. He could almost time the excruciating agony. *Three, two* ... Piercing pain came hard and fast, stealing his breath, causing him to double over with a moan.

In the middle of the ordeal, a hand landed on his back and a soft voice asked if he was okay. He jerked from the contact. "I'm...freaking...peachy," he forced out between clenched teeth.

The surprisingly calm, feminine voice continued. "Should I call 9-1-1?"

"No! I'm...fine." He couldn't afford the drama. The news rat combing the area for something to splash across the front pages of the newspapers and tabloids would have a field day if EMS personnel descended on the shop and he discovered it was Ty in need of care.

"You're not fine." The resolve in the woman's tone indicated she would stay despite his attempts to shoo her away.

Why did everyone think it was okay to bother him? "Leave. Me. Alone." The words came out more scathing than they should have, but hey, he wasn't exactly known for his tact.

"I can't do that, sir."

Warm fingers landed on his neck.

Ty jerked harder at the more intimate touch. "What are you doing?" The pain that usually subsided after a minute, hung on and his knees startled to buckle under his weight.

"Easy now." The woman who couldn't keep her hands to herself guided him to a sitting position against the magazine rack. "Your pulse is all over the place."

Either the awkwardness of the situation or the unwanted attention distracted the pain. The discomfort in Ty's chest lessened and he no longer struggled to breathe. He was finally able to focus on the person crouching beside him. "Your pulse would go crazy too if a complete stranger touched *your* neck."

Soft blue eyes ringed with a darker blue, studied him with concern. "Force of habit. I'm a nurse." Her forehead creased. "At least I used to be."

Ty quirked a brow. "Did you get fired for inappropriate neck-touching?" As soon as the new round of sarcasm left his mouth, he bashed himself for taking his surly mood out on someone who had come to his aid.

The Good Samaritan's long, dark lashes lowered and her concerned half-smile thinned. "I shouldn't have butted in." She straightened to a stand.

The shop clerk approached with a frown. "What's going on?"

Ty's gaze connected with the blue-eyed nurse again. Before he could explain, she did.

"My husband is prone to kidney stones. We're about to board a flight for home so I can take him to our family doctor." She went into a long-winded spiel about how miserable it is to have kidney stones and how she wouldn't wish them on anyone.

Ty's jaw was in danger of unhinging at the blatant lie.

The young clerk stared at the woman with a deer-in-the-headlights look. He clearly had no idea what she was talking about. "I don't mean to be rude, but you need to get him up off the floor."

"I'm on it." The woman extended her hand to Ty.

Ty couldn't suppress a grin. Not only did the short-haired brunette help him with what she could only assume was a heart attack, she was now involved in a ruse of her own creation. He was set to whisper his gratitude when he caught movement at the entrance. "Dammit!" Chaz was standing outside the shop with his head snapping all around.

In another subtle, yet stunning move, his *wife* shoved in front of him to block the view of the guy whose long, bulbous nose poked into his business way too often. The freelance stalker was a giant pain-in-the-neck who catalogued his every move. In exchange for blurry pictures and half-truths, the media paid Chaz big money. Ty stooped to tie his shoes. It wouldn't have drawn attention if he'd actually been wearing shoes that tied instead of square-toed loafers.

"Seriously," the clerk said, "I'm about to call airport security."

Ty peeked around the woman and let out a sigh of relief. Chaz had moved on. "Relax. We're leaving." He clutched the arm of his pretend wife.

As soon as they were in the hallway, his cell phone plinked with the arrival of yet another text message. He'd received a half-dozen in the last hour from his grandfather's private secretary, Rosie. She'd advised him to get to the airport in short order and to head back to Atlanta. Rosie was a tiny, grey-haired woman who was feisty and fun-loving. Over the years, she and Ty formed a special bond. He helped her with whatever she needed, either at work or at her home. In return, she ran interference for him to keep his grandfather none the wiser to his escapades. Somehow the old coot still managed to find out what he'd been up to. The patriarch of the Vincent clan quoted anonymous sources when Ty would ask who narked him out.

Married to Maggie

Anonymous my ass. Everyone had a name. Everyone had an agenda. Everyone wanted money for information. In Ty's case, it was probably his grandfather paying some bloodhound to stay on his trail.

Ty glanced at Rosie's latest message, shoved the phone back in his shirt pocket and fixed a bead of inquiry on the woman with a boyish-yet-feminine hairstyle and eyelashes so long they almost touched her eyebrows. "Who are you?" he asked.

"Maggie Gray," she simply said.

"Well, Maggie Gray, thank you for everything. Your timing was impeccable." Ty's gaze ricocheted between Maggie and the surrounding area. He studied her from behind the fake glasses and finally removed them to get a clear look. She was modestly beautiful. Big blue eyes sparkled with intelligence and a sense of humor. The slow sweep of her lashes reinforced both. He got the feeling that this easy-on-the-eyes stranger could hold her own in most situations.

"No problem. Happy to help."

Ty looked past Maggie to scan the area again. There was no sign of Chaz. "Where are you headed?"

"Dallas." She held up her boarding pass.

"Me too." It was impractical to go back to Atlanta since the conference was almost over. He would adjust his ticket and head back to Texas. Ty winced hard without letting the sound roll out. When he got home, there would be hell to pay and it would take a special kind of shovel to dig him out of the mess he'd made. Rosie couldn't fix this. He eyed Maggie. "What time is your flight?"

"Three-thirty."

Ty watched Maggie shift from foot to foot, repeatedly push her purse strap up on her shoulder even though it wasn't falling off, and open and close her hands at her side. This sudden nervous behavior was in stark contrast to the woman who'd been in control a minute ago. When it came to nursing skills she was confident and in charge; perhaps when things became personal, not so much. *Perfect!*

* * *

'Six foot-four, tousled blondish-brown hair, striking resemblance to Jon Bon Jovi, blue eyes that will win you over in a heartbeat and behaves like the world revolves around him'. Maggie had played those words over in her head again and again, questioning the sanity of the agreement she'd entered into with billionaire T. Loy Vincent, I. She'd walked through Reno-Tahoe International Airport three times, trying to be subtle with her inspection of people passing by, occasionally checking the photo Loy had provided. Actually, she didn't need a picture to recognize Tysen Loy Vincent, III, since he was one of the most photographed persons in the world. The infamous, playboy heir to the Vincent oil fortune graced magazine covers and front pages of newspapers almost daily. He was larger than life; known to woo starlets, top models, even a pickle heiress. Checking the photo numerous times wasn't to jog her memory as to what he looked like, but rather a concrete reminder that she'd lost her mind.

Frustrated that Tysen had slipped by, she'd popped into the gift shop for a bottle of water. To her shock, there he was, in disguise – a poor disguise, at that – in the middle of some kind of episode that had him clutching his chest. *Heart attack* had screamed in Maggie's mind and for good reason, she'd been his grandfather's cardiac rehab nurse for the last few months. Ty inherited his grandfather's good looks, possibly his faulty ticker as well. She'd rushed to help, only to be bitten by his well-known fondness for sarcasm; something else that seemed inherited.

Did she get fired for inappropriate neck touching? Maggie had been tempted to hit the fool with a rolled up magazine. Instead, she was at an airport gate, sitting next to him with her feet crossed at the ankles, trying to stabilize her *own* heart. For reasons she didn't understand, the darn thing was hell-bent on doing a river dance against her ribs.

Ty Vincent was gorgeous and worldly. How would she persuade someone like him to marry her? What had Loy been thinking? What had she been thinking? If she'd taken time to think things through, she wouldn't be in Reno immersed in a sideways scheme.

She feigned surprise when he identified himself and then jabbed him with a smart remark about the hairpiece. He shrugged, ditched the rug in his carryon, ran his hands through his sexy mess of hair and plied her with that well-known, handsome smile.

Their conversation didn't include the normal questions, like why she was in Reno or why he was there. He didn't ask and she didn't offer. And vice versa.

Something indefinable sparkled in his eyes. Maggie's palms started to sweat. Her nerve endings prickled like she was about to be struck by lightning.

Ty shifted in his seat. "I have something to ask you that might sound a little off-the-wall. Your first instinct will be to say no, but hear me out, okay?"

Maggie wanted to come across as cautious and baffled that someone like him would ask someone like her anything. She purposely drew out her response. "Ohhh-kayyyy."

Ty cleared his throat, twice. "I need a…wife. Just for a little while." He didn't bat an eye. "Marry me."

If a person's mouth could drop to their belly button, then Maggie's was there. She widened her eyes, although she shouldn't be the least bit shocked. This was Tysen Vincent. He was known for peculiar behavior. She'd come to Nevada to get him to propose, still, hearing the words come out of his mouth stunned her to the core. She tried to talk…and breathe…but her voice and lungs were rendered incapable of doing their jobs.

This was not real. None of it. Any second now, she expected a TV camera crew to pop out from their hiding places to inform her that Loy and Ty involved her in a prank. She hoped they'd do it soon so she could breathe again.

Ty's serious expression took that hope and ground it to dust. It wasn't a prank, but rather a hare-brained plot that mirrored the first one she was already immersed in neck-deep. No one would believe that she and Ty Vincent bumped into each other at the airport and before she caught her flight home, he asked her to be his wife. Even she didn't believe it. Yet, she was sitting next to him and he was waiting for an answer.

Maggie gnawed hard on her bottom lip, almost drawing blood, while she tried to come to grips with the reality that three men wanted to parade her around as the newest addition to the Vincent family for their own self-seeking reasons. T. Loy Vincent, I, was the grand marshal of the first whacked out parade. Ty wore the crown for the second one. Her father was number three, marching right along with the other two. She understood why the Vincents had lost their minds, she couldn't figure out why her father had lost his. She was his only child, for Pete's sake. The only explanation tendered was that he needed help with a long-standing debt. She deserved a few more details, but the only thing she received was a serious plea for her to lend a hand. Even without all the information, it didn't take an Einstein to deduce that whatever it was had to be big. Maggie cringed at the possibility that she might be a gambling settlement. Her father was known to chance a hefty amount of his income on the ponies. The bad habit was supposed to be under control. Maybe it wasn't. Maybe he was in hock to Loy for thousands of dollars.

Her air and voice returned. "Say what?"

"You didn't hesitate to tell the clerk you were my wife. Why not make it real to help me out? I need you, Maggie." Ty looked determined to get a yes. It was the same strong-minded, devious look worn by his grandfather yesterday. She was of the strict opinion that not only did the Vincents share blood but also insanity.

Maggie sneered with as much disdain as she could muster. At the same time a profound truth hit her between the eyes. Who was she to sneer? She was no better than the three hooligans orchestrating this mess. When Loy offered this strange opportunity, she didn't back away. She did at first because it was too much to comprehend, but she gradually came around thanks to her dad and a sudden termination by the hospital. For the first time in eight years she found herself unemployed. The hospital blamed it on the austerity program they were implementing where each department had to do more with less. Maggie understood the concept. What she didn't understand was why *her* job had been on the chopping block. There were four nurses with less seniority; one nurse – Delia Smythfield – had only been in the unit for six months and was a troublemaker from the day she hired in. Delia was a rich kid who made it known she had more money than she knew what to do with and really didn't need to work. To Maggie's shock, the hospital kept the rabble-rouser and let her go instead. Even her boss and best friend, Nancy, was blindsided by the move. Nancy promised to snoop around to find out why Maggie had been singled out. So far the only thing she reported was that no one knew a thing.

Since Carriage Memorial didn't have a union, Maggie had little recourse. Sure, there were legal avenues she could have pursued to make the hospital squirm but she'd been too hurt to check into them. She'd cried for a week and then pulled herself together to apply at other hospitals only to discover that they too were paring down staff.

"I know it's a half-cocked proposition, but it pays well. I need a wife ASAP to show my grandfather and the Board of Directors that I'm trying to be the guy they want me to be."

Maggie thought it odd that before the proposal she'd informed Ty she was headed to Dallas, he said he was headed there as well, and excused himself to the far corner of the gate with his phone glued to his ear. He'd paced back and forth in front of a set of large windows, occasionally striking a glance in her direction. When he finally sat down beside her, he made idle chit chat and now he proposed marriage. Who had he been talking to? Was this madness his alone, or had it been conjured up by the person on the other end of the phone? Even though it's what she came for, he'd made it easy. Too easy. Disturbingly easy. Maggie silently sighed. His reasons for proposing didn't matter; the only thing that did was that it happened. She cringed at the realization that she and Ty's relationship would soon become a spectacular development that the celebrity gossip and entertainment news industry would latch onto and not let go. They would tout the quickie marriage as a mistake and wager it wouldn't last six months. Ha! The joke was on them; that six-month plan was already in place.

Queasiness settled in the pit of Maggie's stomach. She wanted to close her eyes and not open them until the lunacy proved to be nothing more than a bad dream. Since she was in a busy airport with Ty Vincent, Maggie knew it was more of a wide-awake nightmare that would eventually take a huge bite out of her butt. She gulped hard to loosen the thick knot of reality clogging her windpipe. "No woman in her right mind would agree to something so ridiculous."

"My grandfather has backed me into a corner. So I find myself in need of a wife to convince him…and the rest of the world…that I'm trying to change." Ty laughed with no humor whatsoever.

Maggie twisted her mouth while she pondered the request.

Agreeing to Ty's strategy, while already involved in one with his grandfather, would make her a double-agent of sorts. If she refused Ty's proposal, it would effectively cancel the grandfather's. Essentially, by agreeing to marry Ty, she wasn't just selling her soul to the highest bidder she was selling it to the top two. The knowledge put the squeeze to her heart. How could she enter into something she held sacred with this guy, or any guy that she wasn't in love with? Yes, it was a temporary arrangement, but marriage was something special. It was a gift; not a means to settle an old debt or a way to get an out-of-control grandson to behave.

"I'm serious. Marry me." He squinted hard as though the thought of having a spouse was as unsettling to him as it was to her. "I'll make it worth your while."

Maggie sucked in a breath and held it in an attempt to calm her lungs. Her breaths had been silently jagged since she set eyes on the Bon Jovi look-alike, and now, she had to coax each breath.

In order to sell him that she was just a random person he happened to cross paths with, she had to make him seem like the lunatic. "Out of all the people in the world, why me?"

"Because..." Ty looked thoughtful. "Hell, I don't know. Something about you says you're exactly what I need..." He cleared his throat for the tenth time. "...to pull this off." He nudged against her. "You lied for me."

"Oh God! You *are* serious." She lied to the gift shop clerk and now she was the perfect choice? Maggie wanted to throw up.

Ty squinted again. "Dead serious."

Maggie uncrossed her feet, fidgeted in the chair and touched his forearm. Big mistake! Huge! Something similar to static electricity crackled its way through her veins the second she made contact. She withdrew her fingers and mimicked him by squinting. "Your grandfather is pushing you hard. I get it. I also get that we do things for people we love that we normally wouldn't do for anyone else." *Boy do we!* If it wasn't for the desperation she'd heard in her father's voice she wouldn't be sitting next to Tysen Vincent. She wouldn't be in Nevada and wouldn't be on the verge of becoming a shady character. "One word of advice, play his game if you have to, but don't lose yourself while you're doing it." Maggie flinched from her own philosophical ramblings. The suggestion was fitting, but she didn't talk like that.

Ty opened his eyes wide for a few seconds before he narrowed them even tighter than before. The few frown lines splayed across his forehead multiplied until they were an accordion of creases. "Are you in or not?"

Maggie couldn't stop a nervous laugh and chalked it up as a way to cope. "Am I in or not? Wow. Worst marriage proposal ever."

"This isn't about romance and picking out china, it's a business deal with a few perks. You'll get the Vincent name. More money than you can imagine. Clothes. Cars. A life most women would kill for."

She needed a shot of tequila. Or a pin to stick in Ty's overinflated ego. Since she didn't have either at her disposal, she did the next best thing – an exaggerated eye roll. "Yeah. That's enticing." Despite her calm, cool and collected appearance, a fragile string of hysteria was close to breaking in two.

Ty's frown changed to confusion. "That doesn't appeal to you?"

"I'm sure all of that is great but the thought of pimping myself out to get it gives me a chill." Maggie purposely shuddered.

"I'm just trying to lay it all out, Maggie." Ty lowered his voice when two well-dressed men in business suits sat in the adjacent chairs. He leaned in close and Maggie could smell his cologne, something earthy with a hint of musk. She tried to ignore the spike of delight from his nearness and his scent.

"I'm asking you to pose as my wife. That's it. No sex. No kids. No making me tow-the-line. Nothing. Get it? All I need is a wholesome woman to meet my grandfather's approval. I need you long enough to convince him that I'm trying to live up to his expectations."

Maggie regretted not hitting him with a rolled up magazine when she had a chance. She should've hit her father and Loy with one too.

Chapter Two

"I know I was supposed to be in Atlanta." Ty tried to appear repentant.

His grandfather sighed so long and loud, it echoed through the spacious high-rise office. "You defy me at every turn, Tysen. I've cut you some slack because…" He drummed his fingers on the desk. "…of your dad." Loy Vincent ripped his attention from Ty to idly mess with a stack of papers. In the next heartbeat, the stern look of authority was back and more solid than before. "It's time to stop wallowing in your grief and start living again. It's time for you to return to the responsible adult you were before."

Pain slashed across Ty's midsection at the mention of his dad but he was determined not to let on that it was happening. If he so much as winced from the agony his grandfather would be all over it. Ty tightened his arms into his sides in an attempt to manage the severe discomfort. Physical and mental strife rendered him capable of only two words, "I'm trying."

"You're *not* trying. You're doing the opposite of trying. How do I know? I pay attention; something you should be doing too. You need to pay attention to where your life is headed." The pitch of his grandfather's voice lowered dramatically. Not a good thing. It meant the elder Vincent was about to lower something else, possibly the crescent blade of a guillotine. "I've given you plenty of opportunity in this company and you still refuse to take things seriously."

It was true that his grandfather had given him a taste of everything. He moved Ty around the various departments until he had a working knowledge of wholesale marketing, finance, internal auditing, corporate development, investor relations, supply chain, corporate communications, the list was endless. Ty was currently serving as the company's Vice President of Environmental Protection and Response.

His granddad was partly wrong with his accusation. Oil still flowed through Ty's veins but there had been a shuffle of priorities over the last twelve months. When he was in the office, he worked hard. When he wasn't, he played.

"I need someone with a good head on his shoulders to help me run this company and to eventually take over. That person is not you these days." Loy's guttural groan was another sign of impending doom. "You leave me no choice, Tysen. For now, I'm dismissing you from your position and giving it to Terron Wade. When you get your head out of your rectum, we'll talk."

Anger steamed through Ty. Terron Wade was a first-class jerk. He'd been a thorn all through high school and in college, and yet, his grandfather hired the bastard. Terron was forever trying to outshine Ty. He finally succeeded. Ty drew his hands into fists. It was probably Terron who kept tipping off the press. The lowlife probably had him followed to Reno and reported his findings to his grandfather. "Not happening. You will not move me out and Terron in," Ty said with such hot conviction it burned his throat. He stood up, crossed his arms at his chest and tried to appeal the decision. "I'm your only grandchild, for God's sake."

Loy Vincent sprang from his chair and drew up inches from Ty. "I've warned you over and over that it would happen.

You just had to test the waters, didn't you? Well guess what? I have to back up my words. You are out, buddy." He moved in closer until their noses almost touched. "You've made a mockery out of the opportunities I've given you. Now it's time for some tough love. Pack your things."

Ty wanted to put his foot through his grandfather's expensive desk. Instead, he muttered two little words that would be detrimental to his lifestyle. "I'm engaged."

The angry creases in his grandfather's face lessened. "What?"

"The reason I slipped out of the conference was to give you what you wanted – a granddaughter-in-law." Barefaced lie, but necessary. He owed Rosie big for coming up with the idea of getting married. She pressed him on the issue saying, 'Get married or kiss your job goodbye'. While he was in the airport, he had her run a quick background check on Maggie. The only things Rosie could find was information about Maggie's nursing credentials and that she'd recently gotten a parking ticket. No illicit behavior or videos that would come back to haunt them. She was an only child and drove a Chevy Malibu. Ty had argued with Rosie that asking a complete stranger for a favor of that magnitude reeked of desperation. She was quick to point out that he was running out of options.

His grandfather's mouth was set in a grim line and he cut Ty with a steely-eyed look of suspicion. "Lie to everyone else but not to me. You know I will come down even harder if you do."

Ty made a sound like he was sifting air through his teeth while he tried to assemble something to pacify his grandfather. "Here's the truth, I did blow off the conference. You knew I would."

Loy shrugged. "Yes, I knew."

He sifted more air. "Something remarkable happened when I went to Reno. I met Maggie." He was still lying.

Meeting Maggie wasn't remarkable. Meeting Maggie was… He refused to give the encounter remarkable-status even though it was pretty damn extraordinary that she'd butted in when he needed her and agreed to an absurd deal to become his wife.

"Who the hell is Maggie?"

A strange glimmer filled his grandfather's eyes and Ty knew he had him. "Maggie Gray. A *remarkable* woman who is going to marry me…" *Don't say it.* "…next weekend." Shit. He said it.

Loy's forehead was still creased but now it appeared to be from disbelief. "Did your reckless behavior finally catch up to you? Did you get that girl pregnant?"

Ty's jaw went slack with surprise. Most everyone assumed he was a hit-em and quit-em kind of guy; that he slept his way from state to state. He was well aware of what was said in the newspapers and behind his back, but it hurt to hear his grandfather presume the same things. Sure he lived a high-profile, carefree lifestyle, that included women, booze and late nights but he wasn't the sleaze everyone thought. In fact, his grandfather and the entire world would be shocked to know that he hadn't occupied anyone's bed but his own for almost a year. He stopped sleeping around about the same time… Ty clenched his fists harder to deal with self-disgust. If he'd been with his dad in Houston instead of skirt-chasing in Tulsa maybe his father would still be alive. If he'd gone along on that business trip, he and his father would've been in a bar having a cold one, instead of his father being in the back of a limo when the driver suffered a massive heart attack, killing them both.

Tears burned behind Ty's eyes. Soon it would be a year since that fateful day, but the hurt was as fresh as if it just happened. The pain he'd tried to fend off emerged with more agony than ever. It felt like a jagged blade ripped into his skin and muscle. With all the strength he could muster, he silently withstood the anguish. His knees could barely hold him up, but he refused to grab the desk for support.

"Is she, or isn't she?"

Ty struggled to speak. "She's. Not. Pregnant."

"Then why are you rushing to put a wedding band on her finger?"

Ty finally allowed all his pain and anger to flow into his voice. "You want me settled! I'm getting settled! And Terron Wade can kiss my ass!" Without further words he heavy-heeled it from his grandfather's office, slamming the door on his way out.

* * *

Maggie poured two cups of coffee, sat one in front of her dad and slid into the kitchen chair across from him. "I have news," she said with a thimbleful of joy.

Her father blew a burst of steam from his coffee before taking a sip. "Okay."

Maggie followed suit with a sip. "I caught up with Ty Vincent yesterday." She gulped at the reality.

Richland Gray smirked over the rim of his cup. "What happened?"

"The caper went off without a hitch. Long story short, Tysen and I are now engaged." Admitting she'd scammed Ty filled her with self-loathing and taxed her ability to sit still. She shifted from side to side, crossed her legs, uncrossed them and tapped the side of her cup.

"Good news, right?" Oddly, the question wasn't accompanied by a smile.

"What's so good about it?" She stopped squirming. "I'm engaged to a guy who doesn't love me. He barely likes me and I'm pretty sure he will make the marriage unbearable."

"Maggie, we've discussed the arrangement. This isn't about love. It's about getting Tysen to straighten up so Loy can hand over the business. The board of directors won't approve him as President and CEO until he convinces them he's responsible. Most of them have known him since he was a kid. They're aware that he's brilliant and can do good things for the company, but they also know that he hasn't been himself lately. The majority is rooting for him but a few see Ty as reckless and entitled, and have all but given him the thumbs-down. Ty taking a wife could be a big step in reshaping their opinions." He took another sip. "The bigger issue here has nothing to do with the oil company. Loy is worried about his grandson. He feels that Ty is drowning in grief and won't recover." Her father went on to say that in a way Loy was drowning too, although he'd never own up to it. "Loy not only lost his son, he lost his wife a few years earlier. And now he's frantic that he's slowly losing Ty. Maggie, he and Ty need a life preserver. They need *you*."

She was not a life preserver. She was a nurse. Maybe they were the same thing sometimes, but still, this plan was one whacked-out life-saving technique that should be scrapped. Maggie took another sip of coffee, propped her elbows on the table and steepled her fingers. "Everyone deals with loss differently, Dad. Ty obviously needs more time. If I lost you, I would be consumed by grief for a very long time, maybe forever."

Her father touched her hand. "You lost your mom, yet you found a way to continue to live, Maggie. I know it's a hurt that never goes away. There are some days that I miss Mom so much I don't want to get out of bed. A person can either let heartbreak devour them or they can embrace the memory of their loved ones and keep on living. I chose to live. So did you. Tysen hasn't stopped living, but he's stuck."

"He'll figure things out."

"Listen, sweetheart, the reason Loy picked you is because you had a gentle touch with him in the hospital. When he didn't do what he was supposed to do, you also didn't hesitate to get tough. You understand loss, but you understand that you have to be strong. With careful nurturing and a swat upside the head now and then – figurative swatting, that is – you can pull Tysen out of the muck."

Maggie wrinkled her forehead. "Where's Ty's mom in all of this? Shouldn't she be the one pulling Ty out?"

"The newspapers say she's estranged from the family."

"Families sometimes have difficulties, I get that, but how can a mother be estranged from her son?"

"Long story short, Ellen Peppersmith-Vincent couldn't take the pressure of being married to Tysen's father. So she split."

Maggie frowned. "I'm sure there's more to it than that. There has to be."

"Not everyone is cut out to be a Vincent."

"Yet you have no problem with me becoming Maggie Vincent." Eventually she'd walk away from Ty too. That thought was as disturbing as being thrown into the Vincent shark tank to begin with.

Richland Gray gave her a cheesy grin. "It's not permanent. When the job is done, Loy will be a happy man. His grandson will have his head on straight and he'll be at the helm of the oil company. You can go back to what you love – being a cardiac rehab nurse. Loy said he'll pull some strings to get you into the hospital of your choice. Plus the money he offered is nothing to sneeze at."

Maggie shook her head with a vengeance. "No way am I taking a dime. They both offered a million dollars." She put her hand on her stomach. "The thought of that much money makes me want to barf." Actually, two million dollars was incredible. The way she was supposed to earn it, however, made her want to stick her finger down her throat.

"You're making too much out of this. Think of it as an

opportunity to do something weird yet helpful." He got up and grabbed the coffee pot to refill their cups.

"Try weird and insane."

"You'll be helping Loy and Tysen, but there's potential to help a lot more people."

Maggie lowered her lashes but looked up through them to study her father. "Do tell," she said, convinced that nothing good could come from any of this.

Richland stowed the coffee pot back in the coffeemaker and rejoined her at the table. "You're so focused on the Vincents that you can't see the bigger picture." He patted her hand. "Put that money to good use. Instead of just giving your time to that soup kitchen you help out at, you can stock their shelves. The animal shelters would probably welcome a donation too."

Maggie frowned before a slow smile of understanding curved the corners of her mouth. She did have a soft spot for those whose lives were rocky or filled with despair. That same concern spilled over to her furry friends. She'd always been an animal lover and would have a dog or cat, if the property management company for her apartment building allowed pets. *Hmm.* For the first time in her life, she could make a real difference. Yet marrying Ty Vincent to make it happen still felt wrong and a small part of her wanted to get out while she could. Deep down she knew she wouldn't. She'd suck it up and honor her father's request. She held up her cup. "To crazy but well-intentioned weddings."

"Atta girl."

"By the way, Ty wants the wedding to take place next weekend. You'll need a tux." Maggie ran a hand over her face and began to compile of list of things that would need to be done quickly. She had to buy a wedding dress. Make arrangements for the church. Find an available venue to hold a reception. Then there was the cake, flowers, attendants...

"You met him yesterday, and in seven days you're getting married? A little soon, don't you think?"

"Ten years from now is too soon." A heavy sigh gushed from Maggie. "According to Ty, it needs to happen right away."

Her father hesitated and Maggie was sure he was reconsidering the project. She crossed her fingers with hope.

"I thought you'd date for a month or two, not a day or two." He shook his head with his eyes crinkled. "A spontaneous marriage will set off a charge of excitement...and mayhem. The press will go nuts. Since they weren't aware of you ahead of time, they'll make it their mission to find out everything they can. In a few days they'll know that you're a nurse who loves Japanese food and brushes her teeth with tartar-control mint toothpaste. Before you say 'I do' they'll know who sat beside you in third grade, that you eat a banana and a mozzarella cheese stick for breakfast every morning, and that you have a coffee addiction. You'll become an instant celebrity." He looked thoughtful for a second. "Celebrity suggests something fun. I'm not sure having the media unearth your life will be something you'll enjoy." He tapped the table and connected gazes with Maggie again. "They'll assume you're pregnant." He ran his hand over his morning chin stubble. "Maybe the idea of you and Ty being a couple should marinate for awhile. Let the public soak it in before you shock them with a wedding."

Maggie's mouth snapped open but she quickly closed it. Her father was spot-on. Everything about her life would be looked at through a microscope. While she had no skeletons in her closet, the thought of folks scavenging through her existence like vultures made her shudder. Maybe Ty was smart to suggest they get this done quickly; less time for the buzzards to forage. "Ty said next weekend, so next weekend it is."

"Maggie."

She put up her hand. "It is what it is." Nothing would be marinating. The foraging would begin.

In a way, Maggie wished she was pregnant. It would make what she was about to do seem less deranged.

* * *

Tysen climbed onto the bar stool at his favorite watering hole, aware that Chaz Rosston was lurking outside between parked cars. Maybe he should play nice with him just this once and give him an exclusive regarding his engagement. If he did, Chaz might be inclined to go easy on him and Maggie. Doubtful, but it might be worth a shot. Before he did a tell-all with the rat, Ty needed a stiff drink. Or four of them. "Scotch," he said to the barkeep, Sam Bright. Sam was a childhood friend whose family owned bars all over the state of Texas, a few in Oklahoma too. "You might as well bring the bottle." Ty glanced at his watch. In two hours, he and Maggie had a private meeting with another family friend who happened to be a jeweler. They would pick out rings. The inner-voice that helped him make tough decisions, had been needling him all day. *Don't do it, fool. You'll wreck your life...and hers.*

Sam sat a weighted glass in front of Ty along with a bottle of his finest scotch. They both knew when Ty ordered a full bottle it meant his life was in an uproar, which prompted the question, "What are we trying to drown?"

Ty didn't find the question the least bit amusing because it was loaded with truth. He *was* trying to drown a few things. First and foremost, the painful memory of losing his dad. Next, an early morning phone call from his mother who'd heard through the grapevine that his grandfather was trying to cast him out of the company. He was also trying to drown the fact he was forced to take a wife when he clearly wasn't ready to throw his life in lockdown. It also disturbed him that Maggie *bothered* him. Damn. He had a helluva lot to hold underwater. "You don't have enough time to listen to all the crap going on in my head and in my life."

Sam looked around the bar. Ty did the same. There was only one other patron and the guy was more interested in his bottle of beer than anything else. "I've got all day," Sam said.

Ty poured the glass two-thirds full and chugged the scotch until it was gone. He licked his lips and slammed the glass on the bar. "I got engaged yesterday."

Sam drew back like Ty smacked him with a lie. "No you didn't."

"I did. I lost my mind and popped the question." He couldn't say he caved to patriarchal pressure even though Sam would understand. Sam was from big money too and was familiar with the stress that came with it. While he and Sam's problems were different, their lives were a lot alike.

Sam put a finger in his ear and moved it around like he was trying to remove wax. "I thought I heard you say you're getting married." When Ty raised his eyebrows in confirmation, Sam shook his head. "I didn't know you were seeing anyone on a regular basis."

Ty was tempted to take a swig straight from the bottle. He poured another half glass of scotch and downed it in one gulp. "I wasn't. I bumped into her in Reno."

"You're marrying someone you just met? What the hell?"

"I know, I know. You didn't see that coming. Shit, neither did I." After another belt of alcohol, he added. "One look at Maggie Gray and I knew she was the one." Technically, not a lie. He'd identified Maggie as the one person who could help him.

Sam looked bewildered. "Maggie Gray. Maggie Gray." He snapped his fingers. "Is she from the Connecticut Gray's? Their family made a fortune selling personal hygiene products or something like that."

Ty almost laughed himself off the bar stool, but he stopped laughing when he realized he didn't know a damned thing about Maggie, other than she was a nurse. "Nope. She's from Dallas." Maybe he would wait to publicly announce their impending nuptials until he got to know her a little better. It might be wise to have his lawyer draw up a pre-nup as his grandfather suggested. Even though Maggie verbally agreed to a million dollars to see this farce to fruition, she might try to take the family for a lot more. His grandfather would never forgive him if that happened. Since he was already walking a fine line with the man he dearly loved, he couldn't afford to screw up again. Alcohol crystallized the truth. He *did* love his grandfather and didn't want to hurt him any more than he already had. He swallowed the rest of his whiskey and refilled the glass yet again.

"Tell me about Maggie. How'd you meet?"

"Funny story." Ty motioned to the shelf of liquor behind Sam. "I'm going to need for you to keep it on the down-low, okay?" At Sam's nod, he said, "I'm also going to need another bottle of scotch."

* * *

Maggie shifted carefully in the vintage Louis XVI armchair and watched the jeweler adjust his diamond-encrusted pinkie ring for the tenth time. She glanced at the clock behind him for the *twentieth* time. "Ty seems to be running a bit behind."

"No worries." The grey-haired man positioned two rectangular ivory boxes in front of her, but kept the lids closed.

Maggie twisted her hands in her lap. Ty had asked her to meet him there at six o'clock. It was six-thirty. They were supposed to pick out rings and afterward meet a couple of his friends for dinner. He'd said with the hurried wedding they needed to get things underway as soon as possible – one of those things was to pick out rings. She was there to get things underway, he wasn't.

She spread out her left hand and tried to imagine it with an engagement ring and eventually a wedding band and then folded her hands in her lap as if embarrassed.

Maggie homed in on the clock. With each tick of the second hand, she was getting more ticked. She would give Ty a few more minutes. If he didn't show, she would put the skids to Mr. and Mrs. Tysen Loy Vincent, III.

Come on, Ty. Get your butt here. Tonight was supposed to be about exposing her to Ty's world. To use his words, 'It's time to show you off, Maggie'. In the time since they'd parted, maybe he'd had a change of heart – about everything. A twinge of something indefinable in her chest made her lean back in her chair. Right away she discounted the possibility that the weird feeling could be disappointment because you had to care before you could be disappointed. Maybe it was heartburn from too much coffee. Lord knows she'd had enough she should be sloshing when she walked or bouncing in the chair from an overload of caffeine. Some people resorted to food when they were nervous, she indulged in Arabica blend. Actually, she drank too much coffee regardless of what was going on.

"Do you have a restroom I can use?"

"Certainly. It's in the back. Go through that door and make a left. There's only one bathroom so it won't be hard to miss."

Maggie hoped that when she returned Ty would be sitting in conversation with the jeweler.

When she emerged from the restroom, Ty was still M.I.A. The small amount of irritation churning through her bloodstream gave way to a lot more.

Her cell phone plinked with an incoming text message. Retrieving it from the side pocket of her purse, she verified it was from Ty. 'Running late. Be there in five.' Suddenly, she was more nervous than when they first met. She folded her hands in her lap. Unfolded them. Messed with her cuticles. Crossed and uncrossed her feet. Her pulse decided to do the rumba at her temples. And she broke out in a sweat. Same panicked feeling she'd experienced from time to time in college when she tried to maintain straight A's while working a job that was supposed to be part-time but somehow turned into full-time. It had been overload to the nth degree, just like now. Maggie tried to calm down by pulling in a stout breath. She held it for a few seconds and then released it. The jeweler peered at her over the top of his reading glasses. Maggie was forced to smile.

Exactly five minutes later, Ty burst through the door with an amused grin plastered on his handsome face. He was decked out in a simple but expensive looking white shirt and skin tight jeans that emphasized his trim waist and other spectacular body parts. Maggie silently gasped but her heart thumped so loud she was sure Ty could hear it.

"My future wife." Ty sat in the adjacent Louis XVI chair and scooted it next to Maggie's. He reeked of alcohol and too much confidence.

Maggie almost said, "My future headache". She spared a look at the jeweler to gauge his reaction. The man appeared to take Ty's lateness and state of inebriation in stride. Good for him.

"Sorry. I got held up." Ty leaned so their shoulders touched.

Maggie tensed from the contact. Instead of brushing off his tardiness like she should have, and like Ty expected her to, she said what was on her mind. "I'll give you this one, darling. Next time, I'm conking you on the head." She gave him a fake toothy smile and realized that he made her uneasy, yet calmed her. It was strange how one minute her pulse was going haywire and now…well, it was still going haywire, but it was no longer panic induced.

The jeweler snickered.

"Gustav, have you picked out some incredible rings for my lovely fiancée?"

Maggie instinctively curled her fingers into a fist. Ty grabbed her hand and forced her fingers to open. A devilish grin etched the corners of his mouth. "Let's do this, sweetheart," he whispered loud enough for Gustav to hear.

Let's not. Five minutes ago she couldn't wait to get it over with. Now it was the last thing she wanted to do. When two people picked out rings it meant they'd found the one they wanted to spend the rest of their life with; the one they could joyfully give everything to – their hearts, souls, bodies. In this case, she and Ty would only give each other their physical presence, some of the time. Tysen Vincent would probably continue to gallivant around the country and party hearty like he was accustomed to doing. Maggie would be touted in the newspapers as the long suffering wife. She sighed noiselessly and inserted a smile to convince the jeweler that she was eager to pick something out.

Gustav turned the jewelry cases around and ceremoniously lifted the lids.

Diamonds of every shape and size sparkled with blinding brilliance. Maggie couldn't hold back, "Oh my gosh."

"Excellent," Gustav said, with obvious satisfaction.

Maggie met Ty's eyes. "They're beautiful!"

Ty squeezed her hand before lifting it to his lips and planting a soft kiss on her knuckles.

Maggie flinched. She expected him to play this event to the hilt to sell the idea that their upcoming marriage was for real. What she didn't expect was the warmth that flooded her from a simple kiss to the hand.

"What do you think, sweetheart?" Ty nodded to the jewelry case. "Which one calls your name?"

Married to Maggie

Maggie gradually pulled her eyes from Ty's to browse the rings. Magnificent didn't come close to describing the beauty beaming up at her, but she knew in a heartbeat that none of the rings were for her. She didn't do glitzy. How could she convey that without hurting Gustav's feelings and possibly upsetting Ty as well? "They're all so…" She'd already compromised her integrity by agreeing to be part of the sham, but she still couldn't accept an oversized, overpriced ring that she'd have a problem wearing. "They're too much."

Gustav's silvery eyebrows formed a tight V.

"Money is no object, Maggie. Pick out what you want."

Maggie chewed on her bottom lip. "That's not what I meant." She toyed with the links of her watch. "I need something a little less flashy." She offered a meek smile at Gustav. "Do you have something…smaller?"

"Smaller?" Gustav's frown swept from Maggie to Ty. "Is she serious?"

There was an odd expression on Ty's face. "Are you sure?"

She nodded. "I am."

Ty shrugged. "Give the lady what she wants. If she wants smaller, let's find smaller."

Gustav exhaled noisily and Ty rushed to smooth things over. "What we don't spend on the ring, we'll make up in earrings and a bracelet."

Maggie wanted to roll her eyes. Instead, she said a quiet, "Thank you."

"I'll be right back." Gustav wandered off to a glass display case across the room.

Ty laid his mouth on the side of Maggie's head, sending weird tremors through her. "I'm sorry for showing up late. And I'm really sorry that I had too much to drink." He moved to whisper against the fine hairs of her ear. "I was having a hard time dealing with a few things. Just so you know, you're not one of them. I mean, you are but you're not. I know that doesn't make sense."

Maggie tried to stop the corners of her mouth from tipping into a grin. She failed. The corners didn't just tip they went up as high as they could go. Dammit. "It makes perfect sense."

The jeweler returned with a case of rings more suited to her taste. A simple white-gold band with a small diamond in the center flanked by smaller diamonds on each side caught Maggie's attention. A matching wedding band with a few tiny diamonds completed the set. She was in awe. She didn't want to be, but she was.

Ty's eyes shimmered with something that made Maggie nervous all over again; something warm and possessive. "I take it you've found the one."

Maggie nodded but hurried to clarify. "Yes, I've found the right...ring."

Ty winked at Gustav. "It looks like we have a winner."

Maggie's hand trembled ever so slightly when she pointed to her choice.

Gustav removed the ring from the case and handed it to Ty. Ty smiled, took Maggie's left hand and slid it on. To seal the craziness, Ty gathered her in his arms and shocked her with a gentle kiss on the lips. "My woman," he whispered.

Maggie's impulse was to fight against the pleasure of his mouth and his words, but little bursts of delight detonated inside of her, rendering her incapable of anything but a bigger grin. "So it would seem."

It was every girl's dream to be engaged to a devilishly handsome man who could give her an amazing life. Unfortunately, reality barged in with a reminder that all of this was for show. In six months, the devilishly handsome man and the beautiful ring would be gone. And the special attention Ty was giving her was done out of necessity, aided by alcohol. "We need to pick out a ring for you too."

Ty knew exactly what he wanted – a white-gold band with a rough finish and three small diamonds. "On to the earrings and bracelet," he said.

"We don't have to do that right now, do we?" Maggie suggested. Hopefully he'd agree and she could forget about them altogether.

"Sure we do. Let the shopping begin." Ty squeezed her in a half-hug. "I need to call Quinn to let him know we'll be there in a little bit."

Maggie watched him step outside. Ty was a surprise all the way around. He was warm, loveable, and for appearances sake, happy to be engaged to someone who wasn't a starlet or pickle heiress. Would he be the same guy when he sobered up?

Chapter Three

Chaz must've caught wind that something was up because he'd altered his stalking shenanigans. Instead of snapping a few pictures and dashing off to make the tabloid deadline, he was hot on Ty's trail. The pinhead showed up at the bar, then the jewelry store and was now peeking from behind a red SUV across the street from the restaurant. Ty snickered. After a few glasses of scotch with Sam, he'd decided against giving Chaz an exclusive. Ty had lingered too long at the bar on purpose, and then made his limo driver, Bostwick, drive as slow as he could to the jewelry store. Hell, a snail could've made it there faster. The stall tactic was a way to get under Chaz's skin – small retribution for all the 'Big-Money Bad-Boy' headlines over the past year. Arriving late to the jewelers served another purpose. He wanted Maggie to know he was running the show. If he wanted to imbibe in a bottle or two of scotch, he would. If he wasn't on time, she'd have to deal with that too.

Ty was certain Chaz was foaming at the mouth and had a high-powered zoom lens aimed in their direction. When they left the jeweler via a side entrance, he and Maggie took their time climbing into the limousine, giving the reporter an eyeful. It was time to give the rodent much more – heart palpitations.

If they were going to sell the idea that they were a couple, they had to act like a couple. Ty helped Maggie from the limo, playfully swung her around so her bottom landed gently against the car and brought her hands to his mouth. He planted a kiss on each one. To make the scene even more dramatic he pressed his chest into Maggie's. The surprised look on her face made him grin. "Play along, sweetheart. We're being watched." He'd explained Chaz to Maggie on the ride from the jewelry store.

A moment of confusion was followed by a flash of understanding. "Ahhh! Of course, darling."

Ty lost his bearings for a few seconds. Maggie's next comment snapped him back.

"Should we cheese it up for Chaz?"

God he loved this woman!

Ty drew back at the thought. He didn't *love* Maggie. They were doing a deal together. That's all. He would be wise to keep that information close at hand. But man oh man, the provocative way she was looking at him and her sexy voice rattled his brain.

He frowned to get back on track. "I'd rather hit him with a poison dart."

Amusement danced in Maggie's blue eyes. "Maybe we should hire him to be our wedding photographer."

"Cold day in hell! Chaz can kiss my…"

"Play along, sweetheart."

Damn if she wasn't using his words against him. The woman paid attention.

Ty meant to stage what looked like a deep, soul-connecting kiss to give Chaz some steamy pictures to go with the outrageous headline of the day. He cupped the back of Maggie's head and slowly brought her within kissing range. Maggie darted the tip of her tongue out to wet her lips, morphing Ty's plan into something unexpected. A tremor of pleasure rocked him so hard that he attacked Maggie's mouth like he was trying to devour it. He sucked her lips, drawing a soft gasp from Maggie. When she melted into him, he heard another gasp; it was uncertain which one of them it came from. Ty smiled against her mouth before dragging the fullness of her bottom lip between his teeth. She opened her mouth as if to invite him in and he didn't hesitate. He dipped his tongue in and the intimate tangle of tongues took things to a whole new level. It felt good to kiss Maggie and to feel her soft body next to his; but he hadn't been prepared to get so turned on. He was playing with dynamite, but he couldn't help himself. It took a sharp reprimand from his subconscious before he pulled away.

"Do you think we gave Chaz enough?"

Afraid his voice would reveal too much, he left the question unanswered and latched onto her hand. Her hand tensed in his. "Don't be nervous. Quinn and Tori won't make you jump through hoops to win their affection. Just be yourself."

"I'm sure they're nice, but I'm a stranger – a middle-income stranger. They're used to seeing you with famous women who wear Versace and Christian Louboutin, not someone who gets excited when she finds a bargain on the clearance rack at the mall. One look at me and they'll know I'm a poser. We should clue them in on what we're doing."

Ty tucked a wayward strand of hair behind her ear. "You're exquisite with or without Versace." He meant it. Maggie's tastes were simple, but suited her to perfection. Her short brown hair was silky and swished with her movements and her eyes…a man could get lost. "As far as being upfront," he hesitated, "sometimes it's better to ease into the truth or at least delay it for awhile." He ducked his head into the limo and instructed Bostwick to come back at eleven o'clock. Ty clutched Maggie's hand tighter and tugged her toward the restaurant.

She stopped them a few feet from the entrance. "You

don't trust them any farther than you can throw them, do you?"

"Nonsense. Quinn and I have been friends since kindergarten."

"And Victoria?"

Ty narrowed his eyes. "I trust them, Maggie."

"Sure you do."

Ty took her by the shoulders and gently backed her against the building.

Maggie grinned. "You do like to anchor me in place, don't you?"

Ty laughed from deep in his chest. "Yes."

"About your trust issues…"

"I don't have…" He stopped. "Maybe I don't trust them a hundred percent. Every move I make seems to find its way into the newspapers. I mostly have Chaz to thank for that, but someone is feeding the skunk. Until I know who it is, I'd rather not share the specifics of our relationship." He moved in so close he could smell her lightly floral perfume and the hint of peppermint on her breath. Both made him want to taste those lips again.

Maggie tried to shift away but he stopped her with a firm look. Her blue eyes widened and he smiled. He loved… Ty corrected the thought. He *liked* how her eyes spoke to him. When she was happy, angry, and yes, excited…it showed.

"Maybe you should be more selective with your inner circle and the people you pick up in the airport."

"I'm selective."

She lifted her perfectly shaped eyebrows.

"I'm selective," he repeated with more conviction. "And I trust you, Maggie. Completely." That was mostly true. He was a billionaire's grandson, who'd learned a few things over the years – one of them was to protect the assets. He was sure Maggie would stick to their agreement, but he would still have his lawyer draw up that pre-nup. "End of discussion."

Maggie swept her long lashes slowly over her eyes as though she wouldn't allow him to shut her down.

Ty reinforced his authority with a finger to her lips. "No more talk about my choice of friends...and who I picked to be my wife." He flashed a grin.

A small harrumph stretched his grin wider. "C'mon. I'm starving. Plus, I need something to soak up all the alcohol." He shook his head for effect. "I'm never doing that again." Expecting Maggie to roll her eyes, he was surprised to get the opposite – a soft smile.

"Thank you. For trusting me," she said.

A vague emotion flashed through her amazing eyes, disturbing him in ways he didn't understand. "You're welcome." He intertwined their fingers. "Chin up. Shoulders back. You have an introduction to ace."

"All right, but when this scheme bites you in the butt..."

"Come on, fiancée."

The second they were in the restaurant, the maître de acknowledged Ty with a nod. "Mr. Vincent, it's nice to have you with us this evening."

"Thank you, Enrique."

Enrique was notably professional until he glanced at Maggie. His dark eyes shimmered with interest.

An unfamiliar feeling rushed over Ty. He puckered a brow at Enrique. The displeasure went unnoticed. Ty's eyes followed the same path as the maître de and his heart hiccupped. He'd seen Maggie up close – at the jewelry store, against the limo and in front of the restaurant – but the full impact of how stunning she looked tonight didn't hit him until that moment. Now he couldn't peel his eyes away.

Maggie had styled her short-cropped hair so her bangs swept across her forehead on an angle to hide the corner of one eye. It gave her a sexy, mysterious look. Her lush curves were wrapped in a clingy yet tasteful baby-blue dress with a small slit at her cleavage. The stretchy material highlighted her full breasts, well-defined arms and trim waist. Her long, shapely legs hinted that she was athletic. His attention bounced back and forth from her eyes to the small tease of cleavage. Maggie Gray – *his fiancée*, he thought proudly – would make everyone in the restaurant pause. "Put your eyes back in your head, Enrique."

Enrique snapped his consideration back to Ty. "Yes, Mr. Vincent." He motioned toward the dining room. "Mr. Randel and Miss Caye are right this way."

Maggie leaned against Ty. He squeezed her hand to reassure her that things would be fine. If only someone would reassure him, he'd be all set. Taking Maggie as a short-term wife was as exciting as it was troubling. When she'd agreed to marry him he was filled with an odd happiness. Kissing her caused his heart to jump all over the place. And that sexy blue dress was not helping. At all.

He spied Quinn and Tori at the far end of the dining room, craning their necks for their first glimpse of Maggie.

Ty guided Maggie forward. "Quinn and Victoria, meet Maggie." Quinn's expression surprised the hell out of him. Instead of a generous smile, he greeted Maggie with a half-scowl. Ty wanted to smack him upside the head. Victoria barely smiled too; what was there held no warmth. *Awesome.* Maggie was his fiancée and they were trying to intimidate her with that damn sense of uppity that got under his skin from time to time. Tonight, he wanted to knock their heads together.

Maggie felt the icy wall of not-welcome close in around her. Quinn's grey-blue eyes were about as friendly as wet cement and Victoria's amber eyes were filled with enough frost to make her shiver. The well-to-do hooligans didn't hide their instant dislike or their inspection. They scanned her from head to toe.

It was hard to be congenial under that kind of greeting and

scrutiny, but Maggie pulled it off. She smiled like everything was fine. Although, she reciprocated with a review of her own. Quinn's hair was dishwater-blond perfection, stylishly cut, every strand in place. She stifled an urge to lean forward and mess it up. His sea-green designer golf shirt emphasized his tanned skin. Around his wrist, an overlarge watch with a gaudy amount of diamonds guaranteed to garner attention. And Victoria, well, there was only one word to describe her, striking. Long blonde hair, platinum in color, fell in soft waves to her shoulders. She wore a taupe satin dress with a plunging neckline that revealed a phenomenal chest and framed a huge diamond necklace at the hollow of her throat. Her engagement ring could've doubled as a paperweight. The duo was wealth run amok.

Whatever. They might have money but they lacked class. Ty on the other hand, was the whole package. It was a revelation that rocked her to the core. Ty *did* have it all: looks, charm, class, a sense of humor, a hint of bossiness that was more attractive than it should be, his earthy men's cologne smelled like heaven and messed with her equilibrium, and boy could he kiss. She licked her lips and slanted a sideways glance at the man by her side. He was muscled perfection. Broad shoulders. A chest that made her heart skip, flat stomach, mouth-watering everything. Aye yi yi! She needed to curb those thoughts, but her eyes didn't seem to be connected to her brain and she continued to take stock. His crisp white button-down shirt, Cinch Lucas straight leg jeans, and Durango boots gave him a sexy, casual look. The effect on her pulse, not so casual. It had been wildly thumping in her chest since…they met!

Ty squeezed her hand, bringing her back to the matter at hand. She cocked an eyebrow to silently inform him that he was wrong – his friends *would* make her jump through hoops to win their approval. Since she wasn't especially fond of catering to people who thought they were better than the rest of the world, she'd be pleasant but he shouldn't expect more. She tried to interpret his reply but Quinn butted in.

"So you're the woman who's trying to revoke Ty's bachelor card." He laughed without a trace of mirth.

Victoria followed with an equally off-putting greeting. "When word gets out that you're taking Ty off the market, look out. Half of the women in Dallas will want your head on a platter." The remark might have been construed as teasing if not for the clip of vicious attached to each word.

Again, Maggie shivered like someone dropped an ice cube down her back. In her experience, wealthy people had exceptional manners; she wasn't seeing any evidence in these two. She was actually astounded by their lack of social skills. No 'hello'. No 'nice to meet you'. Just direct notice that she was beneath them and treading on sacred ground. Shaky ground was more like it. Her legs suddenly felt like they were minus the bones and muscles she needed to remain upright. But, in no way would she let her new *friends* see that she was intimidated. She wrinkled her nose with amusement, stepped on her tiptoes to kiss Ty on the cheek and drummed up a laugh. "You didn't tell me that half of the women in Dallas would come after me, sweetheart."

Victoria piped up. "I meant that figuratively, of course."

Maggie couldn't resist, "I know, right?"

Ty cleared his throat. An appeal to let it go?

It would be immature to stomp on his toe. And totally adolescent if she accidentally knocked over Victoria's glass of red wine so it would puddle in her lap. Maggie stretched her hand to Quinn. "I've heard a lot about you." Quinn gave it a skimpy shake. Maggie then put her hand in front of Victoria. A small crease appeared between the platinum blonde's brows. "I've heard good things about you too, Victoria."

Victoria lifted her haughty chin. "I prefer Tori." She took her good old time shaking Maggie's hand.

"Tori," Maggie repeated and bit back a giggle as she wondered what would happen if she was palming one of those joy buzzers that delivered mock electrical shocks. The silly thought helped her to relax. Since these two snobs were important to Ty, she tucked away all thoughts of joy buzzers, for now.

Enrique pulled out a chair for Maggie. "Thank you," she said, wishing she could join him at the host podium instead of sitting at a table where she'd be grilled with questions and drilled with mean looks. She fisted her hands in her lap and braced for a night of interrogation.

"Good evening, Mr. Vincent. Miss," their waiter greeted them with a nod. A bus girl came along with a bowl of torn bread and four crystal dishes of olive oil sprinkled with Italian herbs for dipping.

Ty ordered a bottle of Dom Perignon.

"Excellent." The waiter bowed with approval and rushed off.

Maggie chewed on her bottom lip. A warm feeling replaced the cold chill from just moments ago at the memory of Ty doing the same thing when he kissed her outside the restaurant. Hands down, that was the most delicious, erotic kiss she'd ever had. Ty Vincent might be a spoiled playboy, but he was also a complex, amazing man who turned her knees to jelly. His kisses turned her brain to mush. No wonder the single women in Dallas were hot on his trail.

"Sooo, how did you and Ty meet?" Tori pricked Maggie with a fake smile.

A measure of panic settled in Maggie's stomach. She shifted in her chair and Ty clasped her hand. In that millisecond-moment she decided not to lie or deviate from the truth. "I was buying a bottle of water at the airport gift shop and there he was."

"Aaaaand?"

And you need to get off my back, lady.

The sarcastic thought was swapped for a smile when Maggie remembered how things played out at the airport. "One look and I couldn't keep my hands off of him."

Ty broke out in a hearty laugh. "True that." He lifted their hands to display intertwined fingers. "I've got me a touchy-feely one, Quinn."

Quinn studied Maggie from across the table. "Just like that? You put your hands on him?" His squint said he wasn't buying it. "Ty avoids strangers at all costs and he certainly wouldn't allow one to put her hands on him."

Maggie turned toward Ty in time to see him bearing down on Quinn with a stiff look and a tick at his jaw. She ran her thumb over the top of Ty's hand to make him home in on her and then teased him with big, animated eyes. "Yeah, he flinched. Boy did he. Then we just started talking." Still no divergence from the truth.

Tori chimed in. "And now you're engaged?" Under her breath she added, "Must have something special in the sack."

In a flash the waiter was back with the expensive bottle of champagne. Thank goodness. If Maggie didn't get some alcohol soon she would probably hyperventilate. The waiter popped the cork and poured four glasses.

Maggie didn't wait for a toast. She gulped a mouthful of bubbly, swallowed and let a quiet "Ahhh" roll from her chest. The others at the table were busy getting their glasses filled which gave Maggie a few moments to collect herself. *Buck up, Maggie girl, or these human meat grinders will turn you into hamburger.* Tori's comment about being something special in the sack caused her thoughts to go haywire. She had no idea how she was in the sack; not that it mattered. Ty had been clear – their relationship would not include bedroom activities. If they continued to kiss during the next six months... She slammed on the brakes. She and Ty were not lovers, they were business partners, sort of, and the kissing had been done to make them appear authentic.

Tori stuck her pinkie finger out and took a dainty sip of champagne. "Excellent." She sat her champagne flute aside, blotted her mouth with her napkin, and straightened her silverware before she acknowledged the waiter who was patiently waiting to take her order. "I want salmon seasoned with fresh lemon, not lemon that you cut three hours ago, but newly sliced lemon. Sprinkle it lightly with thyme and serve it on a bed of pasta primavera. If the vegetables in the primavera are overcooked you're taking the whole plate of food back for a do-over. Are you clear on what I would like?" There was one thing crystal clear – Victoria Caye had perfected the art of intimidation.

Maggie tuned out Tori to concentrate on Ty. He seemed absorbed in his menu so she let her eyes drift to his mouth. Mmm. Soft, moist lips. A dimple at each corner. If she could turn the clock back thirty minutes she'd still be enjoying his...

"Maggie." Ty touched her arm and Maggie jerked.

"Huh?"

Ty chuckled as if keenly aware of where her thoughts were. "The waiter would like to take your order."

Hot blood rushed into Maggie's cheeks. Could she be any more obvious?

In a rush of words, she ordered chicken Marsala and a small side salad with poppy seed dressing. Ty and Quinn ordered a heavier meal that included porterhouse steak topped with mushrooms and onions, potatoes au gratin, and green beans almandine.

Ty and Quinn engaged in small talk about the Rangers game from the night before. Tori offered her two cents about the umpire, stating he needed to have his eyes checked. The conversation changed to crude oil and commodities brokers and Maggie was lost. All she knew about the oil industry was that she didn't know squat about it. Tori gave her a smug smirk. Maggie read her loud and clear – that she was way out her league and in no way would she fit in. Well, duh!

Maggie toyed with the tines on her forks and several times adjusted the napkin in lap. She sighed with relief when the food arrived.

Ty tore into his meal like he hadn't eaten all day. Tori picked at her salmon. And Maggie caught Quinn eyeing her between bites of potato.

The waiter delivered a fresh bottle of Dom Perignon.

Ty smiled but waved it away. "We didn't order a second bottle."

"Compliments of the owner, sir."

"Ah." Ty scanned the room and waved to a guy in an expensive black suit who appeared to be watching everyone in the restaurant. Maggie assumed he was the owner and that the gesture of a free bottle of champagne was to keep his rich guests coming back.

"Amazing," Maggie said.

Tori lifted her snooty little nose again. "Good things happen when you're with the Vincents."

And some not-so-nice things, Maggie almost blurted out loud.

Chapter Four

The blare of the alarm clock jolted Maggie awake. She groaned into her pillow and pulled the comforter over her head. Sliding a hand from beneath the covers, she blindly whacked at the clock. It took three attempts and almost falling off the bed, before she shut the blasted thing off.

Maggie lowered the comforter just enough to peek at the time. No way could it be seven o'clock. Under the covers, she indulged in a lengthy yawn. She was so not ready to begin the day; her body still wanted it to be night. After four grueling hours of getting worked over by Quinn and Tori last night, she wanted to block out the mess she was involved in for a little while longer. Spending time with those two was a mental challenge, yet there were knots in her neck and shoulders. She'd tensed and clenched so much in that five-star restaurant, the people at the next table had to assume she had muscle issues. Tonight would be the same, at a more intense level. Loy was throwing a party for her and Ty. Unbeknownst to the elite guests, it was an engagement party. Loy planned to make the announcement with champagne around ten o'clock. She predicted plenty of high eyebrows and a ton of whispers. Maggie rolled to her stomach and buried her face in her pillow. "Shoot me now!"

Married to Maggie

Her cell phone had the impudence to ring.

Maggie inched down the comforter, retrieved the phone from the nightstand and brought it under the covers. "Hello."

"Maggie?"

"Yes."

"It doesn't sound like you."

"That's because I'm under..." She stopped. No use trying to explain that she wasn't ready to face the world, even though the world was beckoning for her to get moving. She shoved away the covers and pulled to a sitting position against the headboard of the bed. "Is that better?"

"Much better. How'd you sleep last night?"

Who slept? Technically, she'd closed her eyes. Maybe she dozed off. Her thoughts were all over the place and would not settle down. She'd lain awake, smiling in the dark, reliving the moments with Ty, trying to make sense of the kissing, trying to convince herself that she didn't enjoy it. The truth was that she did enjoy it, even though it made her feel vulnerable and out of control, which in turn, triggered a whole lot of restlessness. She'd engaged in bed aerobics, rolling to her side, rolling to the other side, flipping to her back. Lather. Rinse. Repeat. And now it was time to get up. "Like a baby," she said, but immediately retracted the fib. "Actually, not very well. You?"

"All that alcohol did me in. I was out the second my head hit the pillow. Then the phone started to ring. My mom called and then my granddad. Damn early risers. They think everyone should be up by seven." He laughed. "Why couldn't you sleep?"

"Too much going on in my head, I guess." If he only knew.

Ty chuckled. "I hear that. We both have a lot to deal with. That being said, I have to tell you something." He paused. "You're going to need a few things for tonight and in the coming days. Granddad wanted me to pass along that he's set up accounts for you at the boutiques at Galleria Dallas. All you have to do is shop till you drop."

Maggie was tickled to know that Ty's mom had called. The rest of the information, not so much. There was no way she would shop till she dropped, especially with Vincent money. She slithered down so she could drop her face into her pillow again to mumble a few choice words.

"Maggie?"

"Umm, yeah...thank your grandfather for the generous offer but I can't accept it. I have money to buy what I need." That was partly true. She had funds tucked away to pay the rent. She'd been a hair away from filing for unemployment but Loy's offer came through first. Maggie put a hand on her forehead. Then came the second deal. Holy mackerel! This wife-for-hire scheme would probably be construed as a farfetched figment of her imagination if she repeated it to...almost anyone. There were moments where even she thought it was nothing more than a hallucination; or rather hoped it to be. Fortunately, she had a small window of time to renege. "Ty, I..."

He interrupted. "Don't be stubborn."

She *was* stubborn. As a mule. As a goat. As someone who wanted to keep what was left of her dignity. She would not allow T. Loy Vincent, I, to clothe her. Once she was a Vincent – *if* she became a Vincent – things might be different. For now, she would spend her own money. The Vincents and their A-list friends would have to deal with her in something nice but inexpensive. She frowned hard when a quote from Coco Chanel came to mind – 'Dress shabbily, they notice the dress. Dress impeccably, they notice the woman'. Her obstinacy was determined to win. "Put yourself in my shoes, Ty. You would fight this too. It's a pride thing."

"I know, but this really isn't about you and me, it's about him. I've given my grandfather so many headaches over the past year that I now find myself wanting to make him happy. I've enlisted you to be part of the effort. Can you hold up your end, Maggie?"

Ty's motivation for this whole pretense seemed to be evolving. He'd talked her into being his short-term wife so he could keep his job. Now it was to make his grandfather happy. Maggie was pleased that he wanted to satisfy Loy, but his changing sentiments put her on her guard. This crazy plan had potential to blow up in both of their faces. She quietly sighed. "I'll hold up my end. First, I'm headed to the gym."

Audible relief filtered through the phone line. "Thank you. The party starts at eight. Granddad wants to meet with us beforehand so Bostwick will pick you up at seven."

Maggie stretched her neck from side to side. "I'll be ready. But now I need to get my butt in gear if I'm going to make my dance class."

"Ahh, yes, belly dancing. Did you see Quinn's face when you mentioned that last night?"

Did you know your eyes were just as big? Maggie couldn't stop a smile when she pictured Ty's reaction. Tori had asked what she did in her spare time. When Maggie said belly dancing, both Ty's and Quinn's eyes rounded to the size of quarters. Tori's reaction wasn't as kind. The platinum blonde curled her lip. "Belly dancing? Seriously, who does that?"

Maggie had countered Tori's superior attitude by deliberately giving too much information. "All that jiggling and shimmying isn't just to entice Ty." She'd nudged against Ty but didn't look him in the eye. "It's an intense workout that sculpts every muscle in my core, even those pesky hard-to-target deep transverse abdominals. You should try it sometime."

Tori made a face like someone forced her to swallow turpentine. "I wouldn't be caught dead at a belly dancing class."

Ty cut into Maggie's current thoughts. "Are you still there?"

"Didn't mean to zone out. I was just going over in my head what Tori said about belly dancing."

"I'd bet a thousand bucks that you grabbed her interest. She'd never admit it though because she's too busy being the much talked about girl who does the coolest, most expensive things. But enough about Tori. I had no idea you were a belly dancer, Maggie. That explains the great hips and tight stomach. Maybe sometime you can show me."

"My hips and stomach? Or how to belly dance?" Maggie clamped her mouth shut. He thought she had great hips?

"Both?"

Maggie masked an unsettling feeling of excitement with sarcasm. "Whatever." She wriggled beneath the covers again when she realized that soon she and Ty would share a residence. They would be in each other's personal space for six long months. At some point he'd see her hips and stomach, maybe a lot more. "I have to go." Maggie hurriedly ended the call.

* * *

Ty tapped the side of his plate while he contemplated exactly what was happening between him and Maggie. He got the distinct feeling he made her nervous. She had a profound effect on him too, other than the obvious physical effect that was difficult to hide. Maggie disturbed his thoughts and senses. The dark-haired little vixen had him thinking about serious relationships. She had him modifying his who-the-hell-cares pattern of behavior he'd adopted over the past year. She had him imagining her in a sexy belly dancing outfit. Maggie was taking him out of his game. Not that he had a lot of game. What he did have, he wanted to keep. He would be wise to think less about her incredible body and how she set him on fire with her kisses, and think more about convincing his skeptics that he was fit to run Vincent Oil. Some of the board members viewed him as weak, while others saw him as a clone of his grandfather; a clone with bastard tendencies like their current CEO but one who had taken an emotional hit that set him back a bit. He wanted to maintain the opinion of those who had faith in him and repair the judgment of those who didn't. Vincent Oil Company needed strong leadership; someone tough as nails, someone with kahoonies the size of boulders, someone settled but not weakened by love. He snickered at how he'd gone from not wanting to play by someone else's rules to wanting to prove he was ready to take charge. All kinds of revelations were creeping up on him. One in particular involved Maggie. Tonight he would show Dallas his bride-to-be. He'd peck her on the mouth, lift her hand in a tender kiss and repeatedly lean into her. He might even smack her on the bottom. He wouldn't have to prod the rich and powerful to take to Maggie because his fiancée was quite capable of winning them over on her own. Maggie was kind and graceful. Beautiful and intelligent. Witty and upbeat. She was also loveable. He hung on that thought. Maggie *was* loveable and it would kill him to behave badly toward the end of the evening. As agreed upon, he and Maggie would split in six months so tonight he had to do something – nothing too drastic – that most folks wouldn't pick up on right away, but later would say 'Oh yeah. Now I remember…' He needed to provide a subliminal hint of impending doom. Perhaps he should engage in some open but harmless flirting. Or hug a former lover a little too tightly. When he and Maggie's marriage fell apart, his somewhat-dodgy behavior would come back to haunt him. There would be whispers. Necessary rumors to make people side with Maggie when she walked away. He had to be seen as the bad guy.

Ty frowned at the idea of upsetting Maggie, both tonight and in six months. He frowned harder at the thought of her walking out of his life when the deal was done. A small spasm of pain in the center of his chest made him close his eyes and lean back in his chair. What the hell?

In a heartbeat, the twinge was gone. Ty attributed it to heartburn. He poured himself a half-glass of milk to coat this throat and stomach. Milk was supposedly a temporary buffer against heartburn. The discomfort, for the most part, was gone. He downed the milk just in case.

He cut a chunk of whole wheat pancake with his fork, dragged it through a pool of syrup and almost had the bite to his mouth. Laying the fork aside, Ty grabbed the newspaper and thumbed through the pages until he landed on the picture that his grandfather had called about before the sun was up.

Ty lifted the newspaper to get a better look at the photo of him and Maggie in a lip-lock outside the restaurant. "Thank you, Chaz." The news hound was freelance so he could sell his pictures to the highest bidder. Ty imagined the newspaper paid big bucks for this one. He chuckled at what his grandfather had to say about the photo. 'I'd rather have seen the two of you holding hands and smiling instead of engaging in foreplay against the limousine. You make a great couple, Tysen. Let's keep it a class act.'

Ty ran his fingers over the picture. He and Maggie had kissed like lovers. Something else in the picture made him crack up laughing – Maggie's hand was on his butt.

He finally took a bite of pancake and examined the picture from every angle while he chewed. The image of them so close together was a sign that he and Maggie were a perfect fit. Instinctively, he denied that conclusion. So she fit perfectly in his arms, it was just body alignment. The more he stared at the way they were tangled up the more *pictures don't lie* wedged in his brain. Still, he didn't want them to be a good fit. Maggie was temporary. If he got hung up on little things like how great it was to have her in his arms and the amazing way she responded to his kiss, he'd never be able to walk away. But he *had* to walk away. He couldn't risk the heartache of loving someone with everything he had and then losing them like he'd lost his dad. That kind of hurt never went away and he wouldn't wish it on anyone. The best plan of action was to keep things as strictly business. No more kissing. No more touching. No more perfect alignment.

As if his wrestling thoughts needed something more than a date on a calendar to cut Maggie loose, they reminded him that the people he surrounded himself with went to the opera and took in art exhibits, attended charity events and hung out at private country clubs. They didn't expose their midriffs, cover their faces with veils and shimmy their hips and torsos to earthy Mediterranean music.

A vision of Maggie in such an outfit made his mouth go dry and his fantasies kicked into high gear. He pictured her magnificent blue eyes teasing him over the edge of a veil while the provocative rhythm of her hips beckoned for him to take her.

The blare of his cell phone suspended the fantasy. He winced when he recognized the number. "Hello, Mother."

"I have a few more thoughts I'd like to share."

She'd bent his ear so much earlier it was a wonder he could hear out of it. "Share away."

"Tysen." The weight of her tone meant she was about to give her two cents whether he wanted it or not. "I have a bad feeling about this rushed marriage. Maybe you should slow down and get to know one another before you promise to love each other for all eternity. It takes time to peel back the layers of a person to discover who they are. Look what happened to your dad and me."

"The troubles you and dad went through didn't have anything to do with how long you knew each other." The discomfort he'd blamed on heartburn, returned.

"I know. But still."

"Relax. Maggie's a great gal. You're going to love her."

Shit. There was the L-word again.

"The question is, do *you* love her?"

Ty wasn't prepared to lie to his mom. He respected her, even though the press would have everyone believe otherwise. He and his mom kept their close relationship on the down-low because she wanted it that way. She hated being in the public eye; or as she put it, trashed in the newspapers. She was a simple woman with a big heart, like Maggie. How she got involved with an oil mogul still wasn't clear. The only explanation she provided was that the second their eyes met, she was a goner. Of course, everything that came with being Mrs. T. Loy Vincent, II, had been too much. After two long, excruciating years, she and his father split; amicably. All she asked for was a modest settlement to start over and equal time with Ty. She also begged his father to make sure the press left her alone. It had taken some swift maneuvering, but his father pulled it off. With her approval, he made it look as though Ellen Peppersmith-Vincent was out of their lives forever. Nothing could've been farther from the truth. Ty visited his mom on a regular basis. T. Loy Vincent, II, or Toy – his mom's pet name for his dad – had been no stranger to her house either. *Toy.* The memory of his father turning his nose up at the name and begging his ex-wife to stop calling him that was bittersweet. Ty chuckled to himself when he recalled the one time he called his dad Toy. His father backed him against the wall and in no uncertain terms advised him to never call him that again, if he wanted to live. Of course, they both burst out laughing. His dad had shook his head and said, 'It's a stupid name but it makes her happy'. Despite their marital status, or lack thereof, his mom and dad had loved each other so much. Ty wanted that kind of relationship…eventually. He wanted someone he could be comfortable with. Someone who understood his demons but wouldn't let him take himself too seriously. Someone he couldn't wait to get home to every night. Someone playful enough to give him a pet name.

Too many seconds must've ticked by without a response because his mom prompted him for an answer. "Well do you?"

Ty snapped back to the question about Maggie. "I love things about her." He fisted his hand and pushed it into his solar plexus to try to relieve the heartburn that was now accompanied by a familiar twinge. *Sweet.* His conscience was most likely prompting the heartburn and thoughts of his dad was bringing on a bigger bloom of discomfort. All he needed now was a headache to finish him off.

"That's not enough. Your marriage won't last ten days if there's no love."

He needed it to last six months. If he played his cards right, it would. "I have to go, Mom. See you tonight."

Ty understood his mom's concerns. If he let her in on the secret six month alliance, she'd try to talk him out of it. She wouldn't buy into that whole spiel that a guy has to do what a guy has to do. He shoved his plate of pancakes aside. Right or wrong, he was marrying Maggie.

* * *

Loy Vincent perched on the edge of the desk and rubbed his chin as though he was having trouble believing she'd pulled it off. "Good job, Maggie."

Maggie shrank in her seat from the compliment that felt more like an accusation.

On the way to the gym, she'd received a call from Loy's secretary, Rosie. Loy needed an update. Instead of sweating from an intense belly dancing workout, she was in Loy's office, sweating profusely by trying not to slip up and reveal that she was also doing a deal with Ty. "Thank you."

Loy continued to shake his head. "How'd you do it? I mean, Tysen isn't an easy person to influence. I knew the moment he laid eyes on you that he'd be intrigued; never in my wildest dreams did I think he'd propose marriage so soon. In fact, I had a few tricks up my sleeve in case we needed them."

"Let's chalk it up to fate, Loy." Maggie extended her elbows so they touched the arms of the chair as a means to steady her nerves. "Everything went according to plan. I tracked him down in the airport. He was in the gift shop having some kind of chest issue and…"

"Not *that* again."

Maggie was glad he interrupted.

"I believe the pain is real but it's psychosomatic at the same time. The loss of his father has him so messed up." Loy winced hard. "He's a Vincent, for God's sake. A Texan. We're rough and tough. We get knocked down, but we get back up fighting. The problem with Ty is that he got knocked down and he's still on the ground." Loy walked to a set of large windows that overlooked the busy streets below and sighed long and loud before turning around. "Help him get up, Maggie."

Maggie understood his frustration; she also felt the need to set the record straight. "Ty is a Vincent through and through, Loy. If you step back you'll see it. He loves you as much as you love him. He also loves Texas *and* the oil business. In my humble opinion, he loves big and he hurts big. He's on his way back up, but you have to let him do it on his terms."

Loy grimaced. "I'm not seeing it."

"Then look closer. Ty loves you. He loves this company." She was getting louder with each word. "Let me repeat – he's a Vincent through and through. A little hardheaded but he's loyal. He's a good man."

"Again, Maggie, I don't see what you see."

Maggie stood up and crossed her arms at her chest. "Are you stubborn, Loy?"

Loy appeared dazed by her impudence and by the question. "I suppose so."

"You can do better than that."

Loy pressed his lips together in a thin line. "I'm stubborn as hell, Maggie, but I don't see how that's relevant. This isn't about me, it's about Tysen."

Maggie dropped her hands to her hips. "This is about both of you. You and Tysen are so much alike it's scary."

A tick at Loy's jaw said she was treading on an icy patch and if she wasn't careful she would fall on her butt. "What I'm trying to say, is that you and your son gave him a good foundation. He's all that you want him to be and he's a chip off the ole block, but he's also his own person."

There was a volatile edge to Loy's voice that made her flinch inwardly. "He's a screw-up. He may love me but he would rather be a skirt-chaser than an oil man."

"If that was true, then why is he getting married?"

"Because I boxed him in and threatened to take away his position. Now he's trying to fake his way into keeping it. Plus, he hates Terron Wade with a passion and would do anything to keep him from moving up."

Maggie couldn't resist. "Or...because he's so attracted to me he can't help himself." Loy didn't as much as crack a smile and she fended off the urge to punch him by asking about the guy that Ty hated with a passion. "Who's Terron Wade?"

"A promising young man that I'm grooming to take over if Ty falls on his face."

If Ty falls on his... Maggie saw red. She pointed to Loy's high-back leather chair. "Sit!"

Loy cut her with a harsh look. "Watch it, Maggie."

"I mean it, Loy. Sit." She'd used that same authority on him in rehab. Since this was Loy's turf he just might have security escort her out. Maggie held her breath.

Loy edged into his chair.

Maggie quietly exhaled. "Thank you. Now I need for you to understand something." She pierced him with an unyielding look of certainty. "If you want me to continue with your little plan then I suggest you stop expecting your grandson to fail. And if I hear you call him a screw-up one more time, I'm done. Got it?" Her pulse thumped hard against her temples and her legs suddenly felt incapable of holding her weight. To steady herself, she placed both hands on the arms of Loy's chair and leaned toward him.

Loy's stern features softened. "Calm down, Maggie, or you'll be the one needing cardiac rehab." He adjusted himself in the chair.

Maggie backed up to give them both space.

Loy drummed his fingers on his desk. "I hear what you're saying, and you're right, I need to give this a chance to play out. Tysen is not a screw-up. He's my grandson." He cocked an eyebrow. "Better?"

Heat had filled Maggie's cheeks the second she'd stood up to him. They were still hot. And her mouth was suddenly parched like she hadn't had a drink of water in days. "It is if you mean it."

"I mean it." A slow curve at the corners of his mouth and the lift of his wrist to expose his watch indicated the meeting was over. "You have shopping to do so you can charm the guests at your engagement party tonight." He wrinkled his nose. "Just don't use that tone of voice with them, okay?"

Maggie grinned but inside she was having a mini-meltdown. He'd said never in his wildest dreams did he expect Ty to marry so soon, well, never in her wildest dreams did she expect to be a wife for hire – one who was getting too emotionally involved with the job.

Chapter Five

"You're doing what?" Nancy's eyes all but popped out of her head as she continued to draw circles with her hips.

"Shh." Maggie's gaze riveted between the instructor of the belly dancing class, and her former boss and best friend, Nancy. "This is for your ears only."

"That won't be a problem." Nancy nodded toward the front of the room. "She has the music up so loud I can barely hear myself think."

The instructor brought her sheer black scarf up below her eyes, the dancers mimicked.

Behind Maggie's scarf she whispered. "You heard right, I'm getting married...on Saturday."

Good thing they were in the back row because Nancy moved in close and put her hand on Maggie's forehead. "Are you burning up with fever?"

Maggie offered the details in a hurry. Tysen Loy Vincent, III. Temporary marriage. No kids. No sex. No trying to fix each other's behaviors. Gah! She might not be burning up with fever, but she was definitely a candidate for serious psychoanalysis.

Nancy's mouth dropped open for a few seconds. "Ty Vincent? Thee Ty Vincent?"

"Yes."

"Have you lost your freaking mind?"

Again, "Yes."

"You are aware that he's...umm...how should I put this? Hot but bad. And not in a good way. He sleeps around so much he probably has an STD."

Maggie gave her friend a pointed look. "He doesn't have an STD."

"You don't know that."

"Yes, I do." Maggie started to laugh...nervously. She lost her place in the workout and it took a few seconds to fall back into sequence. "All I know for sure is that the media tends to inflate things. He might actually be a sweet guy...who has an STD." Laughter jiggled her midsection instead of the movements to the music. "Like I said, I won't be sleeping with him so it shouldn't be a problem."

"Well that sucks. It would've made an exciting bit for your memoir."

"Why would I write a memoir, I'm only twenty nine?" Twenty nine suddenly sounded ancient. Maybe it was a good thing she was getting married, even if it was temporary. Her dating life had come to a standstill, all her doing. She'd grown tired of self-absorbed boneheads. Men who weren't boneheads were already married. Hmm. It seemed that wealthy boneheads only wanted temporary marriages. Essentially, she had zero chance of finding Mr. Right. No job. No love life. No wonder she was easy pickings for wayward plots.

"People love to read about the strange things others do. This, dear heart, couldn't be more strange." Nancy's brown eyes twinkled with amusement. "Only you would find yourself in a love-for-hire scheme."

"It's not a *love* for hire scheme. It's a *wife* for... Oh, God! I'm pathetic!" She and Nancy spent many a night talking about finding the one guy who could make their heart sing. Never did they talk about finding the one guy who could make their bank account sing.

"You're not in over your head yet, but if you wait a day or two, you will be. By the way, don't tell him that you belly dance. He'll try to rent you out for special occasions."

Maggie feigned annoyance with a quirked brow.

"What?"

"He won't rent me out."

"Men have sneaky ways of getting what they want. Just saying."

"You're a hoot." Maggie lowered the scarf, stretched her arms out at her sides and twirled them in slow circles. "Seriously, I have to do this. For my dad. He owes Loy Vincent something big and he's asked for my help." She lifted her shoulders in a shrug. "It's not a problem since I don't have a job."

Nancy shimmied her upper body, her eyes sparkling with animation. "Most people who find themselves out of work file for unemployment. They don't become temporary spouses."

"I'm not most people." Maggie tried to sound confident while wiping a trickle of sweat that collected above her brow. "When have you known me to stick to convention?"

"You are your own person, I'll give you that. But still, Mags, getting married to Ty Vincent is a little more than just stepping outside the box. He's a playboy for crying out loud. He's known to take one girl to bed and take another to breakfast." She shook her head in disapproval. "What the heck is your dad thinking by setting you up to get hurt?"

"That's not what he's doing." Unwittingly, it probably was exactly what he was doing. Maggie refused to dwell on the possibilities of everything that could, and most likely would happen. She'd given her word…to her father…to Loy…to Ty. Nothing was in writing. Maybe she should've gotten an itemized deal complete with signatures. She was sure the

Vincents protected their backsides in *true* business ventures with a paper trail that could go around the earth twice. With this venture they had to assume that anything in print could fall into the wrong hands and all hell would break loose. It was a disconcerting thought that made Maggie lose her place again.

"See," Nancy quipped with a half-grin, "he's already broken your rhythm."

"Keep it up and I won't ask you to be my maid of honor."

"Mags, I want to be your maid of honor when you *really* get married."

"I'm *really* getting married."

"You know what I mean."

"Fine. I'll ask Victoria."

"Who's Victoria?"

"I'll tell you when we're done."

Maggie refused to let Ty Vincent, or anyone else, break the rhythm of her life. She homed in on the music.

* * *

Ty had sent Maggie a text message earlier hoping to rendezvous at Galleria Dallas so he could take her to lunch. She declined because she'd just gotten to the gym. The woman had to eat, plus they had things to discuss.

If she didn't get her butt out of the gym soon, he'd go in after her. Like a complete idiot he'd been standing against his car in almost hundred-degree heat for about fifteen minutes, trying to look cool and collected. His clothes were sticking to him and if he stood there much longer he would need another shower. He checked his watch, looked up and voila! Maggie! His soon-to-be wife had just walked through the automatic doors, deep in conversation with a tall, thin blonde. His pulse kicked up and the extreme temperature was forgotten.

Maggie waved goodbye to her friend.

Ty removed his sunglasses. "Maggie, over here."

She frowned before smiling.

Even with a scowl on her face she was cute. And damned sexy in a pair of skimpy black shorts and white tank top. Whatever Maggie wore revealed the lean as well as the luscious. Desire erupted in him like someone flicked a switch. "No," he said without moving his mouth, trying to flick the switch back off. His subconscious rushed to blame the sudden craving for Maggie on not getting any for almost a year. It wasn't necessarily Maggie he wanted; she just happened to be the one in the picture these days.

Maggie slung her gym bag on her shoulder and walked slowly toward him like she was adjusting to the shock that he was there. "What brings you to the gym?"

The scent of freshly scrubbed skin and shampoo met his nose. "You smell nice."

"You came all the way here to tell me that?"

"Yeah. No," he teased. "I'm here to take you to lunch."

Maggie cocked an eyebrow. "You don't take no for an answer, do you?"

"You have to eat."

She laughed lightly. "True that. But I also have to shop." Maggie fished her car keys from the side pocket of her purse.

Ty latched onto her arm. "There's a mom and pop diner down the street."

Maggie looked at her watch. "If I'm going to make tonight's shindig on time, I need to skip lunch."

"You're not skipping lunch." Ty started to open the passenger-side door of his car but stopped. "You haven't been shopping? I thought…" He raised his hands. "Never mind. What you did with your morning is none of my business. I don't need to know." He was more than a little curious, but hey, she didn't owe him an explanation. They weren't married and neither of them had to account for their time. Even after they were hitched, he wouldn't track her whereabouts and she sure as hell better not track his.

Maggie laughed. "I was delayed."

Ty hoped for more; he didn't get it.

He still had a hold of her arm. "A sandwich or salad won't take long. Climb in."

Maggie's eyes went wide the moment she became aware of his car. "No Bostwick?"

At his grandfather's insistence, he was generally carted around by Bostwick; possibly as a way to keep tabs on him. Today, he'd given his driver the slip.

"No Bostwick." He dangled the Porsche keys in front of Maggie. "Would you like to drive?"

"Uh, no. And I hope not to drive it anytime soon."

"Why not?" He expected her to say because it was too showy.

"Duh. We'll be trading it in for a mini-van."

"No minivans in my driveway," he said straight away.

Merriment danced in Maggie's eyes. "We'll need one for all the kids we're going to have. I'm an only child. You're an only child. It only stands to reason we'd want a slew of kids."

Kids were great but there wouldn't be any in his foreseeable future. He had too much living to do, too many wild oats to sow, an oil business to run.

Who was he kidding? He wouldn't be sowing any oats – wild or otherwise – for quite awhile thanks to playing the part of husband. In a few days his foot loose ways would be put on hold. Although, if anyone queried the women he'd recently dated, they'd find out those days had been put on hold long before his engagement. "You do have an overactive imagination." They shared a laugh and he showed off by speeding down the street.

In minutes they were seated across from each other in a booth at the back of the diner.

Maggie played with her paper placemat, folding the corners, making little tears across the top. "Are you nervous about tonight?"

The question surprised him. "Not at all. You?"

A red-haired waitress arrived at the table and laid menus in front of them. "Howdy, folks." There was a second of recognition that made her mouth drop open but she quickly got her bearings and smiled. "Ahh, Mr. Vincent." She motioned to Maggie. "And…"

"Maggie," Ty said, leaving her last name out of the introduction. The world would find out soon enough.

"I'm…we're…" The waitress seemed momentarily flustered. "Happy to have you." She pointed to a chalkboard hanging on the wall. "Today's special is BBQ pulled pork sandwich, speckled butter beans and cole slaw. Ya 'all want to give that a go or would you like to order from the menu?"

Maggie smiled. "I'll have the special and I could use a cup of black coffee too."

"I'll have the same."

"Ya 'all are making it easy on me. Be back in a jiffy."

Maggie waited until the waitress was well away. "I take it you don't come here often."

"First time."

She giggled but set serious eyes on him and lowered her voice. "Tell me the real reason for the surprise lunch."

Ty caught movement outside the window. "No ulterior motive. Just lunch."

Maggie disqualified his answer right off the bat. "Try again."

The waitress returned with two ceramic mugs swinging from her thumb and a carafe of coffee. She inclined her head toward the window. "Not sure what to make of this, but there are two guys with cameras hiding behind that red SUV. Should I call the law?"

Ty and Maggie looked at each other and both shook their heads simultaneously. "No," Ty said. "They're just a couple of pesky gnats that don't have anything better to do."

"Make no mistake, Mr. Vincent, if those gnats come inside, I'll have Big Jim smack them with a fly swatter." She gestured to a big, burly guy working behind the order window. Big Jim was wearing a hair net which made him seem less threatening. When he moved, however, oversized muscles stretched the fabric of his white shirt. The man looked as if he could knock a couple of paparazzi heads together without breaking a sweat.

Ty read the waitress's name tag. "Thanks, Rita."

"Happy to help, hon." Rita corrected herself. "I mean, Mr. Vincent." She poured them a cup of coffee and sat the carafe on the table for their convenience. "Your food will be ready in a jiffy."

Ty watched Rita leave before suggesting that they give Chaz and his cohort a run for his money by zigzagging around Dallas. "Or we can hole up in my apartment for awhile."

Maggie rejected both ideas. "Not necessary. I can handle a couple of paparazzi. They'll follow me to the Galleria and I'll bore them to tears by trying everything on."

"You don't know who you're dealing with, Maggie. Chaz Rosston is a sly bastard who wouldn't have a problem buying his way into the dressing room and filming you in your underwear." Ty raised his middle finger high enough for the two hooligans outside to see. "Film that, assholes."

Maggie gave him an irked look.

"What?" he laughed.

She pointed to an elderly couple getting out of their car. "They probably think you flipped them off." Maggie pulled in her lips like she was warding off a laugh.

"Maybe I did."

Maggie brought her coffee cup to her mouth but sat it down without taking a drink. "Tell me about the people I'll meet tonight. Will I want to flip them off?"

Ty settled against the booth. "They're mostly a great bunch who will welcome you with open arms, unlike Quinn and Tori. I'm still scratching my head over those two. Anyway, there are a few jerks that my grandfather associates with out of necessity. Feel free to flip them off if they try to trap you into giving too much information. I'll try to stay by your side, but you know how parties go. Now, about holing up at my place – I still think it's a good idea."

"You're forgetting one tiny little detail. I need a dress for tonight."

"No worries." He pulled his cell phone from his shirt pocket, scrolled through his phone list until he found Justine Perthie's number. "Justine, Ty Vincent." He kept his eyes glued to Maggie's while he talked. "Yes, nice to talk to you too." He cut to the chase. "My fiancée needs a dress. Yeah, I know. Most people aren't aware that I'm engaged. It will be announced tonight. Well thank you. It *is* awesome. Keep it quiet okay, Jus'?" He winked at Maggie. "What does she look like? Umm...big blue eyes, beautiful skin – lightly tanned, curvy figure, short dark hair. Her taste in clothes? That's easy. Simple yet chic."

Maggie grinned from ear to ear and his heart went into a thumping frenzy.

He covered the mouthpiece. "Jus' wants to know what size."

Maggie feigned shock by raising both brows. "What size? That's like asking a woman her age."

"Give it to me." The comment made something indefinable flash through Maggie's eyes. Something flashed through Ty too – lust.

"Arranging for a dress over the phone is straight out of the movie, Pretty Woman." Maggie waved away the concept. "In real life you have to try things on. I'm built weird. Too much in some spots. Not enough in others."

Their eyes held.

"What size?" he said firmly.

Maggie sighed. "Eight."

"By the way, you have an incredible body." Ty pointed to the phone as though the remark was meant solely for the boutique owner. Maggie *did* have an incredible body and it would take all his willpower to keep his hands off.

* * *

Ty's penthouse apartment was spectacular with ultra modern decor. Everything had straight lines, was black, red or off-white and pristine as though nothing had been sat on or used. Maggie was surprised there weren't price tags still attached to the furniture and the oversized paintings framed in black. The off-white carpet with occasional threads of black and red was possibly custom-made and was so plush that when Maggie removed her shoes her feet sank in about an inch. The carpet was the only thing soft about the place. There were no throw pillows, knitted afghans, curtains or family pictures.

It was a true bachelor pad with an L-shaped bar. A huge rectangular mirror behind the bar was etched with the Texas Rangers logo.

"Hmm," Maggie said without thinking.

"Hmm? What?" A sly grin bowed the corners of Ty's generous mouth.

"Nice place." Maggie took a sip of ice water. Ty had offered wine but she opted to stick with water. She couldn't get in trouble with water. This was the first time they'd been alone since they met. There had been a few private moments; but someone was always within earshot or picture-taking distance. Until now. She'd balked at coming there but Ty was a Vincent; which meant, she could've argued until she was blue in the face

Married to Maggie

but it wouldn't have done any good. He'd strongly insisted. She'd easily caved. Now she was seated on Ty's expensive sofa, shoes off, wondering how she would fit into his world for six long months. Soon she'd take up residence in this high-priced high-security condominium complex complete with a doorman and entry pass codes for the elevator and doors. She was surprised there wasn't a retinal scanner.

"Nice place, but...?" Ty inquired.

"There's no but."

"Yes there is." His brows vaulted upward calling her on the fib. "C'mon. Tell me what this place says to you."

Maggie jiggled with laughter. "It says, 'The doctor will be right with you'."

"Huh?"

"It has all the hominess of a doctor's office, except for the fabulous carpet." She purposely dragged her toes through the lush nap.

Ty's gaze skipped around the apartment and returned to Maggie.

She held up her index finger. "And it has a bar."

"It does." Ty sat on the opposite end of the sofa with a long neck bottle of beer. "I didn't pick out a thing. No, wait, the mirror was my doing." He took a swallow of beer. "I got a lot of guff about it from…" He cut off the comment and it hung there, unfinished.

"From?"

"No one."

The slight crinkle between his brows said a lot.

"Your girlfriend?"

He didn't answer.

"I know so little about you, Ty, that anything you tell me…even about your girlfriends…will help me get to know you better. Just skip the romantic bits."

"Not many bits to tell." He shifted like he couldn't get

comfortable.

    Maggie rolled her eyes to mock and tease. "According to the newspapers and tabloids, there are lots of romantic bits."

    "Don't believe everything you read. Those vultures aren't as in touch with my personal life as they'd like to think."

    Maggie tried to interpret what that meant and what he wasn't saying. "Good to know. There should be a degree of privacy to a person's life, especially the private bits." She almost said private parts. While she would mean the personal aspects of his life, he might think she referred to body parts and she didn't want to go there. She took another sip from her water glass and Ty took a sip of beer. Their eyes met and Maggie felt a warm flush coat her body.

    "So, Maggie," Ty kicked off his sandals and laid his legs lengthwise on the sofa, almost touching her, "tell me about being a nurse. Why did you choose that field? By the way, did you know my granddad has heart issues?"

    The sip of water caught in her throat. She coughed. "Sorry. Went down the wrong pipe." Was he baiting her with those questions? While she didn't know much about him, except tabloid trash, he probably knew every little detail about her, including that she'd been his grandfather's rehab nurse. And maybe he'd wanted to get her alone to give her a chance to come clean. Maggie squirmed in place while guilt gnawed its way to the surface. She held onto the arm of the sofa and decided to exhaust the next few minutes with mind numbing details about nursing. What happened instead was her passion for patient care came out right away. She heard it with her own ears and smiled. She loved all the things that came with nursing; taking blood pressure and temperatures, handling meds, hooking patients up to IV's, catheters and EKG's. Calming their fears. Enjoying their friendship. She got so caught up in sharing her first love that she almost let her subspecialty of cardiac rehab slip out by mentioning stress tests. Whether Ty would pick up on it, she wasn't sure, but she experienced a moment of panic and nervously took another sip of water, sloshing some on her shirt.

Maggie wrapped up the one-sided gab-fest by saying she couldn't imagine doing anything else but nursing.

Ty's eyes should've been glazed over. They weren't. He appeared to be hanging on her every word.

"So, about my granddad..."

Maggie tried to casually set the water glass on the coffee table but almost upended the darn thing. Again, she tried to maneuver the conversation away from his grandfather by mentioning that she was scheduled to attend a seminar about the six elements of disease management and the science of helping patients change their lifestyles for better health. Although, now she wasn't sure whether she would make the three hour drive from Dallas to Austin to take part in the seminar. A wave of melancholia rolled over her. She missed being in the hospital climate where she made a difference in people's lives versus being eyebrow-deep in a scam, if not handled gingerly, would forever make her seem like a shady character. A con artist. A fraud. Someone not trustworthy. A gurgle of trepidation rolled up from her belly. The noise was just loud enough to catch Ty's attention. A momentary line creased his forehead but in an instant it was gone.

"My grandfather had quadruple bypass surgery and was damned lucky he didn't die."

The man was hell bent on having this discussion.

Ty sat his beer bottle next to Maggie's glass. "I haven't been the best grandson." He lowered his eyelashes so only a smidgen of blue could be seen. A gritty noise followed. The sound of his grandfather's health finally hitting home? "I visited him a couple of times in CCU, but I was too...," he made air quotes, "...busy...to accompany him to rehab."

If Ty *had* accompanied his grandfather to rehab they

would've met long before the airport and there was a good chance none of this would be happening. "Don't beat yourself up. You were there when he needed you the most."

Ty appeared to mull over her words. "I have to stop making him nuts, Maggie. That's why it's so important for me to get married and take the reins of the company. He needs to enjoy life a little before the pressure of the oil business makes him have the big one." He ran his hands across his face. "I lost my dad. I can't lose him too." He did a series of heavy blinks, groaned louder than he did a minute ago and splayed his hand across his chest.

Maggie recognized the same symptoms that Ty experienced in the airport. 'Psychosomatic', Loy had said. Maggie was forever a nurse and couldn't accept that diagnosis. She scooted Ty's legs over so she could move in close. His eye lids flickered open and closed like they were trying to focus but couldn't quite get the job done. "Relax, Ty. Just breathe," she said softly, resting a hand on his thigh, wondering if she should retrieve the bottle of aspirin she kept in her purse for incidents like these. "I know the answer before I ask, but do you want me to call an ambulance?"

Ty grappled to get his bearings. He heard Maggie's words and felt her touch, but the pain was too intense to key on anything but his chest. The episodes were happening more frequently and each one more intense than the last, making him think he was about to have one he couldn't recover from. Not only were the damned things scary, they were also inconvenient and embarrassing as hell.

The pain crested and a few seconds later it was gone altogether. "Don't. Call. Anyone."

"Ty..."

Ty laid a finger across her lips. "Shh. I've had a hundred of these." In restaurants. In elevators. During the national anthem at a Texas Rangers baseball game. In line for the men's restroom. And in a gift shop at the Reno-Tahoe International Airport. "The pain is real, the cause isn't." Admitting that was tough but maybe it was the first step in getting them to stop. He could only hope.

"You don't know that the cause isn't real. You might have an inherited defect or condition that could be fixed with surgery or medication. You just mentioned your grandfather's open heart surgery." Maggie's blue eyes rounded with concern. "Have you been checked out?"

Ty hated that she witnessed yet another incident, but oddly took comfort in her closeness. "I don't have a defect or a condition, and I'm not a candidate for open heart surgery," he said resolutely. "End of discussion." Maggie started to counter; he shut her down. "Seriously. No more talk about defects, ambulances or anything chest related." Although, the mention of chests made his eyes drop to Maggie's.

"I don't want to be a widow," Maggie said, shocking the hell out of him.

She was worried about becoming a widow? She's not even going to be a real wife. Legally she would be, but that was the extent of it. If he *did* have the big one, she'd legally be a widow. Damn. Their plan was becoming increasingly complicated.

Ty had convinced himself he'd brought Maggie to his apartment to iron out the particulars of their arrangement before the big day on Saturday. The more they knew about each other, the less chance the press would have to trip them up. His inner-critic scoffed. *Right*. The truth was that he liked being with Maggie. Liked talking to her. Liked kissing her. Liked the way her body bounced when she laughed. Liked her quick wit. The only thing that gave him pause was that blurry business line that he wanted to cross. "Stop worrying, woman," he said with a grin.

Maggie bent to scratch her leg, inadvertently giving him an eyeful of cleavage.

The dog in him went crazy. He pictured her in that clingy blue dress from the night before that not only revealed her great chest but also emphasized the rest of her delectable body. In no way did that dress say 'business partner'.

Maggie sat back and caught him staring. Her cheeks and neck turned a sweet shade of pink.

The voice of reason poked him with a warning to gear his thoughts and his eyes away from her body. She wasn't there to sleep with him. He'd hired her to help him get his life in order, to make him look good in the eyes of his grandfather and the board of directors. Seducing her with eyes, or any other body part, was a huge no.

His mind tossed around the idea of needing Maggie. How could he have developed this sudden craving for a complete stranger, the craving that blew beyond just lust? He hadn't even known her for a full week, yet he felt stronger with her around, and soon, with her by his side he'd assume control of his grandfather's company. The prestigious position paid well, but it was no walk in the park. It required true leadership skills. He'd have to be on his game 24/7 to deal with the government, the public, commodities brokers, and everything else that came with the business. To be President and CEO meant that he'd have to be as sharp and unrelenting as a five-blade razor and as stinging as alcohol on an open cut. Essentially, he had to become his grandfather; someone who laughed at pain and inflicted his own brand of it when needed. With Maggie in his life, he could be that guy. The thought floored him.

Maggie's tantalizing floral scent invaded the small space between them and to his surprise she was still moving her hand up and down his thigh. The comfort took a quick exit. His eyes skimmed her mouth before dropping to her breasts again. He wanted Maggie. He hadn't wanted anyone in that way for so long that the emotion felt awkward.

"Maggie," he simply said. They stared at one another for a

Married to Maggie

few long moments and in a surprise turn of events, Maggie moved in so close he could feel her body heat, tempting him to the near breaking point.

She's your employee. She's...

In a heartbeat, she was in his arms and their mouth's crashed into each other.

Ty sucked her lips into his. *Mmm.* They were soft and the fine sheen of gloss she'd put on during their trip from the restaurant to his apartment tasted like strawberries. He touched his tongue to her lips and Maggie opened to him. He slid his tongue in slowly to let them both adjust to this special kind of closeness. They'd French-kissed when they were trying to buffalo Chaz, but now, there were no cameras, no gawking public, just the two of them and the kiss was as real as real could be. Ty moved his tongue to explore Maggie's sweetness and she reciprocated with an exploration of her own. The tangle of tongues deepened the intimacy and the sounds of pleasure that came from them both made his body go wild. He held Maggie's mouth in place by putting his hand behind her head. Over the back of her tank top, he moved his free hand up and down, hesitating at the hooks of her bra, before moving on to memorize each muscle, each curve, each inch that was Maggie.

The sensuous sounds continued triggering his heart to thump like it was trying to break free. His jeans grew tight around him. And his breaths were becoming slightly jagged. Maggie had to know how much she affected him.

No raced through his brain while everything else countered with *yes*. His fingers dropped to the bottom of her shirt and he slid them beneath it to touch the tender skin at her lower back. Slowly they inched up.

Ty broke the kiss to catch his breath and to whisper tenderly against her ear, "Oh...sweet...Maggie."

"Ty." The way Maggie said his name sounded like she was

in a trance and he couldn't stop a smile or control his hands. His eager fingers rushed to the hooks of her bra again. Suddenly he had ten thumbs. The hook-and-eye combination was as good as a deadbolt and the treasures being protected, were safe.

Maggie gave him a gentle push, smiled and pulled the white tank top shirt over her head, revealing a sexy white bra edged in lace with a tiny pink heart in the center. It was a push-up contraption that offered him what it held. A shy smile curved her mouth, but there was nothing timid about her slipping the straps from her shoulders. She teased him by lowering the bra to expose the full sweet swell of her breasts, but not low enough to expose her nipples.

Saliva pooled in Ty's mouth and his gaze ricocheted between her chest and those smoldering blue eyes. He ran his tongue over his lips. "Are you sure about this?"

No hesitation. No over-thinking her behavior. Just a slow up and down motion with her head to indicate she wanted this as much as he did.

With his eyes still connected to Maggie's, he removed his own shirt before carefully attacking those frustrating hooks again. Miraculously, his thumbs became deft fingers and that lacy little undergarment with the deadbolt lock was history. He gave it a toss over his shoulder and cupped her breasts.

Maggie's eyes sparkled with approval.

In a flash, they were all over each other. Mouth's tasting. Hands searching. Desire taking a hold and not letting loose.

Maggie ran her hands through his hair while he kissed her deeply and skimmed the tips of her breasts with his palms. She trembled beneath his touch and the thick sounds of delight taxed his ability to go slow.

He left her mouth and trailed his tongue across her chin, down the soft flesh of her neck until he reached the hollow of her throat. He dipped the tip of this tongue into sweet divot

Married to Maggie

then gently nipped with his teeth. Maggie squirmed and her moans increased. The realization that she wanted him as much as he wanted her was overwhelming. She arched into him and his body responded with an uncontrollable thrust against her belly.

"Make love to me, Ty," Maggie whispered so quietly that he wasn't sure he'd heard right. Gently nipping her skin along her collarbone, he worked his way to her ear. He licked the curve and then pulled at the lobe with his lips.

"I want you so much, Maggie," he finally said in a voice strained with passion. Maggie thrashed and made soft sounds of want. Finally, she tenderly mumbled, "Take me now before I think of a dozen reasons why you shouldn't."

"Soon, sweetheart." He was incapable of saying more. Ty lowered his head to her breasts and was about to take her distended nipple into his mouth when a loud, piercing noise cut through the dense haze of desire.

Ty rose up with a groan.

The noise came again. And again. And again. It took a few seconds to realize it was the apartment intercom system.

Ty cursed. Someone would be missing a head in short order. "Sorry, Maggie." He grudgingly removed his hands from her breasts and pecked her mouth on his way to answer the intercom to stop whoever was relentlessly hitting the buzzer.

"Yeah?" he growled.

"Mr. Vincent, you have guests." Joseph the doorman, sounded irritated and nervous.

"Guests that keep ringing the buzzer even though you advised them to stop?" There were only two people brazen enough to ignore Joseph.

"Umm…"

Ty was tempted to tell Joseph to send them away but he knew those two hooligans would make things difficult and wouldn't go away. Joseph didn't deserve the scene they'd make,

which left Ty only one option. "Thank you. Send them up."
He heard the bathroom door close.
Damn. Double damn.

Chapter Six

Maggie splashed water on her face and looked in the bathroom mirror. Reflecting back was a woman with kiss-swollen lips and flushed cheeks. She closed her eyes, crisscrossed her arms across her chest and dropped her head back. She'd removed her shirt, gave Ty access to her breasts and moaned loud enough to alert the entire building. Had she lost her mind? Yes. She sure did. And dammit, it had been premeditated insanity.

How had her life gotten to the point where nothing made sense and where she no longer recognized the woman who used to be mostly reserved; the woman who would've laughed at the prospect of being linked to wealth, the woman who was so guarded she wouldn't have lowered her fences for people like T. Loy Vincent, I, and T. Loy Vincent, III, to step over to separately offer her a deal, the woman who could now be considered a scam artist? She winced at the transformation and how it happened in such a short amount of time. Had there always been a bad girl lurking inside?

Familiar voices permeated the bathroom door.

A low hiss slithered up from her chest and out her throat. She was so not in the mood for Quinn Randel and Victoria Caye. She'd have to put up with those two at the party tonight and she really didn't need an advanced sample of their snobbery.

A rap on the door made her jump. "Maggie?"

"Just a sec." She flushed the toilet even though she hadn't used it, washed her hands and wedged the door open an inch to make a face at Ty.

"We have guests."

"You mean pests."

Ty fixed his weight against the door easing it open despite Maggie's efforts to keep him out. "If I have to put up with them, so do you." He put his pearly white teeth together in a grin prompting Maggie to wrinkle her nose. Ty tugged her into his chest and kissed the top of her head. "Come on, fiancée. Show me what you're made of."

She suddenly had to pee.

Ty looped her arm through his and made her join their guests in the living room.

"Quinn, Tori," she said, forcing a smile. "Good to see you again." Pulling loose from Ty, Maggie planted her bottom in an arm chair since their uninvited visitors occupied the couch. Ty sat in the adjacent chair. From her peripheral she could see him slanting glances her way. Was he still as physically revved up as she was? The sweet ache of desire made her constantly shift in the chair. She tried to home in on Quinn and Victoria, but her eyes wanted no part of them. While she looked straight ahead her thoughts went back to minutes earlier when wanting Ty with every breath she took superseded everything else.

A cackle from Tori distracted her pleasured reminiscing.

"You don't waste any time do you?" Tori's voice was filled with the same annoying sarcasm and indictment as the night before.

Maggie wasn't exactly sure what Tori was referring to but the guilt of her circumstances helped her compile some answers that sadly had to be left unsaid – *yes* she'd moved into

Married to Maggie

Ty's life like she had a right to be there, *yes* she'd be marrying him after only knowing him a week, *and yes* she knew she had all the markings of a gold digger. She leveled an intense stare at the platinum blonde. "Apparently, I don't."

Tori motioned to Maggie's shirt. "It's inside out."

"She just finished her belly dancing class at the gym and we came back here to relax before tonight's shindig," Ty said. It was a logical explanation for the dressing snafu, but Quinn and Tori weren't stupid. He was sure they knew exactly what had been going on and interrupted anyway. But he didn't give a rat's ass what they knew or thought they knew; Maggie obviously did as evidenced by the heightened shade of pink in her cheeks and neck. He hopped from the chair, grabbed the water pitcher from the small fridge behind the bar and topped off Maggie's glass with more cold water. Someone needed to dump the rest of the pitcher on him because he was still warm all over for Maggie, which made it hard to be friendly to Quinn and Tori.

"Mind if I help myself to a beer?" Quinn didn't wait for an answer. He shuffled to the fridge. He uncapped a bottle and downed most of it in one greedy swallow. "Ahhh. Nothing like a cold beer on a hot day." He smacked his lips. "Can I get you one, Ty?"

Ty nodded. He might just need a dozen to put up with these two.

Tori flicked her nails to get her fiancé's attention.

"What can I get you, hon?"

"Wine."

"Shouldn't you two be working?" What a laugh. Quinn and Tori didn't work. They had positions. Even that was a bit of stretch. Quinn's dad owned a chain of cleaning companies that catered to high-rise businesses and condominium complexes. One of the companies cleaned his apartment. Quinn was the Chief Financial Officer, at least in title. Mostly he pawned the bulk of the job off to two eager beaver flunkies who would do cartwheels if he asked. Tori, on the other hand, was heir to a cosmetic fortune and allegedly managed corporate communications for the family's empire. *Right*. Tori occasionally showed up to the office and sat at her desk long enough to delegate her duties too. Sadly, Ty had fallen into the same pattern so it was hard to fault them for their lack of real work when he was just as bad. Although, he was trying to correct his behavior.

"Duh. Helloooo. This is your week, buddy. You're getting married and we wanted to see if there's anything we could do to help out." Quinn sounded sincere. He returned to the living room with a glass of wine in one hand and three bottles of beer in the crook of his arm.

Ty volleyed his attention between Maggie and Quinn, waiting for Maggie to join the conversation. She was strangely silent. A sweet pink blush still coated her cheeks and her amazing lips were still plumped from their kissing. If Quinn and Tori hadn't barged in… Ty stopped the thought. If he let his mind dwell on what he and Maggie had done and where they were headed before being interrupted, he would have difficulty holding a lucid conversation with his friends. "It's going to be a small wedding," he said, not wanting to tune back into Quinn, but he had no choice, "with a small reception."

Quinn's snort said he knew that was a load of hooey. "You're a Vincent. Nothing in your life will ever be small, Loy won't allow it." Was that a warning to Maggie? Or just peer heckling? Quinn downed the contents of yet another bottle in a few swallows. "By the way, you haven't asked me to stand up for you."

Ty mimicked Quinn by finishing his beer and uncapping a fresh one. "We haven't discussed the particulars of our wedding."

Quinn put his legs up on the coffee table and crossed them at the ankles. "Put me down for best man. I suppose

Maggie will want Tori as her maid of honor."

Holy mother of assumption! Ty's gaze rushed to Maggie. He watched her take a sip of water, stare at them through the refraction of the glass and then set the glass down with a clunk.

"You would make a lovely maid of honor, Tori, but if I bypass my best friend Nancy for the favored spot, my name will be mud." There was a no-way-in-hell quality to her tone and Ty had to squelch a laugh.

Tori's expression was priceless. She looked like she couldn't believe Maggie had the audacity to consider someone else.

Ty was pleased that Maggie showed Tori she wouldn't yield to sucking up to win her over.

"Of course you should ask your best friend," Tori said as though she was relieved. Ty knew she wasn't.

Thank God the security buzzer sounded again.

Ty vaulted out of the chair. "Yes, Joseph?"

"Miss Justine has arrived."

He'd forgotten about Justine. Shit. It wasn't a good time for Jus to arrive with a dress for Maggie and there was no subtle, easy way to put her off until later. "Send her up."

"Justine Perthie? From the Galleria?" Tori seemed to come alive. Maggie, on the other hand, slinked down in the chair.

"Yes," Ty replied tightly. "My godmother."

"Oh right. I keep forgetting that she's a friend of your mom." Tori's blonde brows arched as high as they could go. "Didn't she help you dress Rachel Montaigne a few weeks back?"

Ty caught a fleeting look of surprise, and possibly hurt, flash through Maggie's eyes.

The air around them was instantly charged with ions of unease, haughty triumph, regret, you name it. Ty sliced Tori with a firm look of irritation. He couldn't look at Maggie. While he hadn't done anything wrong, he felt like an ass. He didn't make a habit of clothing the women he dated; it was just a stroke of luck – bad luck, it would seem – that he'd needed Justine's services prior to meeting Maggie. He should probably explain that he'd asked Rachel Montaigne to accompany him to an important company dinner and she'd whined about not having anything to wear, but dammit, what happened two weeks ago or two months ago, shouldn't matter.

* * *

Tears burned behind Maggie's eyes and she willed them to stay hidden. She had no reason to cry. It was just nerves from having lost her head by almost sleeping with Ty. Thank goodness for the snobby intruders. Their untimely appearance was actually well-timed. If they had been five minutes later, she and Ty would've... Maggie clenched her hands into fists. Ty Vincent was one hundred percent playboy and she needed to keep that in mind at all times. Instead of getting caught up in his web of smoothness, she would be wise to repeat over and over in her head that everything that happened between had to stay at the business level. No sweet words. No kissing. No sleeping together. No being alone for any reason. And if he wanted to clothe every woman in Dallas, Houston, El Paso or Texarkana, he could and she wouldn't so much as frown.

Maggie straightened her spine and tried to appear excited for the dress Justine would soon deliver. A small knock at the door made her jerk, even though it was expected.

Ty opened the door and hugged a short, dark-haired woman with reading glasses hanging from a chain at her chest.

Maggie had anticipated someone younger, smartly dressed, with a tipped up nose and too much poise. Instead, Justine wore a pair of elastic waist blue jeans and a white tee embroidered with colorful butterflies. When the woman smiled warmly some of the tension in Maggie's shoulders let go.

Maggie soon discovered that Ty had a way with not only women his age, but also those with a few years on them; Rosie and now Justine. She decided she would need to be on her guard every minute. If she wasn't, she'd fall prey to his charm too and end up being just another conquest. Sleeping with him would be incredible, she was sure, but she couldn't risk the pleasure. In six months they would part ways. Ty would be in the driver's seat of a multi-billion dollar enterprise and she'd go back to being Maggie Gray. When it was time to walk away, she wanted to do it with her head held high and most everything intact. Her dignity had been shredded, but her heart was still basically in one piece and she needed for it to stay that way.

"Maggie," Ty said, snapping her from her reverie, "Justine."

Maggie met curious blue-grey eyes. "It's nice to meet you."

"Likewise, Maggie." Justine surprised her with a half-hug. "Congratulations on your engagement to Tysen. He's quite a catch."

Maggie couldn't look at Ty. Not now. Not when her emotions were so scrambled. "Thank you." She toyed with her engagement ring and deliberately omitted agreeing that Ty was a catch. She was still trying to come to grips that Ty dressed his women. It was bizarre and something only the rich would consider doing. She'd never fit into his world, not even for six months.

Justine squeezed Maggie's hand and whispered something in her ear.

Maggie's eyes shot to Ty's. They were filled with question. Hers were filling with the tears that she'd ordered to stay away. She tried to disguise her distress with a smile. "I know," she said to Justine.

"Excellent! Now let's check out the dress I brought for you." Justine unzipped the garment bag to reveal a simple, sleeveless dress in basic black. "This stretchy little number will highlight your hourglass figure while supporting your sweet spots. Every man in the room, including Tysen, will be standing in a puddle of drool." She winked at Ty. "Maggie will soon be the talk of the town and the men will be pawing to be near her."

"Tell me about it," Ty said.

Maggie was well aware of the four people waiting for her reaction. "Not."

Justine patted her on the back. "Go see if it fits, dear, but don't give us a preview, save the vision for tonight when you make your debut."

"You're the best," Maggie said with quiet appreciation. She hurried down the hall and was almost to the bathroom when she heard Tori tender her opinion.

"She's going to meet the world in THAT?"

Expecting Justine to put Tori in her place, she was surprised when Ty beat her to it. "Maggie could make burlap look good, so shut your yapper."

Maggie was torn between smiling and crying, and as soon as she verified that the dress fit and thanked Justine for rushing it over, she was out of there.

* * *

Dressed in a black Hugo Boss suit and diamond-patterned fuchsia tie, Ty paced back and forth on the red brick pavers of his grandfather's circular driveway, sweating like someone turned a garden hose on him. He tugged at his shirt collar, checked his watch for the umpteenth time and messed with the small gold Vincent Oil Company tie tack. He grumbled about the tie. Guys didn't wear fuchsia. According to Justine, it was the right amount of accent to break up the black. He was tempted to yank the darn thing off and open the first few buttons of his shirt. Justine wouldn't care. His grandfather, however, would read him the riot act about looking the part of a billionaire's grandson.

Where were Bostwick and Maggie? They were supposed to be there ten minutes ago. Guests wanting to brown-nose his grandfather before the grand soiree were starting to arrive and Ty was directing them to the back of the estate where an attendant would park their car – there was a sign to go around to the back, but it was ignored since Ty was practically standing in their way. "Come on, Maggie. Get your butt here." When she'd left his apartment earlier there had been a disturbing glint in her eyes that made him worry she might ditch the event. He pulled his cell phone from his suit coat pocket and started to compile a text message. The classy purr of a limousine approaching made him snap the phone closed. To his dismay, it was a Super Stretch Escalade, one of the more elaborate limos on the market with seating for sixteen. Occupied by only a driver and one of the Board members, Ty gestured for the luxury car to proceed to the rear of the mansion.

A flashy black sports car sped up the drive. Before the vehicle reached Ty, the driver stomped hard on the brakes to squeal the tires and leave a black mark on the pavers. A gritty noise snarled from the back of Ty's throat. "Speaking of brown-nosers."

Terron Wade turned off the engine, stepped out of the car like he was royalty and tossed Ty the keys.

"I'm not a parking attendant," Ty silently added *"prick"*, and threw the keys over his shoulder where they landed in a row of crape myrtle bushes.

Terron rolled his eyes, retrieved the keys and brushed the sleeves of his Armani suit coat. "That was mature."

"Can't you read?" Ty gestured to the parking instruction sign.

Terron didn't spare the sign a glance. "You know, Ty,

you're not fooling anyone with this hasty marriage. It's a desperate move to win over the Board." His laugh was sharp and mocking. "They're not stupid. They know as well as you and I that six months down the road you'll be in divorce court."

Terron always hit a nerve. This time, he hit several. Ty clenched his fists at his side. If this wasn't an extra special event, he'd pound the bastard into the ground.

"You'll still be the irresponsible piece of work you were before you pressured some clueless no-name into becoming your wife." Terron squared his shoulders and tipped his overconfident chin in the air. "When I head up this company, you'll be standing in the unemployment line." He leveled a glacial-blue look of hate on Ty.

Temper surged in Ty's chest. "Her name is Maggie, dickhead." He was tempted to give the door of the expensive car a swift kick. With his luck, Terron would record the *irresponsible* act with his phone and play it at the next board meeting. "Move that hunk of metal before I flatten the tires."

"Just remember that when the Board approves me and not you, you're out." Terron climbed into his car and stuck his middle finger out the window before revving his engine and driving away.

Anger surged through Ty so hard he felt like any second he would explode. He paced again, with sharp, jerky steps, while he cussed the jackal who had called Maggie a clueless no-name. The sixth month divorce comment had him plenty pissed too. Terron's private threats to remove him from the company always messed with his head, but now the weasel had gone for his jugular by involving Maggie. Ty had been well aware that Terron was trying to draw him into a physical altercation and it had taken all his strength not to punch the jackass's nose so far into his head that it would take a high-grade suction cup to pull it back out. For a handful of reasons he couldn't so much as trip the bastard – it would ruin the party, Maggie would have a hissy fit that things had gotten violent, his grandfather would come unglued that one of his favorite employees had been assaulted...on his property...by his grandson, no less.

Ty sighed long and hard at the realization that he'd given Terron the upper hand a year ago. He'd been so consumed with the grief of losing his dad that he didn't care what happened. At one point, he almost walked away from everything – the company, his grandfather, the world. He'd booked a flight to the Caribbean and intended to live out his days as a beach bum, drinking beer and soaking up the sun. On his way to the airport that day, something deep inside made him turn around. Ty liked to think it was his dad that kept him from doing anything drastic. Although, marrying for convenience rather than love blew beyond drastic. Marrying Maggie was not only drastic, it was necessary. Maggie was traction. She would help him regain his footing. With Maggie Gray by his side, the possibilities were endless. He'd once again be seen as the level-headed grandson of Loy Vincent. The powers-to-be would finally know the real Tysen Vincent. A true Texan. A shark in a sea of oil. A man of steel who had a soft spot for family.

Maggie would be family.

Ty pushed a bead of sweat from his brow. How would he ever be able to watch Maggie walk out of his life?

A familiar black limousine came through the intricate wrought-iron gates at the end of the drive and a loud whoosh of relief rolled from Ty's chest.

The limo seemed to creep up the drive. "Bostwick, press the damn gas pedal." When the car finally came to a rest in front of the mansion, Ty yanked open the door. "Maggie," he said, trying to play it cool, failing miserably.

"Tysen."

The use of his full name made him lift an eyebrow. Something was definitely bothering Maggie. She'd acted strange after Tori opened her mouth about him dressing Rachel Montaigne. Was Maggie jealous? She shouldn't be. He wasn't marrying Rachel, he was marrying her. He muffled a groan. Why did some women take a smidgen of information and twist it until it was so much more. He sighed. Maggie probably imagined that he dressed his women for certain events only to undress them when the sun went down and then tossed them away in the morning. The truth hit home – he wasn't imagined scum, he was the real deal; slimy froth dressed in Hugo Boss. The facts were there – he'd dressed Maggie for the evening, would've slept with her had Quinn and Tori stayed away and had a set date to toss her aside. He smiled anyway and took her hand to help her from the limo. In the process, he got an eyeful of cleavage and his body responded with a tightening in his groin. Yeah, he was scum alright. "You look beautiful!" Justine had said the men at the party would be pawing to be near Maggie. So true. He would have to protect her from all other slimy froths.

"Thank you. It was all Justine." She pulled her hand away and smoothed the front of her dress.

Ty ran his eyes up and down Maggie. "No, honey, it's all you."

Maggie started to smile but stopped.

"I'm sorry if I hurt your feelings earlier. I can be insensitive sometimes," Ty said.

Maggie waved off the apology but her tone was cool. "You're fine. I overreacted. I have no idea why."

Ty wouldn't let the encounter with Terron crimp his mood. He wouldn't let Maggie's glacial chill do it either. Tonight was supposed to be special, and dammit, it was going to be special. He looked away and took a deep breath. He returned to Maggie and caressed her with his eyes. "I know why," he said, pulling her into the circle of his arms.

"Ty..." Maggie started to resist.

His grandfather made a sudden appearance. "Hey, you two, let's take this inside. We're supposed to have a short meeting before the party begins, in case you forgot."

Ty laid his forehead against Maggie's. "When the party's over, we need to renegotiate our agreement. And I want to know what Justine whispered to you."

Maggie's heart thumped in fast, broken rhythm; possibly an S.O.S. "What do you want to renegotiate?" She had an idea what he wanted because it was the same thing she wanted. In no way could they act on all that want. Want was delicious. It was powerful. Those under the influence sometimes had difficulty making the right decisions. If she gave into it, who knows what would happen. She already had lowered resistance when it came to Ty, giving him her body would mean giving him her heart too. She doubted he wanted both. If she was smart she'd put an end to Ty's mind boggling kisses. The groping had to stop too. And she couldn't allow an amendment to the original agreement. It was six months. No sex. No telling each other what to do. That was it. If he couldn't live with the restrictions he'd set, too bad. Sharing what Justine had said wouldn't happen either, mostly because it wasn't true.

Ty's mouth dimpled at the corners. "Just be ready to say yes."

"I wouldn't hold my breath if I were you." Maggie snickered with sarcasm.

Instead of taking them through the front door where the glass was etched with spindletop oil wells, Ty led the way to a side entrance that required a code so it wouldn't set off an alarm when opened.

Maggie's mouth unhinged at the jaw when she stepped inside. She knew the place was incredible because she'd searched the internet ahead of time. An up-close look at the lavish surroundings was beyond words. It was a to-die-for residence, yet she still couldn't grasp how anyone could live in a place with ten bedrooms, seven fireplaces, a Turkish spa, indoor and outdoor swimming pools, a party room big enough to qualify as an event center, a wine cellar, a theater with seating for a hundred, three separate guest houses, a tennis court, and jogging track, all situated on fifty acres of prime Dallas real estate thick with Texas ash, cedar elms, and desert willows.

"This place takes my breath away."

"It's just a house, Maggie."

"Riiiight."

"The only way you'll get through the evening is to tell yourself that it's just stuff. In my opinion, that's all it is."

"Easier said than done, mister." Maggie's chuckle was skimpy.

Ty lifted his wrist to expose his watch. "If we're not in the den in the next minute, he'll get cranky."

At the end of a long hallway, was a set of heavy wooden doors. Waiting in front of them was Rosie. In their short acquaintance, Maggie decided she liked the old gal who had an unrelenting crafty glint in her eyes.

"Tysen, you look as handsome as ever," Rosie said, stretching up to kiss his cheek. "Maggie, you look stunning." She leaned in to kiss Maggie on the side of the head. "You make a handsome couple if I do say so myself."

"Thank you, Rosie," Maggie replied humbly.

Ty let loose of Maggie's hand so he could wrap Rosie in a bear hug. "You're the best."

After the hug, Rosie pulled something from her pocket. "I've printed name cards for the tables." She grinned impishly and held up a bottle of White-Out. "I've had a little fun."

"What did you do?" Ty asked.

"You'll find out soon enough." Rosie's eyes shimmered with mischief and her laugh was just as devious. "Terron struts around like he's God's gift to the world. Someone has to put the egghead in his place."

Ty pecked Rosie's forehead with a kiss. "I do love you."

"I know, Tysen. I love you too." Rosie winked. "I wouldn't misbehave for just anyone, ya know." She opened the doors to the den. "Your grandfather is waiting." With a squeeze to Maggie's hand she whispered, "Breathe, dear girl."

Maggie would probably need a canister of oxygen pumping through her lungs to get them to work since everything regarding her future husband seemed to rob her of air. In a word, the Vincents made breathing difficult.

Loy Vincent sat behind a mammoth mahogany desk. "Finally." He sprang out of the chair and came around the desk to greet them. He shook Ty's hand, then Maggie's. He kept a hold of her hand and smiled warmly. "Soooo, this is the love of your life?"

Maggie would certainly be given an Oscar in the category for best supporting scammer; Loy would definitely get one for Best Actor in a family drama series. His look of curiosity and surprise was a sell. If she didn't know the circumstances she would've thought this was the first time they'd met.

Loy lifted her hand to his lips. "You're lovelier than your picture, sweet Maggie."

Maggie felt a blush coat her cheeks. "Why thank you, Mr. Vincent."

"Call me Loy."

"Loy," Maggie repeated. "It's great to meet you." Every muscle in her body tensed, every nerve twitched. Although it was a spacious office complete with a wall of books, a fireplace big enough to stand in and countless windows to bring in natural light, the room suddenly felt small and stuffy. Being with Ty and Loy in the same space was a threat to her equilibrium. One tiny slipup and she'd be pegged as a two-timing, money-grubbing con artist. Or she'd pass out.

Loy motioned for them to have a seat. He sat in his high-back leather chair again and clapped his hands together. "Time to run a few things by you. First of all, tonight is a celebration. My only grandchild has found the woman of his dreams."

Maggie expected Ty to cough at the comment. He didn't.

Loy pinned Maggie with a smile that only partially reached his eyes. "It's also a test of strength. You'll be smothered with attention. You'll be pulled at, tugged on, whispered to and whispered about. Stand your ground, Maggie Gray. Draw a line in the sand. Give the people of Dallas only what you want them to know. Cameras and cell phones will capture the evening, so if someone ticks you off, smile. If you're uncomfortable, smile. You get my drift. Smile, smile, smile."

Ty shook his head. "Seriously?"

"Tysen, you're used to the limelight, Maggie isn't. She needs to know what she'll be up against."

"No disrespect, Granddad, but Maggie needs to be herself. Trying to do everything just right is too much pressure. Besides, people can spot a fake from five feet away."

Fake. The word was as grating as fingernails on a chalkboard. It described her to a tee. She *was* a fake and the second she joined the party, everyone would know. Her subconscious pushed her to confess, right now, before it was too late. Maggie opened her mouth to speak but nothing came out. She tried again, still nothing.

"That's where you and I differ, Tysen. You have to prep people to deal with circumstances. If you blindside them, the damage can be staggering." Loy continued to talk but Maggie's brain latched onto 'the damage can be staggering' – five potent words that churned the contents of her stomach and made bile rise in her throat.

Loy and Tysen's differences of opinion became loud and heated. Loy accused Ty of never listening to the voice of reason. Tysen charged that his grandfather tried to control everything and everyone around him. Maggie noticed that Loy's face and neck had turned maroon; a sure sign that his blood pressure had escalated to a dangerous level. He should be protecting his heart, not priming it for another attack. The bossy nurse emerged. "Settle down," she said authoritatively, squinting with criticism. "You look like you're about to blow a gasket, Loy. And Tysen, constantly going against the grain is harmful to both of you. Plus it's exactly what the press is dying to print." She squinted harder. "I'm excited to become a member of this family," she hesitated while the truth sank in. She *was* excited. Scared on so many levels, but excited. "But if there's going to be nonstop chaos then forget it. I can handle the people of Dallas and the paparazzi, what I can't and won't handle is the two of you fighting."

Loy's aged blue eyes grew wide and he went slack jawed. Thankfully, his color lessened to a less harmful shade of red.

Tysen's dazzling and slightly arrogant eyes also doubled in size. "Wait a minute, Maggie, you can't..."

Maggie cut him off. "Yes I can." She stood up and hooked gazes with Loy. "You said to stand my ground. You meant where everyone else is concerned. I think it applies to the two of you as well. If you're going to go at each other like this, I'm walking out that door."

To her surprise, Loy started to laugh. "Well, well, well. Beautiful *and* a backbone." He leaned back in his chair. "You're a lucky man, Tysen."

Tysen stared at Maggie like she had some nerve. The look she returned let him know she had at least one nerve – and they were getting on it.

"Yes I am." Ty's mouth bowed into a smile. The edges of Maggie's mouth didn't bow, not even a little.

Chapter Seven

"Mr. Tysen Vincent and Miss Maggie Gray," sounded through the party room's built-in, amplified speaker system so clearly that everyone was forced to stop what they were doing and set probing eyes on the guests of honor. The leader of the band hired to play dinner music announced their names a second time in case someone in the bathroom, or within a fifty mile radius, had missed the broadcast. Too bad Rosie hadn't messed with speaker wires instead of whatever she'd done with the White-Out. Ty smiled and gave a small wave. Maggie followed his lead. Instantly, they were walled-in by the crowd.

Rachel Montaigne pushed her way into the center and was the first to offer congratulations with a smile that didn't reach her eyes. "Tysen. Maggie. I'm so happy for you."

About as happy as a grizzly bear that had a trout yanked from his grip. Ty introduced Maggie to the woman who wanted to be Mrs. Tysen Vincent, III, more than anything else in the world. "Maggie Gray, Rachel Montaigne."

He felt Maggie stiffen and saw a flash of recognition fire through her eyes. Maggie looked down at her dress and then her gaze slid to Rachel's. Ty wanted to say something comforting but there was no chance of that happening.

"Nice to meet you, Rachel," Maggie said, with a good-

Married to Maggie

natured expression pasted on her face. Ty was sure there was nothing good natured running through her thoughts.

"Rumor has it that you and Ty have only known each other since Friday," Rachel spat in more ways than one. Spittle hit Ty's face. The people around them gasped from the comment. "And now you're getting married? Tell me it isn't true. I mean, really. Ty you'd never do anything so impulsive."

Where in the hell was everyone getting their information? When Ty found out who the leak was, he was going to beat them to a pulp.

Maggie didn't waver. "For appearances sake, it would seem that we've only known each other a short time." She put her hand on her heart. "Anyone in love can tell you that they've forever known the person they are meant to be with."

Ty was blown away by the remark.

A crease formed between Rachel's perfectly plucked eyebrows. "Huh?"

A dark-haired guy standing next to Rachel clarified Maggie's comment. "As soon as you saw Tysen you knew you were in love. You knew he was the one. Aww, that's so sweet."

Maggie grinned from ear to ear. "It's true, Dad."

Ty thrust out his hand but caught himself before he said, "Happy to meet you, Mr. Gray". He couldn't let the onlookers and gossipers know that he was meeting his future father-in-law for the first time.

Richland Gray winked. "I'll have a beer with you later, son."

"Sounds like a plan."

Rachel coughed to grab the spotlight again and made a face like she'd been forced to swallow a tablespoon of dirt. "You knew right away that he was the one? That's the stupidest thing I've ever heard." She used her elbows to part the crowd so she could stomp off.

Maggie clutched Ty's hand with a death grip. It was a sign

she needed him; maybe not forever, but she did right now. He pondered the fib she'd told that she loved him the moment she set eyes on him. It was a disturbing thought.

One by one, he introduced his future wife. Everyone, with the exception of Rachel, was abundantly interested in the newbie. Maggie adapted well. She handled herself with poise and graciously answered their questions. And she smiled.

The band leader again took the microphone. "Dinner is served. Please find your places. They're marked with name cards."

"You're doing excellent, Maggie," Ty whispered.

"Tell that to my quaking knees."

One side of the large room was filled with round tables covered with white linen table cloths edged in white satin, deep purple cloth napkins and candles shimmering in small crystal votive cups. Vases of fresh cut lavender roses sat in the center of each table as the focal point. Loy certainly had style and Maggie was in awe.

They made their way toward a table with a much larger vase of flowers. Ty drew them to a halt in front of one table in particular and pointed to a specific name card. He laughed at Rosie's modification. Terron Wade was now *Terror* Wade.

Maggie felt the hair on her arms prickle, although she had no idea why. She soon got her answer. A tall guy with piercing blue eyes invaded their space. He was reasonably attractive with perfectly gelled dark hair, blinding white teeth and a grey-striped Armani suit. Despite his striking appearance there was something instantly off-putting about him. Maybe it was the blend of too much cologne and hair product. Or maybe the arrogant set of his shoulders.

Ty's laughter died away and was replaced with a look of disdain.

"What the..." The guy snatched the name card from the table and tore it in half. "Laugh at that, jerkwad." He stuffed the pieces of card into Ty's coat pocket.

Terror Wade, no less. Maggie inadvertently mumbled, "Hmm," drawing his attention.

Terron met her eyes before shifting his attention to her chest.

Maggie wanted to impale his foot with her four inch heels. Remembering Loy's words, she smiled.

Terron took his time meeting her eyes again. "A word of advice, get out while you can."

Ty squared off in front of his archenemy. Maggie stepped between them. If she couldn't spear Terron with her heels, Ty couldn't drill him with his fists. "It's time to eat," she said.

Terron was the first to back away.

Maggie put her hand into Ty's. The gesture seemed to calm him down. He tightened his hand around hers. "It's our engagement party, lover boy, no fights allowed." She'd dropped her voice for his ears only but someone beside them had a keen sense of hearing.

"That's right. No fights."

Maggie turned to find Ellen Peppersmith-Vincent. Curiosity beamed between them. She quickly noted that the countless pictures that peppered the newspapers for years had not done Ty's mom justice. Ellen was eye-catching beautiful with strawberry-blonde hair and intelligent blue eyes. She had flawless skin and was built to perfection. No wonder Ty was so gorgeous. He'd had a drop-dead handsome father and an even more stunning mother. "Hello," Maggie said, suddenly more nervous than when she was immersed in the crowd of socialites.

"Mom, this is Maggie."

Ellen's expression was unreadable at first, then a small smile. "Happy to meet the woman who has finally won my son's heart."

Maggie froze in place. She had Ty's hand, not his heart.

She decided in that moment that she couldn't lie to his mother; not for all the money in the world. If Ellen Peppersmith-Vincent flat out asked if she and Ty's relationship was solid and true, Maggie would discreetly reveal the facts and then numbly watch her world unravel. "He's easy to love, Mrs. Vincent." Ty's mouth dropped open. Ellen pulled back a fraction of an inch like Maggie had disclosed something shocking. Maggie felt a hot blush rush to her face.

People gawked and walked around them to locate their tables while Ellen studied her further. "Please, call me Ellen." She leaned into Maggie with her shoulder. "Sometime we need to have coffee." Ellen raised eyebrows at her son. She did the same to Maggie. "So we can talk about what it will take to be a Vincent. I'm a poor one to offer advice, Maggie, but if you're willing to listen, I'm willing to share."

Ty groaned.

"Coffee it is," Maggie quipped joyfully.

"Great." Ellen looped an arm through Maggie's and one through Ty's. "Let's be seated before your grandfather blows a blood vessel." She nodded to where Loy stood with a prominent vein bulging in his forehead, pretending he wasn't annoyed.

Maggie had known Loy long enough to recognize that he was being driven to madness by their delay, and quite possibly by the presence of his former daughter-in-law. She also knew she'd discover Loy and Ellen's relationship in short order.

"Loy," Ellen said without a hint of friendliness.

Loy returned the greeting with the same level of goodwill. "Ellen."

Sweet, Maggie thought. She'd have to tread carefully so she wouldn't alienate Ellen by being overly congenial to Loy and also so she wouldn't tick off Loy by being too friendly to Ellen. She quietly sighed. When the night was over she was going to open a bottle of whiskey. She hated the taste but she needed its effect in a big way.

* * *

Ty had grudgingly released Maggie to his mother's care. Girl talk his mother had said. So why was he worried to have the two of them together? It wasn't like Maggie would nark him out regarding their less-than-real marriage because it would not only make him look bad but her as well. Maybe it was more that she would unconsciously say something to make his mom suspicious. His mom would understand their plan if it was exposed; she wouldn't like it, but she would understand. She knew only too well what it took to stay in good graces with T. Loy Vincent, I, and wouldn't judge Ty accordingly. She would, however, judge Maggie – that bothered the hell out of him.

He bellied up to the bar while keeping his radar locked on his women. "More," he said, handing his empty glass to Kylee, a friend and barmaid from Sam Bright's bar. Kylee made extra money as part of Sam's bar staff rental service.

"Scotch, I assume?" She asked.

Ty grinned. "Yep." When the drink was sat before him, he downed it in one swallow. "Hit me again."

"Whatever you say, Ty. Don't blame me in the morning when your tongue has grown fur." Kylee produced another glass and then wandered to the opposite end of the bar to fill another drink request.

Quinn and Tori joined Ty.

Tori blocked his view of Maggie. "Sorry we're late. We just left the hospital. My grandmother had another spell."

"Sorry to hear. Is she going to be okay?"

"She'll be fine. They're going to up her blood pressure meds."

Quinn scanned the room. "What did we miss?"

Ty moved so he could keep an eye on Maggie and then

distractedly answered Quinn. "Terron got a dose of Rosie."

Quinn made a weird sound when he turned to order drinks. Ty swung around to see what caused it. "What?" Ty asked.

"Oh nothing."Quinn's expression was a dead giveaway.

Tori sliced her fiancée with a mean look before doing the same to the buxom blonde behind the bar. "Don't even think about it, Quinn," she hissed angrily.

"No idea what you're talking about." Quinn leaned on the bar. "I'll have a gin and tonic, Kylee."

Tori used the pointy toe of her shoe on Quinn's shin and stomped off to blend in with the crowd.

"Trouble in paradise?"

"Always." Quinn focused on Kylee again with a flirty grin.

"No, Quinn," Ty said under his breath. If Tori saw Quinn give Kylee the eye again things would get ugly.

Quinn raised and lowered his eyebrows, took a drink of his gin and tonic and withdrew his attention from behind the bar when Kylee seemed more interested in cleaning beer mugs than him. "What happened with Rosie and Terron?"

Ty turned his back to the bar so he could scan the room for Maggie. He spied her and his mom laughing it up with one of his buddies, Trigg Sinclair. Satisfied that she was fine, he explained Rosie's White-Out prank to Quinn.

Quinn cracked up laughing. "Priceless."

"Yep."

A crowd of people worked their way in front of Maggie. Ty fidgeted until they moved. In the blink of an eye, his fiancée was gone. He watched Trigg walk away too when the socialite from hell cornered his mom. "Be back in a few."

"Mom," he said, approaching from the side. Ty didn't wait for the dreadful woman to stop yapping. He slung an arm around his mom's shoulders. "Hate to steal you away, but the caterer really needs to speak with you." His mom grinned up at him with silent thanks and scampered away.

"Sorry, Ruth, you know how caterers can be." Ty put his teeth together in a toothy smile and left before she could rope him in with conversation.

Now, where the hell was Maggie?

He worked his way through the crowd.

"Ty, my boy." Trigg Sinclair popped out of a circle of guys and grabbed his arm. "Let's talk bachelor party. Golfing, maybe?" He laughed, almost spilling his drink. "Day trip to the Caribbean? Strippers? Tell me what ya want, buddy."

Ty was too distracted to enjoy the company. "Can't talk right now, Trigg. Call me and we'll set something up. Right now I have to find my woman. I promised not to leave her alone since she doesn't know anyone."

Trigg's eyes flickered with amusement. "I met Maggie. She's hot, man. How'd you get so lucky?"

Ty slapped Trigg on the back. "I have no idea." His attention riveted to the top of the winding staircase where he caught a glimpse of a little black dress.

He heavy-stepped it to the stairs only to be stopped again by another close friend, Jake Garrison.

"I can't believe you're getting married, Ty. What's up with that?"

Ty thought about Trigg's remarks regarding Maggie. "It's self-explanatory, Jake. Have you seen her?"

"I have. You scored big."

"'Nuff said."

"Damn, you fell fast."

"It happens." Ty shook Jake's hand and took off up the stairs.

Standing near the door of the nearest bathroom was Maggie. His heart hitched at seeing the woman who would soon be his wife. Voluptuous. Beautiful. Hot Maggie Gray.

It took a few seconds to register that she wasn't alone.

Terron Wade towered over her by a good foot. She smiled up at the buffoon and Ty saw red. In a few long strides he joined them and accused Maggie of treason with his eyes.

Maggie took a clumsy step backwards. Ty advanced forward. "I let you out of my sight for two minutes and I find you with him?"

Maggie puckered her brow. "I'm not *with* Terron."

Ty was so mad he was shaking.

Maggie put her hands on her hips. "Apologize. Now," she commanded without raising her voice, but there was no mistaking the lethal undertone.

"Already fighting. Who could've seen that coming?" Terron mocked with a snide laugh.

Ty dropped the f-bomb under his breath. Twice.

"I'm not kidding, Ty, rescind the accusation." Maggie held steady even though she wanted to scream and pummel him with her fists. Ty watched her through half-closed eyes. She crossed her arms at her chest, determined not to back down. The only reason she didn't tell him to kiss her butt and leave, was that Terron *did* hit on her and she felt guilty of wrongdoing even though she'd done nothing to entice him. The sly fox had had tested her loyalty to Ty by complimenting her on her dress and saying she was complete perfection. Ha! She was about as far from perfect as a woman could be. She could barely walk in the four-inch ankle strap heels, almost twisting an ankle on the way up the stairs. And the dress? While it was incredible, there was far too much of her and not enough dress. She had a few razor nicks around her knees from shaving in a hurry and a pimple was erupting in the center of her forehead. A pimple. Really? She hadn't had one in years. It had to be stress wreaking havoc with her insides and now with her outside. She was perfection all right. Her bullshit meter pegged Terron as one of the biggest and worst BS'ers she'd probably ever meet. As she waited in line for the bathroom, he said he would make a better husband than Ty. She'd laughed at the brainless comment and then Ty showed up, scaring the bejesus out of her.

Maggie gave Ty one last chance to express regret. "You have thirty seconds, mister." Expecting him to hold out until the last millisecond, she was surprised when he softly said, "I'm sorry, Maggie."

Ty's whole demeanor changed in an instant. In pure Vincent style, he took control with a smile that made Maggie go weak in the knees. "I know you're madly in love with me, Maggie. You know it. I know it." He jerked his thumb to Terron. "This dipstick, however, doesn't know anything, and if he doesn't get his candy ass away from you ASAP I'm going to toss him over the banister."

Terron put his hands up in surrender and snickered, but then wagged his finger back and forth from Maggie to Ty. "I know this love thing is a freaking joke, but I'm not about to get in a fist fight over it. Besides, everything will be exposed soon enough." He left without another word.

Ty glowered until Terron was down the stairs.

"We'd better watch out for him, Ty."

Ty took a deep breath and pushed it back out before pulling her into his arms and touching her forehead with his. "Forget about him, Maggie." He claimed her mouth and kissed her slowly and thoroughly. Maggie melted against his chest. She was so caught up in the moment that she vocalized her enjoyment with a moan. Someone tapped her on the shoulder, making her jump. It took a moment to come out of the heavy fog of hunger to realize it was Loy.

"Tysen, Maggie, I get that you're in love, but seriously, you shouldn't be sucking face in public and ignoring your guests."

Maggie and Ty said, "Terron," simultaneously. He'd probably bumped into Loy at the bottom of the steps and narked them out.

Loy shrugged with confirmation. "I don't know what

Terron's deal is lately, but he's starting to get on my nerves."

"Starting to? He's gotten on mine since kindergarten."

Loy dodged further discussion about Terron with a clear directive. "Mingle tonight. Kiss tomorrow."

Maggie grinned. "Sorry. No kissing tomorrow. I promised Nancy we'd spend the day together. By the way, she felt bad that she couldn't make it tonight. She had plans she couldn't get out of. Anyway, tomorrow she and I will be going to belly dancing class, wedding dress and maid of honor shopping, enjoying sushi, and we'll probably finish the day by watching chick flicks and drinking wine."

Loy laid a hand on Ty's shoulder. "You need to show your face at the office tomorrow anyway so we can go over a few things."

Ty didn't look pleased. "We have wedding plans to talk about, Maggie."

Loy cut in again. "Forgot to tell you, I reserved the church and the country club." He smiled at Maggie. "I hope that's okay." As an afterthought, he said, "I'll need a guest list."

If this was an authentic marriage centered on love instead of an arranged alliance, she'd make Loy back off. "That's fine." Maggie winced quietly at the uncertainty rolling through her and how she felt like laughing and crying at the same time. Things were changing between her and Ty at a rapid rate and she didn't know what to make of them or how to slow them down. There was a tug of war going on inside. Part of her was thrilled that their time together was temporary, the other part longed for it to be permanent. She was head over heels in lust with the man; no doubt about it. When he was near, she wanted to kiss him and rip his clothes off. She'd even entertained the possibility that what she felt for him went beyond lust; which was complete hokum. It was just her body reacting to his extreme good looks, his devil-may-care personality and incredible scent. That wasn't love. It was hormones. Maybe the pull of the full moon had something to do with it too. It was shining through the windows like a giant search light.

Maggie decided the only way to stop desire from taking over was to construct a few road blocks. She blinked up at Ty. "On Wednesday, we can finalize our plans and compile a guest list."

"Wednesday?" Ty looked at her like she'd sprouted horns. "It's Sunday, Maggie. I'm not waiting until the middle of the week to see you."

Maggie wouldn't back down. "Tomorrow belongs to Nancy. Tuesday belongs to the soup kitchen and animal shelter. You can have Wednesday."

"Penciling me in, are you? Guess again, almost-wife." Ty's sexy laugh turned Maggie's resolve into a heap of goo and flicked her pilot light to the highest setting. She lowered her eyes and looked up through her lashes. "Wednesday, Ty."

Chapter Eight

Ty tried to concentrate on the pile of legal documents setting in front of him, but his mind was torn a thousand different ways. He'd told Maggie before the party that once it was over they needed to make some changes to their agreement. After the last guest had left, he tried to persuade her to go back to his apartment to talk. She'd sassed him with a reminder that he was on schedule for Wednesday. The wily vixen was doing whatever she damned well pleased and had an ally to back her up. Make that two allies. In front of her father and his grandfather, she'd yawned and said she could barely keep her eyes open.

'Stop smothering her, Tysen,' his grandfather had said. Richland Gray smiled. Richland was a quiet man who watched everything but said little. They'd had that beer as promised, with Maggie anchored between them. Ty refused to let her out of his sight with Terron skulking about waiting for another opportunity to stir up trouble.

Richland, Maggie and Ty had made small talk mostly. At one point, Maggie's father put his hand on Ty's shoulder. "I'm happy to have you as my son-in-law," he'd said.

Ty liked Richland.

What he didn't like was being tag-teamed by two men who

went out of their way to make him give Maggie some space. Wednesday, for crying out loud. Maggie was going to be his wife soon. They had things to discuss. The only way that was going to happen was to spend time together.

The sparkle of victory in Maggie's eyes had been an indication that there was more going on than just exhaustion and he aimed to find out what she was up to. It had better not involve Terron Wade. If he found out... He stopped when he felt his blood pressure rise. Maggie wouldn't join forces with that scumbag. No way in hell. She was a sweetheart that didn't have a complicit bone in her body. His thoughts hung on that conclusion. Maybe Maggie had horns to hold her halo up, but she wouldn't stab him in the back.

Damn insecurities. Good thing his grandfather and the Board members couldn't hear what was going on in his head; they'd know what a mess of a man he really was. Even his mom wasn't privy to certain thoughts. Maggie was a different story. She'd figured him out from the get-go. She knew he had issues. Big issues. In a way, he was glad she knew so he didn't have to pretend to be something he wasn't. If they were going to make this marriage seem real he needed...Ty leaned against the window frame and stared down at the endless traffic forty floors below. He ran his hand over his face while his brain shuffled the words of his last thought; arranging, adding and omitting things, until it was pared down to three simple words – *he needed Maggie*. Ty growled at all the chaos and innermonologue going on inside. It was making him crazy.

His grandfather stuck his head in Ty's office. "Ready?"

Ty was ready all right – for a straight jacket. "Yes." He was hungry for the distraction of work, which would involve formulating a strategy for dealing with the Texas legislature and the public regarding pipelines, eminent domain and environmental issues. Landowners whose land held deep significance to their families were trying to stop the construction of a pipeline that would carry oil across the country. Ty understood their concerns and those of the company. It was a sensitive issue if mishandled would give the company a black eye for a lot of years. He was up to the challenge and would work his hardest to come up with a compromise suitable to both sides. He finally smiled. When it came to business he didn't back away from the tough stuff. He was hit by another profound thought – when it came to matters of the heart, he was the first to cut and run. Relationships qualified as tough stuff, but unlike work, the rules were different and there was no clear path. He'd take work over personal relationships any day.

His cell phone plinked with a message: Having a blast shopping with Maggie and Nancy. Love you, Mom.

"What the...?" What was his mom doing with Maggie?

When he frowned, it prompted his grandfather to ask, "What's going on, Ty?"

"Nothing really. Mom's out shopping with Maggie and her friend. Weird."

"You should be happy that your Mom and Maggie are hitting it off. And your mother knows how to handle paparazzi if they show up." Loy offered a half-smile. "Your mom and I haven't seen eye to eye over the years, but I have a deep respect for her, Tysen. She's a no-bullshit kind of woman. So is Maggie." He chuckled. "I pity those poor bastards if they try to intrude on their shopping expedition. Your mama will cut them off at the knees and Maggie will kick them to the curb."

Ty studied his grandfather. "How is that you know so much about Maggie?"

"I make it my mission to find out everything about anyone who touches this family."

* * *

Maggie couldn't believe that she and Nancy were sitting in a Japanese restaurant eating spicy tuna and drinking sake with Ellen Peppersmith-Vincent. It was surreal and surprisingly easy. Ellen was nothing like the media's portrayal. She wasn't selfish and didn't have tyrant tendencies. Instead, she was warm and enchanting. Maggie was also over-the-moon-happy to find out that Ellen wasn't estranged from her son in any way, shape or form, as the press would also have you believe. She and Ty had a loving relationship, tightly guarded but that was their business. Her relationship with Loy was something altogether different. Ellen described it as civil with occasional bumps. Basically, Loy hadn't forgiven her for walking away from his son and from the oil empire. She still had considerable shares of stock and was the mother of his grandson so he had to put up with her whether he wanted to or not.

Over a sip of sake, Maggie reflected on the shopping trip. At the bridal shop, she'd combed through racks and racks of wedding gowns and had stowed at least ten in the dressing room. Dress after dress got the gong from Ellen and Nancy. When she was down to three, she was ready to throttle them both.

Maggie had stepped from the dressing room wearing a flashy gown with thousands of shimmering beads and a ton of lace. It was a beautiful design, but a bit much, both in price and style. Right way she'd received a thumbs down. The second last dress; floor length with princess sleeves, a few satin bows and a diamond shaped beaded brooch below the bust line was also a no. Ellen had rolled her eyes and said, 'Don't come out again until you're wearing something that is completely you'. Maggie feigned annoyance but inside she'd smiled. Ellen was easy to like. There didn't seem to be a stuck-up bone in her body, she had a quick wit and a quiet self-assurance.

The last dress Maggie tried on had been the winner – a silk, form-fitting design that showed off her curves. There was only a smidgen of lace and a single strand of beading at the circle neckline. It received oh's and ah's; not only from Ellen and Nancy, but also from another bride-to-be and her entourage of bridesmaids.

With Maggie's dress out of the way, they had to choose something for Ellen and Nancy. Nancy had gone first. She'd slipped into a hideous dress in pumpkin and teal, pranced around the dress shop like she was a movie star, blew kisses and said 'Dahling'. They'd laughed until they had tears in their eyes. The owner of the shop was not amused, which made it all the more funny. Finally, a spectacular dress in dusty red called Nancy's name. The neckline dipped low enough to tease yet was elegant.

Ellen's turn on the hot seat. Maggie quickly learned that her future mother-in-law enjoyed shopping for herself as much as she liked the news media. Not. At. All.

'Not without a drink', she'd said. Pools of watery emotion had filled the corners of her eyes and a big dose of reality slammed into Maggie. What she and Ty were doing was for real. The proposal. Engagement party. Dress shopping. Vows. Living together afterward. Real. Real. Real. A sick feeling for duping everyone, most especially Ellen, had settled in the pit of her stomach and unshed tears for being so stupid burned behind her eyes. She'd gathered Ellen in a hug. "It's going to be fine. Trust me," she'd whispered. Now those words were eating her alive. Things would be fine for six months and then the plan was for them not to be fine. She couldn't bear to think about the fallout if Ellen found out this was all a sham.

Ellen had dragged them to a bar a block from the bridal shop where they shared two bottles of wine. An hour later, a wee bit tipsy, they commenced shopping. Ellen tried on suits until she was sick of trying them on, finally ditching the suit idea and going with a simple red sleeveless, pleat neck dress by Valentino. She bought matching red shoes with modest heels.

Nancy snapped her fingers in front of Maggie. "Off in dreamland?"

Maggie laughed and took another sip of sake. "Yes."

Ellen laid a hand across Maggie's. "I was worried that Tysen was making a mistake. Now I know he'll be in good hands."

The sip of sake Maggie had just taken burned at the top of her throat but she couldn't cough or show signs of distress. She and Ty were scamming everyone, including Ellen and Loy. And she and Loy were scamming everyone, including Ty and Ellen. It was a whole lot of scamming that made her want to run away. Far, far away.

Their waiter laid the bill on the table and Maggie snapped it up. "My treat," she said at the protest of the other two. "Seriously, let me pay." The three of laughed and tussled over the tab until Maggie held it over her head out of reach. They were still laughing when Nancy's cell phone plinked with the arrival of an incoming text message.

Nancy's expression changed from jovial to serious in a flash.

"Everything okay?" Maggie asked.

Nancy looked at Maggie with something vague swimming through her green eyes. "Uh…yeah." She stood up, slung her purse on her shoulder, tossed a wad of bills on the table to cover the tip and said she'd call Maggie later in the evening. She shook Ellen's hand. "I had a blast hanging out with you and Maggie today. We'll have to do it again sometime." On her way out of the restaurant, she looked over her shoulder and met Maggie's eyes before she continued her exit.

Strange. Hopefully nothing serious happened at the hospital since every incident, good or bad, fell on Nancy's shoulders. It was a lot of pressure for one person. There were times when Nancy had all she could do to keep it together in front of her staff. A few nights a week they would meet for drinks and vent about the things that went on at Carriage Memorial. Or they'd rendezvous at the gym for an evening belly-dancing class to work away the stress. Sunday morning was the only day-class offered, and Maggie was glad that she and Nancy had taken advantage of it yesterday. It appeared that Nancy needed a class right now to shake off whatever the heck was going on.

Maggie finished her sake, filled with worried thoughts. Worried about the hurt she would inflict on Ellen when it appeared that her son's marriage had fallen apart. Worried about Nancy who seemed to have too much resting on her shoulders. Worried that the stress of her own situation would be too much to handle.

Ellen also got a text message, from Ty. He wanted to meet up with them. Ellen laughed. "That boy is whipped, Maggie."

No. He isn't. He's playing a part, too damned well. It dawned on her that she was playing her part equally well. Maggie responded the only way she could, with laughter. "He's a bit of a control freak." As soon as the remark was out, she clamped a hand over her mouth. She'd forgotten for a second who she was sitting with.

Thankfully, Ellen chuckled too. "Genetic legacy of the Vincent men." She ordered more sake and sent Ty a text telling him to bug off.

Maggie realized, much to her dismay, that it hadn't been lip service – Ty *was* easy to love. Ellen was easy to love too. Dammit all to hell, so was Loy. And she was in over her head.

* * *

"Bug off? Not." Ty pulled into the parking lot of Maggie's apartment building and through the constant movement of the windshield wipers he stared up at her window on the fourth floor. It had been raining off and on for the last few hours. The tropical storm that had been closely monitored by the weather experts had lashed Houston, moved further inland and was now lashing Dallas; inundating them with dangerous lightning and so much rain that the streets were starting to flood.

The storm outside the car was nothing compared to the one inside. Ty drummed his thumbs on the steering wheel, contemplating how he would get Maggie to agree to twelve months instead of six. Of course more money would be involved, but still, he remembered her reaction when he'd offered the first deal. Shit. He was over-thinking things. All he had to do was lay it all out. She was a reasonable woman. If she couldn't do a year, maybe she'd consent to nine months. He was flexible. Hopefully she would be too.

Ty climbed out of the car and sloshed his way into the building.

Standing by the elevator, soaking wet, he eyed the elevator buttons. What if Maggie told him to kiss her ass? He would. He'd kiss whatever she wanted him to kiss, including her sweet ass.

While Ty waited for the elevator, a few people dashed into the building, also soaked to the gills. Instinctively, he turned away, bracing for the flash of a camera.

To his surprise, no cameras.

The elevator doors pinged opened and Ty crowded in with the others.

"Nasty as hell out there," the guy standing next to Ty said.

"No kidding," he responded, trying to shield his identity by blending in with the group.

The guy locked his radar on Ty. "Are you who I think you are?" Before Ty could sidetrack the question, the guy snapped his fingers. "Jon Bon Jovi."

"I wish." Ty chuckled. He'd been told he bore a striking resemblance to the famous rocker, but he didn't see it. His hair was possibly the only thing that came close. He was blessed with a thick head of hair, a result of good genes from both sides of the family. The guy who cut his hair encouraged him to wear it long and layered, which bugged the hell out of his granddad.

"Seriously, dude. You could be Jon Bon Jovi's stunt double."

Ty smirked. "Again, I wish." He forked a hand through his hair to push back the droplets of rain water that kept rolling into his eyes.

"Well, if you ain't Jon, you come damn close." He shook Ty's hand. "I could've sworn we had a celebrity in our midst. There's a white news van outside and guys creeping around the building. Funniest damn thing watching them try to juggle their big cameras and an umbrella."

The elevator doors opened at the fourth floor and another guy in the group got it right. "You're Ty Vincent."

Ty stepped out of the elevator without a denial and hurried down the hall to apartment 408.

At Maggie's door, he stood opening and closing his hands, trying to decide whether to knock, or wait until Wednesday.

He took a few steps back toward the elevator and stopped. He had to see her to strike a new bargain. A heavy sigh rolled from his chest. This was nuts! He was Ty Vincent. He didn't chase women who didn't want to be with him; although, he couldn't remember a woman not wanting to be with him. Maggie Gray was different from most women. Was that the allure? Did he want her simply because she didn't want him? When they kissed it felt like she wanted him.

Ty braced against the door frame. If his dad was still alive none of this would be happening. They would be drinking a cold beer and watching the Rangers kick the hell out of whomever they were playing. Life would make sense. As it was, nothing made sense. Thoughts of his dad flicked the pain switch. Razor-sharp anguish sliced across his chest making him double over. In the process, the unimaginable happened. He thumped his head hard against the door.

Maggie opened the door straight away as though she had been peering into the peek hole, watching him lose it. "Ty?" In the blink of an eye, she was in tune with the situation and guided him inside.

Ty didn't resist. Mentally he did. Physically he was incapable.

Maggie led him to the couch, ran to the kitchen for towels and knelt in front of him. She blotted the water from the bottom of his hair and neck and softly spoke. "I know you miss him, Ty, but there's more going on here than just missing your dad." She touched his chest. "You have to get checked out. If you don't, one of these days you'll find yourself buzzing along on I-635 in the back of an ambulance with the lights flashing and sirens blaring. Please get checked out." A small amount of hysteria threaded her voice. "Please!"

It took a few agonizing minutes for the pain to fully go away. Ty closed his eyes and let the f-bomb ricochet through his brain at least a dozen times. When he opened his eyes, he was stunned to see tears in Maggie's eyes. To deal with the wayward emotion wracking them both, he took the low road. "Stop bossing me, Maggie. Remember our agreement? You can't tell me what I should or shouldn't do."

Maggie sniffed before bringing a doubled fist into view. "Tysen, I swear to God if you don't stop blowing this off I'm going to slug you."

Ty raised his eyebrows. "Still bossing, Maggie." He half-smiled. She didn't.

"To hell with our agreement." Maggie stood up. "This thing – you and me – can't happen. There's too much at stake. After spending the day with your mom, I am now painfully aware of the people we'll hurt when we divorce. I don't even want to think about how angry they'll be if they find out it was just a scam." Her voice quivered and Ty realized that Maggie was trying to borrow Rosie's bottle of White-Out. Any second she was going to cover her virtual signature on their agreement. Tears rolled unrestrained down her cheeks. "Your mom is awesome, Ty. She's so sweet. I can't hurt her." She used the back of her hand to wipe her nose. "I can't do this. I thought I could, but I can't." She slumped onto the couch.

Panic roared in Ty's ears. "You're not backing out, Maggie. I won't let you. I need you. You said you would see this through. Don't leave..." His words stuck in his throat and the ache in his chest from a minute ago was back, stronger than ever. "Uhhhhhhhhhh!" He clutched his chest and rolled, head first off the couch, striking his cheek bone on the sharp end of the coffee table.

"Oh no you don't, Vincent. I won't let you use those chest pains to bait me into keeping that stupid agreement."

"Maggie, I..." He curled into a fetal position.

In a flash, she was on the floor next to him, tears flooding her eyes, whispering soft words of regret for upsetting him. "I'm sorry, Ty. So sorry. I'm calling 9-1-1." She sprang up and grabbed the phone.

"Don't!"

"I can't ignore this any longer. These episodes aren't just psychosomatic, they're real. If I don't do something..." A glazed look of fear accompanied her sobs.

Something miraculous happened – either that or he died. The pain stopped. Not a lessening, a complete stoppage. No off shoots or after-shocks. Just a chest without agony. Along with it, a strange sense of peace. "Put the phone down, Maggie," he said quietly, yet firmly. "I'm fine."

Maggie shook her head. "You're not fine." Heavy tears continued to spill from the corners of her eyes and her nose was full like she had a bad cold. "You need help, but not the kind I can offer."

Ty pulled up from the floor, snagged a clump of tissues from a box on the lamp table and handed them to Maggie. He waited for her to blow her nose. "Sweetheart," he said tenderly, "I want the kind you can offer. I want everything you have to offer. I want..." Ty took her in his arms and laid his forehead against hers. "...you. I want to make love to you, Maggie. And then I want us to get married and see what happens."

Maggie pushed against his chest to put some space between them. She wiped her eyes with the heel of her hand and sniffed back the last of her tears. "Do you know how crazy that sounds? People don't get married first and then see what happens. Some people do, not those with their right minds."

"You completely missed that I want to make love to you." Ty pulled her back into the circle of his arms. "How about this – marry me because you want to. Marry me because when we're together it feels right."

Maggie gasped.

Ty couldn't contain his smile. "I knew it. You want to marry me. Admit it."

"The only thing I want is to keep my sanity."

"Bullshit. You want to marry me...and...you want to sleep with me. Losing your mind over me is hot, Maggie." Ty worked his hands to the small of her back and pushed his hips into hers.

"No I..."

Ty lowered his head and sealed her mouth with a hungry kiss. God she tasted good! He kissed her deeper, sliding his tongue inside her mouth, drawing a moan. He felt her tremble and he pulled her tighter; so tight she wouldn't miss the evidence of his desire, the effect that was almost instant whenever he touched her, or kissed her, or even thought about making love to her. His body...and soul...seemed to react to Maggie on its own.

Maggie sighed with resignation. Fighting the truth was

hard on them both. He wanted her and she sure as heck wanted him. Whatever Ty wanted, he could have. Her body, her hand in marriage, anything and everything, was his. She would pay a stiff price, but she could no longer deny her heart or her passion. She needed this man. Needed him with every ounce of her being. Damn the repercussions.

With shaky hands she started to unbutton Ty's wet shirt. The dampness swelled the button holes, making the simple task of undoing buttons feel monumental. She tugged and pushed, to no avail. Soon she would rip the darned shirt off. Or would resort to using scissors. Either way, that shirt was coming off.

Driven to madness, she took a half step back. "Strip out of those clothes," she commanded, relishing the power but noticing the urgency in her voice.

Ty's face was serious and tight, but his blue eyes sparkled with passion. In a rush, he struggled to get the wet shirt over his head. Maggie helped tug it up and off. While his arms were still in the air she gave his mouth a brief peck before descending to his chest where she planted small kisses and soft nips to his skin. Enveloped in delicious heat, she backed away to pull off her own shirt. Ty stood bare-chested, roving his gaze slowly over her, prompting her to unhook her bra. She let it fall to the floor. His sharp intake of breath left her no choice but to unsnap and lower the zipper of her jean shorts so she could slide them from her hips to pool at her feet. Maggie felt reckless but ready to enjoy what his amazing eyes, mouth and body promised.

"Maggie." Ty's voice was raw and gritty.

Maggie saw his Adam's apple bob in his throat.

"Are you sure?" he asked.

Her response came out as a hoarse whisper. "Yes." She was sure but she vowed not to become just another notch in this famous playboy's belt. She would be his wife and wouldn't walk away in six months. No way would she willingly divorce him. She wasn't wired that way. They'd deal with all of that later. Right now, she wanted to deal with more pleasant circumstances.

Ty scooped her in his arms. "Which way?"

Stormed by desire so thick and rich, it kinked her vocal chords. All she could do was nod in the direction of the bedroom.

Before they made it past the couch, a series of persistent knocks at the door jarred them both. Ty groaned but didn't put her down or stop the trek to the bedroom.

The knocks continued.

Ty propped Maggie against the hallway wall, splayed his hands across her naked breasts and moved in with a heat-seeking kiss.

Maggie moaned from the joy of Ty and secretly hoped whoever was at the door would get the hint that this was not a good time.

The door vibrated with continued banging. A voice accompanied the heavy noise. "Maggie."

Maggie winced. Ty followed with one much louder.

"Just a sec." Maggie drew away from Ty with him mumbling that at least it wasn't Quinn and Tori this time.

She rushed to the heap of clothes, slid into her t-shirt and shorts and tossed Ty his shirt. Taking a stout breath, she undid the chain lock and unlocked the deadbolt. "Nancy. Hi. I thought you were going to call."

"Sorry, Mags, this couldn't wait." She trounced into the living room, dripping wet. "I had to deliver the news in person." Nancy's face dripped with rain water and concern. The moment she spied Ty lurking near the hallway, her eyes widened. "Ohhh. Umm…"

"It's okay, Nancy, really." It wasn't okay, but hey, her best friend wouldn't have come out in this kind of weather unless it was important, extremely important. Water ran off of Nancy like she'd brought a rain cloud inside. Maggie grabbed her arm and tugged her to the kitchen where the water would fall onto the linoleum instead of the carpet. She fished more hand towels from the drawer, handed them to Nancy and leaned against the counter. "So what's up?"

Nancy shifted from foot to foot. "Nothing that…" She stumbled over her words and she cleared her throat. "…can't wait." Her eyes dropped to the floor.

Crap. Something had happened at Carriage Memorial. Something bad. Maggie draped an arm around Nancy. "You obviously need to talk." She tried to smile. "What are best friends for?" The lovemaking would be put on hold yet again. It would be immature to stomp and throw a fit, but Maggie wanted to do both.

Ty could take a hint. He didn't want to, but it appeared he didn't have much choice. "I should go," he said, hoping Maggie would stop him.

Before Maggie could respond, Nancy did. "It's probably best if you did."

Ty jerked at the comment. Maggie jerked too.

"Nancy?" Maggie said.

Nancy wrung her hands and she continued to restlessly shift in place. "I don't know how to say this, Maggie, there's no easy way."

"Are you sick?"

Nancy shook her head. "I'm sick all right, but not in that way. No, honey, this isn't about me. I wish it was." Anger tipped her words and she cut Ty with a look of loathing.

"Then who?"

Ty heard the weave of panic in Maggie's voice. He made a move toward her and to his shock Nancy stepped in his way. What the hell?

A thousand thoughts skittered through his brain. Nancy knew about the deal between him and Maggie, so that couldn't be what had her all worked up.

His past?

His grandfather warned that there would be a day of reckoning. Maybe that day had come. For the life of him he couldn't think of one thing he'd done that was so earth-shattering to cause Nancy to draw and quarter him with her eyes. Yes, he'd been a skirt-chaser and was known to occasionally drink too much. Hell, his track record wasn't unique. Most bachelors had one that mirrored his.

"Loy." Nancy sighed like it had taken a lot to say his name.

"What about him?" Maggie's brows had knit to the center.

Ty matched Maggie's frown.

Nancy shot him a look that said 'one false move and I'm taking you down'. He stayed put. "He's been up to no good."

Ty made light of the comment. "When isn't he?"

"Not funny." Nancy dropped the rest of the bomb, leveling the place with emotional destruction. "He's the one who got you fired, Maggie. It took some digging to exhume the culprit, but I dug until I got answers. Loy Vincent went straight to the top. He used his wealth and influence against you."

"That doesn't make sense. Why would he…" Maggie stopped. She looked at Ty with sudden tears and he felt the world cave in around him. He was surprised when she shook her head repeatedly and defended his grandfather. "Loy is a shrewd businessman but he wouldn't have me terminated." She shook her head harder. "He wouldn't."

"He did," Nancy stated matter-of-factly. "It sounds like something from a soap opera, but trust me, it happened. He convinced the powers-to-be to hand you your walking papers." Nancy gathered Maggie in a hug. "I'm sorry to be the one to tell you. As your friend, I had to before you marry the devil's spawn."

Maggie drew away from Nancy and walked to the opposite

end of the kitchen, her eyes volleyed between her friend and Ty, like she was trying to adjust to this new set of circumstances.

Ty wanted to offer some sort of comfort, but what? If he made a move, she'd straight arm him or Nancy would do it for her.

Maggie's posture went stick straight and her hands curled into fists at her side. "Ty, I think you should leave."

Ty moved his head slowly back and forth. If he left, he was sure their agreement would be kaput. There'd be no marriage. No wife. He'd be back to square one. Or it would be the final nail in his coffin and he might as well hand over his office key Terron. "No, Maggie. We need to sort this out together."

"*I'll* sort this out."

A cool wall of indifference beamed from her pigheaded blue eyes.

"There has to be some kind of mistake. My granddad wouldn't do this to you. He can be heartless from time to time but why would he get you fired? He didn't even know you until I told him we were getting married." His grandfather had connections far and wide, and those connections would do almost anything for Loy Vincent, but it was doubtful that they would sever someone like Maggie from their payroll without good cause. "Sorry, Nancy, someone has fed you some bad information."

"You're right, it is *bad* information." Maggie's anger filled the small kitchen.

"Calm down, sweetheart. There has to be a logical explanation."

"Don't tell me to calm down. This is happening to me, not you."

"You're wrong. It's happening to us." If his grandfather *had* gotten Maggie dismissed from her job, there would be big trouble. Huge. The old man messed with his life constantly but he wouldn't stand for him messing with Maggie's. When he found his grandfather and pulled the truth from him, he'd give him an earful and possibly walk out of his life...forever. The hurt of losing people he cared for yet again was almost too much to bear. He'd lost his dad. Losing Maggie was inevitable. And it sounded like he would soon lose all ties with his grandfather. The crippling pain that he knew would come didn't disappoint. It came hard and fast. Pain slashed across his chest while his lungs seized and he couldn't breathe. He closed his eyes and slumped against the wall.

In a tone filled with suspicion and derelict of real concern, he heard Maggie order Nancy to call 9-1-1. He would've balked, but it wasn't possible. He couldn't talk, walk, or breathe.

Chapter Nine

With a wobbly hand, Maggie filled an insulated mug with coffee and propped against the kitchen sink. She took a sip and almost spit it back out. Instead of putting in the usual three scoops of grounds she'd put in six, hoping to catch a caffeine buzz that would jolt her into full consciousness. After the devastating news that Loy Vincent convinced the hospital to let her go, Ty went into another chest episode; the worst one yet. She and Nancy grudgingly followed the ambulance that carried him to the hospital. She predicted he'd take the trip, she hadn't expected it to be this soon. Good thing Nancy offered to drive to the hospital because Maggie basically lost it on the four mile trek. She'd cried so much that her eyes were still sore this morning, so was her rib cage. When they'd reached the hospital and emergency personnel wheeled Ty out of sight, she'd fallen apart again. She'd dabbed her eyes and blew her nose so much the volunteer behind the desk had to put out a fresh box of tissues. She'd paced and cried. Nancy tried to smooth things over by saying that maybe she did get bad information. She also reminded Maggie that Ty was in good hands, that he'd be all right. Nancy gave up and perched in a chair with a magazine. She'd flipped through the pages until Maggie had driven her wonky with all the walking back and forth. She finally made

Maggie sit and they had a heart to heart talk which lasted until four in the morning. Nancy was now privy to every thought Maggie had about Ty, including that she cared deeply for him. When Maggie asked what she should do about it, Nancy lifted her eyebrows. 'There's only one thing you can do', she'd said. Maggie still hadn't figured out exactly what that was.

Before they left the hospital around four-thirty, she received an update on Ty and was offered a chance to go back to see him. She'd tiptoed into his room and found him asleep despite all the hustle and bustle happening at the nurse's station right outside his door. The nursing staff was a hive of worker bees, buzzing around from room to room giving their patients strict attention. She'd wanted to sit quietly in the chair beside him but if he woke up and she was there, she'd have to be nice and she didn't feel like being nice. She was mad at Loy, but Ty was guilty by association. She was torn between wanting to slug him and kiss him. Instead, she slipped out of his room before Loy showed up. When Loy's powerful voice reverberated around the quiet wing of the hospital, she'd peeked out and spotted him at the nurse's station. She'd tiptoed away.

This morning she was exhausted and none of her anger had gone away. In the shower, with the water turned to the highest setting, she'd fisted her hands and covered her eyes with them, and let the bulk of her anxiety out in one long continuous groan.

Maggie peered at her phone over the top of her insulated mug. She was tempted to call her dad and inform him that whatever debt he owed that grey-haired goat was effectively paid in full. A job for a gambling debt. Of course, Loy got the better end of the deal. The Vincents got everything they wanted. Money. Cars. Lavish homes. Prestige. You name it, it was theirs. One thing Loy would not get – her as a granddaughter-in-law. One thing Ty would not get – her as a wife. The bastards could get on their knees and beg. She was fairly certain that wouldn't happen since neither of them knew the meaning of the word beg. If they did, they'd probably hire someone to do their begging for them.

Maggie took a deep breath and blew it back out. Today she would concentrate on something other than disgustingly well-off madmen and their dog-eat-dog tactics to keep their wealth. In a nutshell, that's what the last few days had been about. It wasn't to get Ty to behave or to heal his broken heart, it was about money. Loy needed for Ty to assume the helm of his empire to insure that the Vincent Oil Company would stay in Vincent hands so it would continue to thrive and keep them filthy rich.

Maggie grimaced when she realized just how easily she'd fit into their money-grubbing gambit. With little resistance they reeled her in. Not only did she fall for their evil ways, she fell for Loy's evil grandson. Together, Loy and Ty were the dynamic duo. Loy manipulated her life. Ty manipulated her heart.

She sank to the kitchen floor and laid her head against the cabinets for support. She'd fallen head over heels for Ty; was completely and totally in love with the jerk. But he didn't love her. Truth be known, he'd been in cahoots with his grandfather from the start. She thought that whole marriage proposal scenario at the airport was a little too convenient. That's what she got for agreeing to the swindle to begin with. Powerful people got away with illicit deeds and their consciences didn't bother them a bit. It was the meek and lowly that felt the guilt of having tried to con their way into something that was supposed to be helpful.

From the table a few feet away, her cell phone rang. Maggie pulled up from the floor and glared at the small device like it was the source of all her problems. She would not answer the blasted thing. Not today. The world could kiss her rump.

It stopped ringing for two seconds and began again.

Nope. Not answering. Totally immature on her part, but it was the only way she could block out anyone who might ruin her day; not that it wasn't already in the toilet.

The incessant ringing stopped for a whole minute and a half. "One more time and you're toast." Maggie shoved the blasted thing in her purse. She stretched her neck side to side, topped off her mug with more coffee and hustled out the door, determined to stop the pity party. Today she would do something meaningful. She would work in a hot kitchen and prepare meals for folks who had their lives turned upside down for one reason or another; folks who needed the soup kitchen to be their temporary bridge over rocky waters. Working there was a humbling experience and it put her life in perspective. She didn't have any problems, not really. She was fortunate to have the big three: food, clothing and shelter. Some only had one out of three, without the soup kitchen they wouldn't even have one.

Maggie hurried across the parking lot to her car. From the side pocket of her purse, her phone had the nerve to ring again.

"Keep it up and you'll become a Frisbee in short order." Whoever was calling would not win. It was probably Loy with an update on Ty. She didn't want to know how he was doing. If she didn't know, she couldn't care. He was in capable hands, thankfully not hers. Besides, as wily as the Vincents were, those chest pains were almost certainly staged.

* * *

"There's no need to take my blood pressure again." Ty edged away from the shift nurse. "I'm fine."

"That's for your doctor to decide." The nurse wrapped the Velcro contraption around his arm and gave the bulb a few pumps while batting her eyes.

Ty almost rolled his. He hit re-dial on his phone. He would

continue to bug Maggie until she either threw her phone at the wall, breaking it into a thousand unfixable pieces or until she tossed it in the nearest sewer drain. He was prepared to do whatever it took to get her to talk to him, even escape the hospital in the backless gown with his ass cheeks showing and an IV needle stuck in his arm. Hopefully it wouldn't come to that.

She still didn't answer. "Come on, woman!"

The nurse who had moved from taking his blood pressure to taking his pulse drew back in surprise.

"Not you," Ty said, irritated with both the nurse and the hellcat with the most amazing blue eyes who was ignoring her phone.

"Tysen!" Loy Vincent stormed the room with his commanding presence and a Styrofoam coffee cup, making the nurse glare. She cautioned him right away. "You're in CCU, sir, please lower your voice."

Surprisingly his grandfather took it down a notch, but not without making a face first.

If Ty wasn't so annoyed, he might've at least cracked a smile at the nurse who had the kahoonies to shush T. Loy Vincent, I. Not many people could get away with backing him down. Ty decided in that moment, that nurses were awesome. They wielded a lot of power. This woman did. Maggie sure as hell did.

"I'll come back in a little bit to *try* again to get your pulse." She did that bit with her fingers to her eyes and swung them toward his grandfather to warn him she was watching him. Hilarious. But again, Ty wouldn't ease the tension with a laugh.

Loy waited for the nurse to get out of earshot. "I've been worried sick, Tysen." He scowled toward the door. "They've told me very little." He lifted the IV hose and winced. "Are you okay?"

"No. I'm not okay," he said hotly.

Loy's expression tightened. "Oh God, you don't need open heart surgery, do you?"

"No, but that would be easier to deal with."

Loy's voice fell a few octaves. "Something worse?"

"Hell yes it's something worse."

"Tysen, whatever it is, we'll get the best doctors."

Ty lost his ability to be civil. "Listen grandfather," his tone was loaded with impatience, "I'm not sick. I'm pissed."

Lines of confusion creased Loy's forehead. He studied Ty. "You're in the hospital because you're pissed? That doesn't make any sense."

Ty struggled to sit up straight and set off some type of alarm. The nurse who succeeded in quieting Loy minutes before hurried back in to mess with the IV tree. She checked the heart monitor too. When she was finished she put her hands on her hips and accused Loy with her question. "Are you responsible for this?" She didn't wait for an answer and turned to Ty. "Stop wiggling around or I'll be in here every few minutes."

Ty plied her with a genuine smile of appreciation for putting up with him. "I'll try."

She straightened his blankets and again glared at his grandfather on her way out.

"That woman despises me. But she's sweet on you, grandson." He puffed out a breath. "I used to have that touch."

"You've been a bully for as long as I've known you." Ty didn't tread softly around the truth with his granddad, and vice versa. If anything, the two were brutally honest with each other. It caused problems sometimes. Other times, it was helpful. Ty hadn't fully addressed the huge issue hanging between them so it remained to be seen what his honesty would bring.

"Yeah, well, stress makes you hard around the edges."

Ty studied his grandfather. He was still a good looking man for an old fart. When you got past the eyes that could reduce most people to rubble with just a look, you could see that time had taken a toll. There were permanent creases in his forehead and endless crinkles at the corners of his eyes. Under his eyes, dark circles. The man didn't sleep much. Running a profitable oil business and trying to keep the public, government, Board of Directors and stockholders happy was a balancing act; one that could cause an adrenaline rush or an ulcer. Factor in the hot Texas sun. A faulty ticker. And a grandson who tested the waters way too often. No wonder Loy Vincent looked and behaved like he'd been through hell and back. Although, none of that stuff was as harmful and hurtful as the loss of his only child. Ty suddenly had a pulsing knot the size of a grapefruit in his throat.

Loy wasn't known to linger too long on any one subject. "About the reason you're here…does this have anything to do with Maggie?"

Ty lowered his lashes so he was looking through thin slits. "It has everything to do with her. You got her fired!" He hadn't meant to be so loud, but his voice boomed off the four walls.

Loy didn't flinch at Ty's burst of anger. "Oh, that." He exhaled and inhaled dramatically. "She was a casualty of downsizing. I'm on the hospital Board."

"Oh that?" A surge of fury took over. "Oh that?" Ty repeated in the form of a shout. "How can you be so nonchalant about ripping someone's livelihood out from under them?" Each word was louder than the last until he was sure everyone on the hospital floor and in the parking garage across the street heard him.

"Calm down."

"I can't calm down! I'm so mad I want to scream!"

"You *are* screaming."

Ty fisted a handful of blanket. "You pretended not to know Maggie when I told you we were getting married. I should've paid attention to that annoying gleam that you get when things go your way. I should've paid 'effing attention."

Loy rested his elbows on his thighs and laid his face in his hands. "I did know Maggie beforehand. I'm familiar with her father too. Nice guy."

"Before I wring your neck, I need for you to explain what the hell is going on."

"How did you find out that I had a hand in letting Maggie go?"

"Is that what you think is important?" Ty squinted to drive home his point that it wasn't right. No matter how the man would spin it, it just wasn't right.

"I'm sorry, Ty. Maggie's a good gal and you obviously care about her."

"You have no idea."

"Well then, tell me about you two."

Ty seldom discussed matters of the heart, especially when it pertained to women. Mostly because until Maggie he hadn't felt anything stronger than lust or friendship. "I love Maggie. I know it's sudden, but I do." His voice cracked. "But now, I can forget about her loving me back. I'm sure we're done." He closed his eyes and ran his hand over his tired face. "I need sleep."

Loy touched Ty's shoulder. "Tysen, for what it's worth, I'm sorry."

"Whatever." Ty kept his eyes closed.

* * *

"It's over, Dad." Maggie turned her coffee cup in circles without meeting her father's eyes. "I'm happy that it is." Unshed tears burned deep behind her eyes.

Richland Gray lifted her chin. "You don't look happy." He gently ran his thumb back and forth across her cheek.

Maggie shrugged dejectedly. "I'm happy to be free from

the agreement, but I'm sad about losing…" Instead of saying Ty, she said, "Ellen."

"Ellen, huh?" He scrunched his face with question. "You bonded with Ty's mom?"

"Yes." A quiver threaded the one-word answer.

Richland pulled Maggie into the comfort of his arms. "I'm glad you're out of that despicable agreement too. What woman in her right mind would want to marry Ty Vincent? He's nothing but trouble. I'm glad you like Ellen though. She's okay in my book."

Through a cloud of tears, Maggie blinked up at him. "Trouble doesn't come close to describing him. His grandfather is even worse. They have a peculiar DNA that makes them mess with people for their own gain."

Her father jiggled with a small laugh. "Maggie, darling, *lots* of people have that DNA. Some just aren't as obvious."

His emphasis on the word *lots* made Maggie feel guilty since she'd engaged in some underhanded schmoozing to become Ty's fiancée and to gain the public's approval. Crap. She had the same sordid DNA. "Real subtle, Dad."

Richland Gray's mouth dimpled into a smile. "Not only beautiful but perceptive too. Now, what are you going to do about this mess? I mean, the whole world knows you're engaged. And you have the dress. By the way, did you see the paper this morning?"

She hadn't seen it. Didn't want to see it. She'd cancel her newspaper subscription to keep from seeing anything Vincent related, if she had to. What she would do about she and Ty, she hadn't a clue. Maybe nothing. Maybe it would all go away if she didn't do a thing. Or maybe she'd wake up and discover that this was all a bad dream.

Earlier, while helping to prepare pots of chili con carne at the soup kitchen, she came to the conclusion that Ty was not worth the effort to try to fix things. She'd silently called him shallow, self-serving, an egotistical bastard and a dozen other names that fit him to a tee. If she could keep that perspective it would be easier to go on with her life. Someone put her to the test right away. Velma, one of the soup kitchen administrators, had sidled next to her. "Congratulations on your engagement to my all-time favorite heartthrob, Tysen Vincent." Velma pretended to swoon. "He's our biggest anonymous donor of food and money." She rested a hand on Maggie's shoulder. "Essentially, that makes you one of the biggest donors too. Awesome, huh?" Not so anonymous, it would seem. Maggie was floored by the news. She remembered mentioning the soup kitchen to Ty but he didn't as much as bat an eye and she'd chalked it up to what most guys suffered from, nothing-on-their-minds-but-boobs syndrome. Velma didn't stop there. "The Vincents are world class philanthropists."

They were world class all right. World class pains in the butt.

Maggie pushed away from her father and held her hand out to display her engagement ring. She turned the ring around several times and slipped it off.

From out of nowhere, she started to cry; not just salty tears, full body-wracking sobs. Thank goodness her father was there to tell her that everything would be fine. He was delusional, of course, but it was a relief not to suffer alone.

Chapter Ten

Ty knocked on Maggie's door. He heard shuffling on the other side and a small groan. She knew he was there. He knocked again. "Open up, Maggie. You promised me that we'd be together on Wednesday. It's Wednesday."

The sound of the door chain being slid open and the deadbolt being unlocked were good signs.

Maggie inched open the door. There were dark circles under her eyes, she had a serious case of bed-head and was dressed in a short cotton nightie with pictures of dogs on the front. Ty grinned. Even in her disheveled state she was sexy as hell. "Can I come in?" He wasn't sure of the exact time, and he wouldn't look at his watch to make her feel bad, but it had to be just after twelve o'clock noon.

She ignored the question. "You're out of the hospital."

"Yes, and you'll be happy to know I don't have a heart condition. Well, at least a medical one." He splayed his hand over his heart. "I do have an ache right here that doesn't seem to go away. It's for you, Maggie."

"Fancy words." Maggie tried to close the door. "Wednesday is cancelled."

Ty shook his head. "You can't cancel Wednesday, nobody can." He stuck his foot in the door to prevent her from shutting him out completely. "I'm not letting you welch on a promise. Throw on some clothes, Bostwick is waiting."

Maggie chewed on her bottom lip. "I thought I made it plain that we're through."

"Yeah. No. You didn't." He tried to smile and keep his voice even. "Let's discuss it over lunch. I said we needed to renegotiate our deal and you never gave us a chance to do that."

"That's because you were too busy seducing me."

"Me? Seducing you? I think it was a mutual seduction, Margaret."

Maggie pulled her lips in.

Ty moved his head up and down. "I see that you agree."

"Don't call me Margaret."

Ty lifted his shoulders in a shrug. "Then get your butt moving and stop playing the victim. Yes, you got a raw deal from my grandfather. I'm not happy about it either, but his actions opened up a world of possibilities for you. For us." She didn't move a muscle, making him add, "Margaret."

"Bastard."

"And then some. Now hurry up or I'm carrying you to the limo in your pajamas."

"Hardhead."

"Takes one to know one." Ty pointed to the bedroom. "You have two choices, Margaret: get dressed or let me ravish you." He tried not to smile when she made big eyes at him.

Maggie's heart was doing double-time. It was pumping so hard that she felt her pulse at her temples. She hadn't expected to see Ty so soon. Actually, she hadn't expected to see him at all. She'd let the thirty or so text messages he'd sent go unanswered, a strong hint that she didn't want to see him or talk to him, no interaction whatsoever. Obviously he couldn't take a hint. If there was a flashing billboard that read "Leave Maggie alone", he'd probably ignore that too. Bonehead.

Numbskull. Tyrant.

She dressed in a soft pink, two-button short-sleeved shirt and a pair of faded jeans. Dampened her hair and gave it a little body with the blow dryer. Brushed her teeth and swished minty mouthwash.

Ty appeared around the bathroom door. "Come on, Margaret. By the way, we need to make a stop at the courthouse to get our marriage license."

She lifted an eyebrow to convey her annoyance. "You're really pushing it, Tysen."

Instead of volleying back a smart remark he pulled her into his chest, lifted her chin and stared deeply into her eyes. "I'd rather piss you off and have you fight back, than to have you kill me with your silence. I called you and sent text messages and you didn't respond."

Maggie said the first thing that came to mind. "Stalker."

Ty shuttered his eyes, lowered his head and sealed her mouth with a kiss.

Maggie tried to refuse him but he restricted her movements by tightening his arms around her. She wouldn't enjoy his kiss. No way would she enjoy it.

Ty was gentle at first but he sucked her lips into his, stirring her passion from its hiding place. Maggie groaned. She didn't want him to stir anything, especially her passion.

He loosened his hold so he could stroke her jaw line with his thumb. Oh God! He knew exactly what to do to cripple her resolve and how to turn her into a heap of goo. Slowly, that incredible thumb made its way across her chin, down her neck to the hollow of her throat where it lingered. She felt his heat emanate into her throat. The warmth moved slowly throughout her body until it found her core. She had no choice but to tremble.

Ty continued the complex assault by urging her mouth open with his tongue. The erotic kiss made her lose her bearings. She was close to losing her inhibitions too. He laid his mouth against her ear. "Baby, you're mine. All mine."

She groaned to fight the pleasure. Maybe she moaned. She was in a thick, dense Tysen-fog so it was hard to tell. Somehow she managed to wedge a hand between them and give him a push. "Lunch," she said. "I'm starving."

"Me too." Ty's blue eyes shimmered with unspent passion. "Not for food."

Maggie swallowed hard. "Too bad. Food it is."

* * *

Maggie smirked at Ty's obvious aversion to eating anything wrapped in seaweed. He shouldn't have let her pick the restaurant. And she shouldn't be enjoying the faces he was making every few seconds.

"Fermented soybeans. Broiled eel. Tuna, crabmeat and avocado rolled with salmon." Ty stuck his finger in his mouth and pretended to gag as he ran down the menu.

"Don't be a baby." The word baby took Maggie's thoughts back to her apartment, not more than twenty minutes ago Ty had whispered that very word, in a very different context; a luscious, mind-boggling context.

"You're mouthy," Ty countered.

"Get used to it, Vincent." She messed with her menu. "I'm getting white tuna and cucumber."

Ty inclined his head to where an Asian gentleman wearing a starched white chef's hat was entertaining his customers with an onion volcano. "Whatever he's cooking, that's what I want."

"Okay, but the waiter is going to think you're weird when you order an onion volcano."

Ty scrunched his face. "The steak, knucklehead, not the onion volcano." He looked thoughtful when he closed his menu. "So…you're saying we're staying together?"

"I didn't say that."

"Yes you did. And you're still saying it…with your eyes. You want to be with me, Maggie."

It was painfully true. Maggie did want to be with him even though she knew full well it would be a threat to her mental health. She'd not only have to deal with Ty but also Loy. She coughed the word "bullshit".

Ty almost laughed himself off the chair and Maggie wanted to push him the rest of the way.

Under the table, Ty twined their legs. Maggie tried to pull loose, unsuccessfully. "I need sake," she said to a passing waiter.

The guy was caught off guard but he grinned. "I'll advise your waiter."

"Thank you," she said.

"Maggie, can we stop fighting? Please?"

Ty sounded as desperate as she felt. She sighed in surrender. "Yes. We can." She'd deliberately behaved like a juvenile as a way to turn him off, but it was getting old, even to her.

He took her hand and kneaded the top with his thumb. Maggie didn't want his touch, yet she did. Gah! It was grueling wanting something so bad, knowing it wasn't good for you. Even in those moments when she thought they were finished, she longed for his touch. It was sheer lunacy.

Ty looked thoughtful but continued to play with her hand, gently tapping her knuckles, running his fingers down hers, messing with her fingernails. Maggie grinned at the memory of Ty telling Quinn that he had himself a touchy-feely one. Pfft. He was the one who was all hands.

Ty stopped the hand manipulation. "Can we get this renegotiation out of the way?"

She needed to say no, "Yes" slipped out instead.

Ty grabbed her hand again, this time he turned it over to expose her palm. He lifted it to his lips while keeping his eyes locked with hers. Goosebumps coated every square inch of Maggie.

Their waiter arrived with the sake. "Are you ready to order?"

Maggie drew her hand away, rattled off her food choices and pointed to Ty. "He'll have an onion volcano."

Ty playfully rolled his eyes. "I'll have the steak and shrimp combo. Rice. No noodles." Only after the waiter was well away, did he move his chair closer to Maggie. "Before we're interrupted again, here's my proposal." His luminous blue eyes sparkled and Maggie knew she was sunk.

"I'd like for you to stay with me for..." He paused.

Maggie's heart flipped in her chest while the gas pedal of her pulse was stuck in turbo, pumping excitement through her veins, blowing past the mental stop signs that she kept in place. "For?"

"A year."

Maggie's speeding pulse slammed to a screeching halt. "A year," she repeated, dazedly.

"It would be better than six months, don't you think?"

"Sure. Fine. Whatever."

Ty sensed her disappointment. He felt his own too. He couldn't offer forever. Not yet. He had too many personal things to fix. Until he got his head on straight, he would only offer time in small increments. "Thank you. You won't regret it."

She wrinkled her nose. "Too late. I already do."

"You're such a drama queen, Margaret."

Maggie bristled and Ty refrained from grinning so she wouldn't clobber him right there in the restaurant.

"What's this sudden penchant for calling me by my full name?"

"I like your fire, *Margaret*." He pushed her bangs to one side and lifted her chin. "You're so cute when you're pissed."

She used her forearm to nudge him away. "Wow. I'm going to be freaking adorable for three hundred and sixty five days."

To gear Maggie away from sarcasm, Ty changed the subject with small talk about the weather. It was hotter than hell in Dallas and the extended forecast called for it to be a scorcher on their wedding day, with only a slight chance of showers.

"Good thing I bought a sleeveless wedding dress." Maggie lifted her eyebrows up and down.

"Tell me more."

Maggie wagged her finger back and forth. "You'll just have to wait and see."

The conversation turned into easy conversation about an array of subjects. He talked about his love for baseball and Maggie shared her love for animals, particularly dogs.

"Someday I'll have a Bassett Hound. If my building allowed pets I'd already have one."

"Why a Bassett Hound?"

Maggie smiled big. "Because they're devoted, sweet-tempered, affectionate animals."

"So am I."

She laughed. "I can housebreak a Bassett Hound."

"Ha. Ha. Aren't you funny?"

"Yep."

"By the way, my friends want to have a bachelor party for me tomorrow night." He must be getting old because he didn't want any part of a bachelor party. He didn't want to fly to Cancun via private jet. He didn't want strippers. All he wanted was to hang out with Maggie.

"Sounds like fun."

"I don't think it's going to happen because we need to put

our heads together and compile a guest list." He smirked. "Nothing like getting a last minute invitation to a wedding and having Loy Vincent expect you to be there." He meant it as a lighthearted comment, but it dawned on him how spot-on it was. His grandfather would expect everyone who was anybody to be at the wedding of his only grandson. If they weren't, he wouldn't be pleased; which meant, they would drop everything to make him happy. It was unreasonable. Ty made a silent pledge that when he had the reins at Vincent Oil, he would run the company as efficiently as his predecessor, but he wouldn't rule with an iron fist.

Maggie pulled out a small notepad, scribbled a few names and handed it to Ty. "Now you can go on your bachelor party."

"This is your guest list?"

"Uh huh."

"Your dad. Nancy." He read a few other names and quirked an eyebrow. "Seriously?"

"Not a long lineage as you can see."

What he said next was beyond the scope of his common sense. "We may have to jump start that lineage."

"Riiiight." Maggie scooted her chair away. "You wanted six more months. I'm giving you six more. That's it."

"You also said you wanted to trade the Porsche for a minivan."

Maggie sucked in her bottom lip, and Ty wanted to latched on to that plump mouth and kiss her senseless. He noticed her left hand. No ring. How had he missed that important detail? Trying to keep his temper in check, he dug his fingernails into his palms. "Where's your ring?"

Maggie casually sipped her sake and stared at him over the rim of the glass.

Ty slumped back in his chair, more hurt than mad. He shouldn't be, but dammit, he was. "Fine. Don't wear the damn thing."

Their food arrived and Ty was never so happy to see a slab of meat in all his life. He went at it with a vengeance, stabbing the steak with his knife, cursing without making a sound.

"Ty?"

Ty's head shot up when he recognized the voice from hell. Delia Smythfield. Tori's friend. Shit. He'd hoped to never bump into that pain in the rump ever again. Delia was a stunning blonde with piercing green eyes and a body built for sin. She had a flirty, fun veneer. Underneath, there was nothing fun. When things didn't go her way she had the temperament of a rabid raccoon. And she slung the f-word around like it was part of her normal vocabulary. He'd taken her out a few times, at Tori's request. Hated every minute of it. When he finally told Delia to piss off, Tori didn't speak to him for a week.

"Delia," Maggie said flatly.

Ty's head snapped to Maggie. She and Delia were familiar? "You two know each other?"

"Maggie and I worked together at Carriage Memorial until she got the boot." Delia slid into a chair, uninvited. She slanted a haughty glance at Ty, but focused the bulk of her attention on Maggie.

Ty frowned hard.

"Imagine my shock when I opened the newspaper this morning and saw your engagement picture. I didn't even know you were dating. It said you're getting married *this* weekend. That had to be a typo, surely."

"Not a typo," Ty said matter-of-factly, while he stared at his fiancée too. Maggie lowered her head, but he could see her gnawing her bottom lip so hard he expected it to spurt blood.

The waiter arrived and handed Delia a menu. "Can I get you something to drink, miss?"

"She's not staying," Ty said straight away.

"Vodka and cranberry," Delia said in that slow, purring voice that she used to snag men. She tapped her fingers on the table, a fraction of an inch from Ty's. "Put it on his tab." She laughed like she'd one-upped him. What next? Was she going to tell Maggie that she'd slept with him? She'd told everyone else. It was a lie; one he brushed off because who the hell cared? No one. At least until now. He had an inkling Maggie would care.

Maggie was extraordinarily quiet.

"I would normally ask how you met, but I already know," Delia quipped like she kept tabs on him.

Ty continued to frown. "Oh yeah?"

Maggie choked on a sip of sake.

Delia laughed. "Duh. You met at the hospital."

Ty studied Maggie closer. She wouldn't meet his eyes and was now wringing her hands in her lap. "We didn't meet at the hospital."

"Ohhhh. I thought you met when Maggie was your grandfather's rehab nurse."

It only took a millisecond for him to put two and two together. *Son of a bitch!*

Chapter Eleven

It had been a week of extraordinary blunders. Seeking Ellen's advice about her son would probably be her biggest.

Maggie sat in Ellen's driveway with the motor running, her head resting against the steering wheel. Why she was there, of all places, she had no idea. All she knew for certain was that she felt a special connection with Ty's mom. Maybe it was because she missed her own mom so much, or maybe it was Ellen's kind heart and wicked sense of humor.

Without lifting her head she fumbled for the key and turned off the engine.

The sun was starting to set, but the temperature still hovered in the high nineties making the inside of the car stifling hot almost right away. Maggie made another blind swipe for the button to lower the window.

There was no breeze. No air movement whatsoever. Just heavy heat that felt like she was covered in a wool blanket.

"Are you going to get out of the car or what?"

Maggie startled. "Ellen," she said.

Ellen's expression was warm but curious. She didn't ask why Maggie was there. She didn't ask anything. "I have wine," she simply said.

Maggie was thankful not to be interrogated right off the

bat. There was a better than good chance that Ellen already knew about the unrelenting chaos of she and Ty's relationship. There was also a good chance she'd heard about her son throwing a wad of bills on the table at the restaurant before storming out, leaving Maggie and Delia staring wide-eyed at one another. How could she not know? Everyone seemed to know everything. Every move she and Ty made. Every move they didn't make. Every breath they breathed. Every time they'd held their breath. Everyone knew. Their short relationship had been photographed and documented. The morning newspaper carried a picture of Ty giving someone the finger, Chaz Rosston, most likely, with a caption beneath that read: Big Money Bad Boy – Is the wedding off? Is Maggie Gray carrying Tysen Vincent's love child? A little birdie says yes to both.

A little birdie? Try a network of crows that were more than happy to feed on the Vincent family drama and tweet it to anyone who would listen.

It *was* safe to assume the wedding was off. Ty had been so angry and accusing in the restaurant, it was hard to imagine she would walk down the aisle on Saturday, or any day for that matter. She should be marginally happy that things had fallen apart, instead of feeling weak and on the verge of tears. This fragile behavior was so not like her. She was a cardiac rehab nurse, for crying out loud. Nursing was not for sissies. It took strong people to deal with folks who fought their health issues. Some patients – like Loy Vincent – tested the medical community to the breaking point. He didn't want to follow the rules and had tried to push her around. *Not in this lifetime, bucko.* Maggie wondered how she could be so tough with her patients but a complete wimp in her personal life. Thanks to the Vincent men she was falling apart at the seams. She tried to rationalize the breakup with the old saying that *everything happens for a reason*. She and Ty's relationship had been based on a lie.

Well, karma was a bitch and had caught up with them.

"Come on, Maggie, you look like you're about to pass out."

Tears blazed like a hot bonfire behind Maggie's eyes, but she was determined not to fall apart. Not again. Certainly not here. If she was lucky her tear ducts were swollen shut from all the bawling she'd done yesterday.

The second she climbed out of the car, Ellen draped an arm around her shoulders and led her inside the spacious two-story brick house.

"Welcome to my oversized home." Ellen snickered. "This was Toy's idea. Six bedrooms. Three full baths. A game room." She rolled her eyes. "I don't need a game room and I can only sleep in one bedroom at a time. I do love the pool though." She shook her head. "No matter how hard I tried to live a simple life, my sweet Toy wouldn't allow it."

Maggie squeezed her hand. "I wish I'd known him."

Ellen gave her a broad smile. "Toy was mouthwatering gorgeous. One look at the man and I wanted to rip off my clothes." Her grin stretched wider. "I'm sure that conjures up a creepy vision for you, but it's true. He had looks that were out of this world and he had a big personality to go with it. You either loved him or hated him." Ellen released a soft sigh. "He was easy on the eyes and hard on the nerves. My son is the spitting image of him in every way." She motioned for Maggie to have a seat on a sage green sectional sofa. "With that disclosure, it's time to kill a bottle of wine. Maybe two." She laughed her way to the kitchen.

Maggie wanted to curl up on the couch and close her eyes. Instead, she looked around. The love seat was also sage green but the recliners were a soft shade of cinnamon. Sage brocade throw pillows – some square, some round – were tossed on the furniture while large striped pillows in cinnamon were propped against a stone fireplace. Indoor palm trees, a dragon tree, corn plants, and a collection of smaller plants filled the rest of the space. Ellen had turned her expensive surroundings into a tasteful but comfortable home.

Maggie felt some of the tension in her shoulders give way. Ellen returned with a bottle of merlot and two glasses. She popped the cork and poured two glasses.

Maggie took the offered glass and set it aside, afraid that even a few sips would make her lights go out.

Ellen removed her sandals and put her feet up on an extra-large ottoman. She motioned for Maggie to do the same. "Let's talk."

"I don't know where to start."

"At the beginning. Tell me everything."

At the time, coming to see Ellen made perfect sense. Ellen knew Ty better than anyone. Plus she had the wisdom of having dealt with Loy. Now Maggie questioned the sanity of drawing Ellen into the madness. "You know that moment when all hope seems lost yet you seek comfort in the enemy camp? Yeah. That." She laughed, nervously.

Ellen laughed too. "Dear girl, this is not the enemy camp. Not even close." She sat up straight and studied Maggie. "You and I share a common goal – we both want to see Tysen happy."

"That's not the goal."

"Yes it is. Continue."

Maggie lowered her head and looked up through her lashes. "Don't toss me out on my head when I'm finished, okay?"

"Won't happen."

The incredible tale of woe and wonderment began, slowly at first, but the more Maggie talked the more the valve of information turned until she wasn't just reliving all that happened over the last few days, she was baring her soul. Ellen's mouth dropped open a couple of times, but she remained quiet, letting Maggie finish.

"That's it. A year's worth of drama fit into six days." Maggie's sigh was heavy with regret.

Ellen's blue eyes gave little away. She propped an elbow on the arm of the sofa and ran her fingers over the dimple in her chin. "I'm going to kick my son's ass," she said offhandedly.

Maggie did not see that coming. She didn't mean to rat out Ty or pit mother against son. All she really wanted was an objective third party; someone who could sift through the mud and clear up a few things, someone who would give it to her straight, someone who would take her by the shoulders and give her a good shake. She'd been a fool to think Ellen was that person. Ellen was equally tied to the mayhem and in no way could she be unbiased. "You can't do that."

"Kill joy."

Maggie was torn between a groan and a chuckle. "Gahhh." She put her face in her hands. "I'm a candidate for some serious therapy. I've allowed myself to get sucked into something I had no business being in. I let Ty and Loy use me. It's been a mess from the get-go but there have been some spectacular moments. I want to walk away and not look back, but a small part of me wants to stay. Am I losing it, or what?"

Ellen nodded with a strange look in her eyes. "I can top that. Loy is the most amazing prick I've ever met." She clunked her wine glass on the lamp table beside her. "I can't stand him but I love him. Does that make any friggin' sense?"

Maggie finally took a sip of wine. She understood the challenge of feelings regarding Loy. He'd screwed up her life so much she no longer recognized it, yet she didn't hate him…darn close, but no, there was no hate. "He got me fired so he could bend me to his will. Instead of wanting to put him in a headlock, I find myself wanting to understand him. How whacked is that?"

"Now you know what I've been dealing with all these

years." Ellen refilled her wine glass and offered to top off Maggie's. Maggie waved her hand over her nearly full glass. Ellen took another drink, caught a drip of wine with her tongue and then frowned. "Loy got you fired?" She shook her head like it would clear whatever was going on inside it. "I was listening, I swear. It's just that my brain seems to skim over things these days thanks to pre-menopause." She chuckled. "It's a time lapse thing. Luckily my mind backs up to latch onto the important stuff. I'd be in big trouble if it didn't. Anyway, I digress. What the hell was Loy thinking?"

"That I'd be putty in his hands if I didn't have a job."

"That conniving bastard. When I get a hold of him…"

"No, Ellen. I have to fix this myself. When the time is right, Loy and I will have words. I just needed someone to listen."

"I can't promise not to knock his block off. If he so much as looks at me sideways, I'm taking him down."

Maggie guzzled her glass of wine. She quite innocently set the stage for World War III. "Let's talk about something else. Did you know that I help out at the soup kitchen a couple of days a week?"

"That's awesome, Maggie." Ellen shared that she found it difficult to volunteer without paparazzi descending on the scene. "I tried to help with a blood drive once but my presence took away from the great cause it was supposed to be. So I've stayed away and now donate money instead of my time."

"You know, Ellen, if you want to help out at the soup kitchen, I can make it happen and I promise you that if the media butts in, we'll deal with them in a special way." Maggie giggled. "After they do a sink full of dirty dishes they can snap a few pictures."

Ellen studied her for a long moment. "Loy has misjudged you." She held up her wine glass so they could clink them in solidarity. "Beneath that soft exterior lurks a kick ass woman."

"I'm not so kick-ass. I allowed Loy and Ty to buy my services. I fought the idea of marrying Ty. And now…" The tears she'd held back, spilled out.

Ellen leaned in. "And now…?"

"It's all I think about. It's all I want. When he's near I want to clobber him. When he's not around it feels like a part of me is missing. I've only known him a handful of days but it's been long enough for him to get under my skin." She winced for sounding like a blubbering, lovesick fool. Ellen handed her a box of tissues. Maggie took a few tissues, blotted her eyes and blew her nose.

"Sex changes the dynamics of every relationship, dear girl."

Maggie wasn't even mildly jarred by the comment since she'd accepted that Ellen said what was on her mind. It was one of the things she liked about her. "We haven't had sex." A strange sound worked from Maggie's throat. "We almost did a couple of times but we were interrupted."

The corners of Ellen's eyes crinkled. "Really?" At Maggie's reluctant nod, Ellen laughed. "That tickles the hell out of me."

"Huh?"

"My son is so much like Loy it's scary. Things come easy to those two. What they want, they get. The fact Ty's had to wait – even at your expense – is music to my ears." She took an overlarge sip of wine and shrugged. "What can I say? Sometimes a mom knows when her son needs to be taken down a notch." She cocked an impish eyebrow. "Make him work for it, Maggie."

Maggie felt the color rise in her cheeks.

Ellen gave her a pointed look. "No need to be embarrassed. You and I are friends before we're anything else, okay?"

Maggie nodded and blew her nose again. "I won't be making him work for it, because we're no longer together. The engagement is off and so is the wedding."

"Au contraire. Loy called earlier and asked who I wanted to invite to the wedding." Laughter jiggled Ellen's well-toned frame. "He's running around like a chicken with his head cut off. He's so excited, Maggie. I am too. My son is getting hitched and I'm going to have a daughter-in-law; one that will give the boy a run for his money."

* * *

"Cancun and strippers would've been a helluva lot more fun," Trigg Sinclair said, trying to keep his glass of beer steady so it wouldn't slosh on his shirt and also trying to balance the paper boat holding two hotdogs with mustard and onion so he wouldn't wear them too.

The bachelor party made their way toward Vincent Oil Company's box seats at the Rangers Ballpark.

Trigg had grumbled at the concession stand that they could've placed an order and had the food delivered. He also whined repeatedly that they should've gone to Cancun. He'd said it so much that Ty and the rest of the guys were ready to put duct tape across his mouth.

"Damn, Trigg, you're turning into a real hag. Stop your bellyaching." Quinn smacked him on the back and half the beer in his glass sloshed over the side.

"Thanks a lot, dirtbag."

Quinn laughed with a wicked gleam in his eyes. "Besides, why would Ty want to go to Cancun with strippers in tow when he has Maggie to belly dance for him? The thought of those sweet hips gyrating is hot!" He elbowed Ty.

Jake Garrison, the quietest of the four, frowned. "That's crossing the line, Quinn."

Ty laughed but he wasn't feeling particularly amused. He didn't want anyone picturing Maggie gyrating anything. But that was the least of his irritation. Angry thoughts had been piling up since he'd blown out of the restaurant yesterday. He felt volatile but on-hold; like someone had lit the fuse and the fire was taking its good old time getting to the dynamite. He would feel much better if he could just explode. After the scene at the restaurant, he'd headed to the bar to see two old friends, scotch and Sam Bright. Until the wee hours of the morning, he drank whiskey and bent Sam's ear. He finally crawled into bed sometime around four thirty in the morning, so trashed he should've been out before his head hit the pillow. His mind, however, was so revved and his feelings so torn he couldn't shut his eyes. In the darkness of his room, his thoughts went wild. He was angry at Maggie. He loved Maggie. She should be locked up. He wanted to marry her that instant. How could she conspire with his grandfather against him? Maggie Gray was a real piece of work. She was two-faced and heartless. He thought Delia was bad. Ha! Delia couldn't hold a candle to Maggie. By six o'clock, he ran out of steam. He closed his eyes. Thankfully, they stayed closed. The second he woke up, all that troubled him before he fell asleep, was back, making him even more nuts.

"Tori's in a tizzy. She has no idea what to get you and Maggie for a wedding present and she harped all morning that she has nothing to wear to the wedding. That woman has more clothes than the Galleria. What is it with women?"

"When you find out let me know." Ty's sarcasm made Quinn's eyes flash with interest.

Quinn held onto the back of Ty's shirt and motioned for the other two guys to go on. "We'll be there in a few."

Trigg frowned. "What are you doing?"

"None of your business," Quinn said. The second the others were out of sight, the questioning began. "What's going on, Ty?"

"Nothing." Ty didn't want to tell anyone anything; except for Maggie, he wouldn't mind telling her a thing or two.

"Bullshit. I know you. You're wound so tight I expected you to punch Trigg when he wouldn't quit his bitching. And I baited you with the comment about Maggie's belly dancing. You laughed but the icy look you gave me said if I didn't shut up you'd kill me without a second's thought. Now that it's just you and me, talk. Tell me what happened."

Ty ran his hands over his face. "Nothing a bottle of scotch won't fix."

"Not a good enough answer. Try again."

Ty leaned against a steel girder. "Don't dig, Quinn." In no way did he want to discuss Maggie. She'd questioned why he wasn't upfront with Quinn and Tori. At the time, he didn't know. Now he knew. He didn't trust Quinn the way good friends were supposed to trust each other. He didn't trust anyone. Not only did his world fall apart yesterday, but someone had tipped off the press. The morning paper had a running account of everything. They knew where he'd been and that he'd ordered steak and shrimp. There was even a bit about Maggie's severance from the hospital with a hint that Loy may have played a part in getting her terminated. Someone close was doing a tell-all with the media. When he discovered the culprit, he wouldn't just give them a piece of his mind, he'd give them a piece of his fist too. An even more noxious thought hit him in the gut. What if Maggie was the guilty party? Maybe she and Chaz had partnered up to ruin him once and for all. Instead of just two-timing him with a double deal, she was possibly three-timing him with the press. Of course, if it was Maggie, he couldn't use his fists, but he sure as hell could cut her out of his life, forever.

"Don't bottle this up. We're friends. Friends share."

"If we're such good friends, why didn't you and Tori welcome Maggie with open arms? Why did you make her feel like she was second rate?"

Quinn didn't take time to think about his answer. "Habit."

"Habit? That's all you've got?" Ty dropped a cluster of cuss words.

Quinn stood with his arms crossed. "Are ya done?"

"I don't know."

"I haven't changed, Ty. I'm still the same asshole I was in school. I'm comfortable being an asshole. You, on the other hand, have developed this annoying nice-guy attitude. Ever since your…"

"Ever since my dad died? Is that what you were going to say?" A twinge in his chest warned of impending pain. Perfect. Just freaking perfect. The chest episodes were just one more thing that would eventually make headlines. He was amazed that the media hadn't already picked up that story, especially with that 9-1-1 call and his overnight stay at the hospital. The newspapers knew he had steak and shrimp at the restaurant but no idea that he had an IV hooked up to him? Somewhere in that information was a clue as to who was selling him out, he just didn't have the time or focus to figure it out. All he knew was that once the press caught wind of his heart issues, they would spin that gem a thousand different ways: heir to oil fortune on his deathbed, six months to live, his playboy days have caught up to him, all the money in the world can't save him. On and on and on. Truly, he didn't care what they printed. The Board of Directors, however, would care. Oh would they care; especially those who were against him filling his grandfather's shoes. Those untrue snippets would make their case against him. He was getting to the point he didn't give a rat's ass whether they approved him or not. His dad wouldn't… Ty jerked hard like he'd been hit upside the head. The reality was that his dad wouldn't approve of Ty risking the future of Vincent Oil by letting it fall into Terron Wade's hands. Plus, a no-vote from the Board would destroy his grandfather.

The twinge in his chest intensified.

Over the last twelve months his mom encouraged him to embrace the memory of his father instead of letting it hurt him. She was right. One hundred percent right. Maggie's words at the airport came back in a rush too. 'Play the game if you have to but don't lose yourself while you're doing it'. At the time, he'd been too tense and impatient to listen, but now he heard the wisdom. It only took a fraction of a second to determine he *had* lost himself – long before he met Maggie. And it was time to find his way again. Time to honor his dad's memory with hard work, not grief and pain. Time to recognize that everything his grandfather did – right or wrong – stemmed from love of family.

Everything running through his thoughts – at a hundred miles per hour – was earth-shaking yet empowering. Ty was suddenly pumped with adrenaline and ready to do whatever it took to prove his love and loyalty.

An even harder twinge put him to the test. *Bring it on*, he silently dared.

To his surprise, nothing happened. No slicing pain. No moment when he thought he'd been ripped wide open. Nothing.

He fisted his hands, waiting.

Still nothing.

Quinn gave Ty a small push. "For a year now, you've been someone else. You're so damned nice I want to puke. Since you met Maggie you've gotten worse. You've been going around smiling like you've lost your mind."

"I'm not smiling now." That sounded stupid as hell. Ty finally laughed. "This is the most 'effed up conversation ever."

He offered Quinn some truth. "I can't be the guy I used to be. I don't want to be that guy. I'm just now starting to understand some things. The people I have in my life and the relationships that I have, are special. I want to keep them. If I want to smile like I've lost my mind, that's my deal. I won't apologize. If you can't handle who I am, then I guess you'll have to find a new best friend." The elephant that had taken up residence on his shoulders didn't seem so heavy. Everything he said, he meant. His relationships were special, including the one with Maggie. He wanted her so much. Not just the soft, sexy woman with the extraordinary blue eyes and great hips. He wanted the woman who was willing to go out on a limb to help his grandfather, the woman who unselfishly agreed to marry him so that he and his grandfather would be on good terms. The awareness that Maggie would give him a year of her life to make his life better was the final slap upside the head he needed. She was not two-faced or heartless. She wasn't three-timing him with the press. She was a *care package*...sent to him...by his dad. Emotion clouded his eyes. "Thanks for the talk, Quinn. You have no idea how helpful it was. I've got to go."

* * *

Maggie stood in front of the full-length mirror posing in her wedding dress. She didn't want to return something so incredible. Maybe she would keep it as a reminder that someday she would find her Mr. Wonderful. He wouldn't come with a conniving grandfather, snooty friends, or plans to call it quits in a year. She would meet him as a single woman, not a divorcee. They would fall in love, have a proper wedding that they planned together and when the time was right, they'd have a few kids. Maybe they would buy a minivan. Most of all, they would be in it for the long haul. If she was lucky, she'd have an amazing mother-in-law like Ellen would've been. Before she could be overtaken by a sob, her cell phone rang from the kitchen where it laid on the counter. Maggie let it go to voicemail without verifying the caller. Loy had called three times while she was with Ellen. She didn't answer his calls then and she wouldn't answer them now. She wasn't in the proper frame of mind to deal with him. For now, she would follow Ellen's advice, 'let the bastard sweat'.

She ran her hand down the front of the dress and carefully slid it from her shoulders.

A thunderous knock on her door made her jump like she'd been caught doing something illegal. She hurriedly pushed the dress back on the hanger, pulled on her jean shorts and tee, and ran to the door to smash her eye against the peek-hole.

Tousled blondish-brown hair filled her line of vision. Maggie backed away from the door with a measure of panic. She wrung her hands and walked to the kitchen. After a few moments of clenching and unclenching her hands, she returned to the front door. Another loud knock made her flinch.

"Open up, Maggie. I know you're in there. I saw your car in the parking lot and I can hear you breathing."

There's no way he could hear her breathing, especially since she was holding her breath.

"Are you here to reclaim the ring?" Maggie put her ear to the door and strained to hear his reaction – a sharp intake of air that was followed by deep silence. Her gaze dropped to her left hand. "I'm sorry. I didn't mean that. It just came out."

"Open the door before I take it off at the hinges."

"Leave my door alone."

"Then open it."

With the speed of a snail, she slid back the chain lock and unlocked the dead bolt.

The second she turned the knob, Ty's weight against the door opened it with so much force she went reeling backwards. He caught her before she fell.

"Maggie," he said softly.

She stiffened in his arms.

Ty brought her hand up to display the ring and a smile curved his mouth. His eyes sparkled with an indefinable emotion. "It's time for us to stop fighting." He swooped down and claimed her mouth and Maggie trembled from sheer joy. Ty was right. It was time to let whatever this was...happen. She allowed him to envelope her tightly in his arms and suck her lips into his.

A dizzying current raced through her, destroying any latent resistance, making her surrender to her feelings. She wanted this. Wanted him.

Ty urged her mouth open with his tongue and plundered her with hunger. He tasted and explored, drugging her with desire. Each movement of his mouth fanned the flames until she was hot. So very hot. She wanted to rip off her clothes and his, so nothing would separate them. She wanted to feel his bare chest against hers, heartbeat against heartbeat.

Ty unsnapped her jean shorts, slid them from her hips and toyed with the elastic of her underwear.

He kissed her deeper.

Ty's breath's came in short pants. Maggie struggled to breathe too.

They parted and stared into the depths of each other's eyes, both looking for answers and for the green light to continue.

Ty's voice was filled with the strain of self-control. "If you need for me to stop you'd better say so right now, sweetheart."

Maggie wanted Ty with every fiber of her being. Needed him more than air. Before she could compile a list of reasons why this shouldn't happen, she urged him on. "Please don't stop."

Ty's blue eyes sparkled with victory. He scooped her in his arms and carried her the short distance to the bedroom. He stood her by the bed and hauled her against him. Trailing soft kisses across her cheek, he moved to her ear. "I haven't done this in a while."

Passion shot through Maggie with a velocity that would've

Married to Maggie

knocked her backwards if he didn't have her securely in his arms. Ty's moist breath rustled against her ear lobe. "Don't hold it against me if things don't go exactly as planned." He chuckled softly into her hair but Maggie detected a faint thread of nervousness in his laugh.

"It's been forever for me too," she admitted just as quietly. "If a certain *something* doesn't happen, don't be disappointed." With fumbling fingers, Maggie pulled the tail of Ty's shirt from his jeans, undid his belt and knew there was no turning back. In a heartbeat she'd eased down his zipper.

"I could never be disappointed with you, Maggie." Ty's words were raspy and filled with hunger.

Maggie brushed her lips across his mouth in appreciation. "I love you" was on the tip of her tongue but she tucked it away. It would be liberating to say what was in her heart but if Ty didn't offer the same, it would hurt. At the moment, the only things she wanted to deal with were his incredible mouth and the anticipation of making love.

In one fluid move, Maggie pulled his shirt up and over his head. Ty's eager hands did the same to her t-shirt.

Without breaking eye contact, Ty pushed his jeans from his hips, down his legs and kicked them aside.

Maggie took a full step back and provocatively slipped the straps of her black lacy bra from her shoulder. She lowered her head but looked up through her lashes to gauge his reaction.

The rakish lift of his eyebrows egged her on.

Maggie leisurely unfastened the hooks of the bra and let it fall to her feet. In just a pair of black lace boy-cut underwear, she grinned shamelessly and began to move her hips just like she did in belly dancing class. Her slow, flowing hip lifts made Ty's eyes go wide. She added pharaonic arms, reaching, sliding them up and down, keeping her fingers soft. With short, isolated movements of her torso and hips, her unrestrained breasts shifted with her. Maggie lowered her arms and extended them outward, turning her wrists in circles before motioning to Ty with her index finger.

Ty's eyes were wide and his state of arousal was magnificent. "Mmm, Maggie." He closed the short gap between them and nuzzled her neck. "So sexy." In that moment, she felt sexy, wanted, and she was on fire.

Ty eased her down onto the bed and lowered himself above her, his knees locking her in place against him. He smiled, brushed her lips with his before burying his face in her neck. He whispered against her skin how much he needed her and feathered soft kisses across her throat.

Maggie gripped his shoulders when he gently nipped her collar bone with his teeth. When he cupped her breasts and gently squeezed, she moaned repeatedly.

Her pleasured sounds seemed to rev his actions. He lowered his head to capture her nipple with his lips. Slowly, he pulled the distended bud with his tongue. When he moved to her other nipple and gave it the same great attention, Maggie thought she would die from a combination of fire and joy.

Ty kept his hands in place but inched his tongue slowly down to Maggie's flat belly. The firm muscles she'd gotten from belly dancing tensed under his mouth. He reared up with a smile. "Trust me, sweetheart." He dipped his tongue in her belly button.

"Tyyyyy." Maggie said, her chest raising and lowering rapidly from her ragged breathing.

Ty moved up and graced her mouth with a series of rapid kisses while fiery sensations pulsed through him, his want so unbelievable he expected if they didn't hurry, it would be over for him soon. With one hand he held Maggie, with the other he slipped on a condom.

Before he took his next breath…the night fell apart.

A sequence of low knocks made them both groan.

How was it possible that again when he was about to fully

love Maggie, someone decided to show up? The only conceivable explanation was an airplane had to be flying over Maggie's building with a banner that read – Be a pain in the ass today. Drop by apartment 408. Do it now!

Ty couldn't hold back the stress of being fully charged with need and the mental smack down that he would have to wait. "If that's Quinn and Tori, I'm going to beat the shit out of them." If it was Nancy, it would be up to Maggie to beat the shit out of her. He made a snap decision that once whoever was at the door was dealt with, he and Maggie would relocate to a hotel room where privacy could be guaranteed with orders at the front desk not to give out their room number.

Maggie held him tightly in place. "Let's not answer."

Ty gently squeezed her breasts and pecked the tip of her nose with a kiss.

The pest continued to knock, harder.

Ty growled.

"Maggie, I need to talk," came a pitiful sounding voice from the opposite side of the door.

"No. No. No." Ty sighed with exasperation and rolled away from Maggie. This was so not happening again.

Maggie was out of bed and into her clothes in a hurry. She rushed toward the door. Ty cut in front of her. "I'll get it." He finished tucking his shirt in his jeans.

"My apartment. My door. Besides, I showed up at her place earlier. It's only right she show up at mine."

"You went to my mom's? Why did you go there?"

Maggie shrugged. "I needed to talk."

What he did next was as good as a flick to Maggie's forehead – he put his hands up in surrender. "You win."

Maggie recoiled at the anger in his voice. "What does that mean?"

"It means I freaking don't understand any of this. Things are getting out of hand in a big way and if I had an ounce of sense, I should just walk away." He ran a hand over the back of his neck like he was trying to work out a kink. "I thought my life was screwed up *before* I met you."

Maggie was stunned. A minute ago they were caught up in desire so hot they could've burned the place down, now Ty was backing away like she'd done something wrong. Her mind and body were still reeling with the pleasured effects of his hands and kisses and it was hard to gear down to understand this sudden change in circumstances. "Ty, it's okay," she said tenderly. "We'll make it happen. I promise."

"It's not just the sex. It's everything. You did a deal with my grandfather. You did a deal with me. Now you're going behind my back and visiting my mom. Why are you driven to make my crazy life even more insane?"

Maggie went numb in an instant. Gone was the passion. Delicious memories of being naked in each other's arms were erased. Wanting to tell him she loved him was replaced with the need to tell him to jump off the nearest overpass.

Another knock made the hair bristle at the nape of Maggie's neck. She glared at Ty and nudged him out of the way. Before she turned the doorknob, she took a breath. "Ellen," she said, welcoming the friend who had the ill fortune of birthing a blockhead.

"Thank God you're home." Ellen sighed. "I needed to get to you before Loy did."

A high probability that her life had just gone from bad to worse made Maggie feel sick…and dizzy. She grabbed the door to steady herself. "What happened?"

"I screwed up. You didn't want me to say anything to Loy, but the more I thought about him firing you, the madder I got. I drove to his house and told him off." Ellen puffed out her cheeks. "Bad move. I'm now banned from the wedding."

"Oh no." Maggie had wanted someone with a friendly ear to listen to the chaos. That's it. She hadn't meant to deepen a family rift. "I shouldn't have said anything." Consumed with guilt, she met Ty's gaze. His blue eyes were now a silvery shade of titanium and just as cold.

Ellen became aware of her son. "Ty?"

Ty ignored his mom and advanced on Maggie. "You couldn't leave well enough alone, could you? This," he moved his finger back and forth between them, "whatever the hell it is, is strictly between you and me. Not you, me, my mom and grandfather." A low growl charged the air that separated them and Maggie took a step back. Ty moved when she moved and his eyes thinned until they were almost closed. "When my mom and grandfather have words, it gets ugly. They go at each other like a cat and dog confined in a closet." He injected her with a bigger dose of blame. "You, of all people, should know better. My granddad has heart issues, for crying out loud. What are you trying to do, kill him?"

Maggie was overwhelmed with so many different emotions she didn't know whether to give in to tears or hit him with a lamp.

"Check that temper, Tysen," Ellen ordered without raising her voice. "Maggie and I had a couple of glasses of wine and talked about the men in our life. What's the big deal?"

Ty stood with his arms crossed, glaring from his mom to her.

Whatever worry or anxiety Ellen came with seemed to be gone, or at least tucked away. She placed her attention solely on Maggie with a sudden mischievous glint in her eyes. "I do believe I've *interrupted* something."

"Trust me, you didn't interrupt anything important." Maggie tried to sound convincing while giving Ty the mental jab he needed.

Ty's response came as a hefty wince. He latched onto his mom's hand. "It's time to go. We'll leave your car parked and I'll drive you home so *we* can talk." He slung a hard glance at

Maggie.

Maggie was a mix of anger and regret, but she would stand her ground. The inner-voice that sometimes kept her steady and other times landed her in trouble, prompted her to put out a feeler. She touched Ellen's shoulder. "I could use your help tomorrow if you have time. I have to drop by the florist to pick out flowers." The comment was meant to soothe Ellen and disturb Ty.

As predicted, a glimmer of happiness and conspiracy lit Ellen's expression.

"No need to pick out flowers," Ty said with all the flexibility of a steel beam.

They didn't need flowers at the wedding? Or there wouldn't be a wedding?

Ty tugged his mom out the door and closed it behind them.

Maggie slumped against the door, folded her arms around her and closed her eyes. This on-again off-again arrangement was about as pleasant as running barefoot through a field of stinging nettles and the smidgen of gumption she had left wouldn't allow Ty or Loy to toss her aside without a fight. They'd begged her to help them and that's exactly what she intended to do. When she agreed to their individual whacked-out plans, she'd shelved her integrity and risked her good name. Cutting her loose was not an option. If they did, the press would not be kind. Loy and Ty would take a hit but they'd bounce back, whereas, she would not.

Maggie flung open the door and ran down the hall. She caught up to Ty and Ellen at the elevator. The doors were on their way closed. She shoved her arm in and the built-in safety feature reopened the doors. She stood halfway in the elevator and halfway in the hall with her hands on her hips. "A deal is a deal, Ty. Like it or not, you and I are getting married. You are not backing out. I won't let you. You had better be at the rehearsal tomorrow night and you better show up at the ceremony on Saturday. Understand?"

Ty looked mad enough to eat nails. From the corner of her eye Maggie caught Ellen's smirk.

Maggie's heart pounded in her chest while the thunder of power roared in her ears. She backed out of the elevator and allowed the doors to close.

* * *

"She's good for you, ya know?"

Ty cast a squinty-eyed glance at his mom as he opened the passenger side door. "So is broccoli but I still don't like it."

Ellen Peppersmith-Vincent rolled her eyes and started to climb into the Porsche but stopped. "You're a brilliant man, Tysen, but sometimes you can be…" She twisted her mouth to the side as if searching for a delicate way to be forthright.

Ty toyed with her, even though he was in no mood to jest. "A genius?"

"You know what they say about geniuses – borderline insane."

Ty released a small laugh. So did his mom.

"Hardheaded. Now that's a word, isn't it?" Ellen quipped. She finally got in the car and put down the window.

Ty crouched so they were eye to eye. "So I'm a brilliant, borderline insane, hardhead who doesn't like…broccoli?"

Ellen lifted her shoulders in a shrug. "Broccoli. Maggie."

The light taunting was over. Soon the serious conversation would commence. He didn't want to hear it, yet he wanted to hear all that she had to say. It was the whole point of driving her home.

By the time they got to the first stop light, it was go-time.

"I meant what I said about you being brilliant, Tysen. As far as IQ, you've run away with the brains in this family and that's quite a feat since your grandfather is an intelligent…ass." She grinned devilishly, but when she spoke about his dad the radiance in her eyes changed to a soft sadness. "I was in awe of your father's mind. He knew stuff I could only dream of knowing. The man oozed confidence and was the master of the deal. When Vincent Oil wanted or needed something, he made it happen. But he had something more incredible than intelligence – he had a great capacity to love. You are your father in every way. You're confident, loyal, have an intelligence that would shock your grandfather if he paid attention, and you possess business skills that will keep Vincent Oil healthy and make them a force to be reckoned with for years to come." Her voice trembled ever so slightly. "Your father would be proud. He'd also be over the moon that you allowed someone as special as Maggie into your life."

Ty merged onto I-635, trying to deal with thoughts of his dad and thoughts of Maggie – both were pains in the chest, just differently. He drew his arms close to his body while holding onto the steering wheel as a way to handle the things going on in his head and his chest. He made the mistake of sparing his mom a quick look. Those blue eyes bored into his soul, making her privy to everything.

"Ty, I've said it before and I'm saying it again, don't let your father's memory cripple you. Let him be your strength. It's also time to stop fighting your feelings for Maggie. Your father once told me that I helped him become the man he needed and wanted to be. Let Maggie do the same for you, son. Let her help you. You need her. And she needs you."

Ty remained quiet while he tried to handle the serrated knife of pain cutting diagonally across his chest and the comments aimed at his heart.

A quarter of a mile up the road he merged onto the exit ramp. The pain had mostly subsided. "You think the Vincent men are smart?" His mouth twitched with a smile. "I think the

Peppersmith's, one in particular, got the lion's share of brains."

"What can I say, women are smart creatures." She patted his arm. "We need to be since our men are brilliant but extremely thickheaded at times."

In no time, they were parked in his mom's driveway.

"Come in for a cup of coffee?"

Ty shook his head. "You've given me a lot to think about." He hopped out of the car, opened the passenger door and enveloped his mom in a hug. "I don't know what's going to happen between me and Maggie. Whatever decision I make I'll have to live with and so will you. Just don't get mad if it's not the one you'd like me to make."

"It's your life. You have to do what's right for you." She stretched up to peck his cheek with a kiss. "Just don't leave Maggie standing at the altar, if you get my drift."

"Again, don't get mad at the way I choose to handle things, if you get *my* drift."

Chapter Twelve

Maggie sat at the kitchen table in her pajamas with a bad case of bed head and dark circles under her eyes, staring at the folded sheet of paper setting in front of her. In just over twenty four hours she'd either be married or she'd be the laughing stock of Dallas. She flipped open the paper, made a face and flipped it closed. It was tempting to rip the certificate that would declare them man and wife into bits of confetti and toss them out the window to scatter the ground below. She stared at the document with such heated intensity that it should've singed the edges. A sigh whooshed from someplace deep, possibly her soul. She couldn't singe the paper or so much as put a wrinkle in the blasted thing just like she couldn't skip the rehearsal and wedding like she'd planned in the darkness of her room last night when she couldn't fall asleep. She wasn't a quitter.

A low rap at the door made Maggie perk up. She peered into the peek-hole, slung the door open and drew Ellen into a swift hug. "Wasn't sure I'd see you today." She didn't add anything more because they both knew what the carefully worded greeting meant.

"You'll most likely see me every day for the rest of your life," Ellen quipped jovially, but she didn't fully meet Maggie's eyes. Ellen's way of saying things were iffy but she was holding onto hope that they'd get better?

Ellen sniffed the air. "Coffee?"

Maggie inclined her head toward the kitchen. "Just made a fresh pot."

Ellen dropped her purse on the sofa and rushed to the coffee pot like coffee was the one thing that could sustain life. She gestured to the tufts of hair spiking Maggie's crown. "I'll help myself to a cup while you hit the shower. Where do you keep your cups?"

Maggie pointed to the last cabinet. "I thought I'd go out like this." She fluffed her hair and wrinkled her nose with amusement. "Chaz Rosston and his cronies would love it. Tomorrow's headlines: Big Money Bad Boy and Messy Maggie." She giggled. So did Ellen.

Ellen wrapped her hands around her coffee cup and took a careful sip. "You're so different from any of the girls Ty's had in his life. You actually have a sense of humor."

It was meant to be a compliment yet it served as a reminder that Maggie wouldn't have an exclusive with Ty. He'd probably fill his nights with the likes of Delia Smythfield or Rachel Montaigne, discreetly of course; perhaps not too discreetly the closer it came to ending their twelve month contract. Melancholia filled the pit of Maggie's stomach but she made herself smile in spite of it. "Laughter is the best medicine." Right now, she needed to laugh her butt off to keep from permanently creasing her forehead.

"Time to dazzle Chaz with your beauty instead of hair that's scaring even me."

Maggie chuckled. "Make yourself at home." She dashed to the bathroom and turned the shower to the hottest setting. Like hot magic fingers, the water massaged the tight muscles in her shoulders and neck. She moved her neck from side to side and gave herself a pep talk. Today, she would win that Oscar. She would smile until her face hurt. She would look and act the part of Ty's fiancée. Only a handful of people would know that things were amiss. Her father had called last night to catch up. While she'd kept her despair to a minimum, she gave it to him straight – there may or may not be a wedding. He wasn't surprised and he'd offered his take on things, 'You can lead a horse's ass to water, but you can't make the butthead drink.' He'd said that Loy contacted him to vent. Things were not going as planned and Loy was ready to strangle both Ty and Maggie. She told her dad that it would be hard for Loy to strangle her while she was busy strangling him. They ended the call with some heavy thoughts – her father had said he'd been thinking about the pressure he'd put her under and he felt like the worst father ever. He also said Maggie's mother would not approve. If Maggie decided to skip out and move to Ohio, she had his blessing. All that stuff weighed heavy on her mind and she hadn't been able to sleep. And this morning, over her fourth cup of caffeine, she decided after she picked out flowers she had an important stop to make.

* * *

"If you snap at Janelle one more time, Tysen, I'm going to toss you out the window." Loy Vincent sat in the chair across from Ty with an irked expression. "She's been a good secretary to you like Rosie has been to me. She doesn't deserve your bad mood."

In the big scheme of things, you're the reason I'm snapping at Janelle. Ty had to bite his tongue to keep that surly thought inside. He didn't want to engage his grandfather in a battle of words, even though it needed to happen. "You're right, she doesn't." He closed the manila folder filled to capacity with environmental policy documents and pushed it to the corner of the desk. He'd been trying to sidetrack his sour disposition with work.

"Give her a break and be nice." Loy idly toyed with Ty's business card holder. His annoyed appearance morphed into a knowing smirk. "Nerves on edge?"

Ty crossed his arms and leaned back in his chair. "Maybe."

"I was married to your grandmother for fifty years so I know a little bit about nerves and I have a fairly good idea where you're at right now." A fleeting look of sadness flashed through his aged eyes.

The loss of Loy's beloved Genevieve Pannaway-Vincent had almost done his grandfather in. Gennie. His grandmother. The amazing blue eyed beauty conquered Loy's heart right before he went into the Air Force. As soon as his service to his country was done, they married and became a power couple whose romantic escapades made the world take notice. They loved hard. Played hard. And together, became a business phenomenon. Best of all, they had T. Loy Vincent, II. Sadly, cancer ripped Gennie from their grasps way too soon. And an accident took...Ty barricaded thoughts of his dad's tragic demise. He felt incapable of dealing with the pain today. He zoned back into his grandfather's presence. "I need a stiff drink."

"Marriage ain't for sissies, Tysen. Although, there may be times you'll want to invent a business trip just to get away for awhile." Loy chuckled but there was little merriment in his eyes to back it up. "After a day or two away you'll find yourself pining for the old ball and chain."

Ty downed a sip of lukewarm coffee and made a face. "No ball and chain for me, thank you very much." The comment was bait. A golden opportunity for his grandfather to come clean about the pact he had with Maggie.

Nothing.

Ty tried again to reel him in. "I can't believe I proposed to a woman I met in an airport. What the hell was I thinking?"

The shark bypassed the hook. "Where you met Maggie

isn't what's important. How you feel about her and about this job, are the only things that matter. Search your heart, Tysen. If you think the two of you can make a go of things then by all means marry the girl. If you're just tying the knot to please me and the Board, forget it. Your marriage will crumble right away." Loy ran his hands over his face like he was drained and his semi-pleasant tone sobered. "No more freaking drama. No more headlines that will sully the Vincent name. No more slow torture. My head can't take it. My heart sure as hell can't. Marry Maggie, or don't. Your decision. I'll be at the rehearsal tonight. Hopefully you will be too. If you do something stupid and reject Maggie, you'll be missing out on a great gal and if you don't become CEO it's because you truly didn't want the job in the first place." He stood up, puffed out his chest like he'd delivered an ultimatum and left without saying more.

There it was – everything laid on the line. Well, mostly everything. The old man still hadn't confessed to orchestrating the marriage and probably never would. His grandfather must've felt the tug of the fishing line and decided the only way to stay in the water was to distract Ty by mentioning the CEO position. His mom's assessment of Loy was accurate – he was an intelligent ass. He was also an expert manipulator. Ty threw his business card holder across the room. Cards scattered and the holder crashed against a mahogany file cabinet. He expected Janelle to rush in to see what caused the racket. She didn't.

Ty rubbed his eyes. He wasn't just physically tired, he was also mentally fatigued. He went to take another sip of coffee and remembered it was barely warm.

He headed to the break room. On the way, he spied Janelle at the copier. In a few long strides he stood beside her. She flinched and drew back. Dammit. He hated when people reacted in that way. Yes, he was intense. Yes, he possessed more confidence than should be legal. Yes, he was lucky that life was not a struggle…generally. Despite his good fortune, he was a nice guy. Compared to Quinn and Trigg, he was a saint. That made him what? The best of the worst? "Hey, I'm sorry for being a jerk, Janelle." He heaved a sigh. "You were a victim of all the shit…" Janelle's eyes widened and Ty adjusted his words. "You were the victim of my insomnia. I couldn't fall asleep last night."

Janelle straightened the stack of copies she'd made. "It's fine, Mr. Vincent. We're all prone to sleepless nights and bad moods."

"I promise it won't happen again."

"Maybe you should find a place to take a nap." A polite smile curved her mouth. "The boss won't care." Her smile slowly grew. "You have a big night ahead of you, and speaking from experience, tomorrow will be a blur."

For lack of something better to say, Ty went with, "A nap sounds good."

"I'll be at your wedding, Mr. Vincent. Since you'll be busy mingling I might not get a chance to offer congratulations, so…best wishes from me and Dewey."

Ty had only met Janelle's husband once and for the life of him couldn't remember what Dewey looked like; another niggling reminder that he was too self-absorbed. Along with a hundred other things, he needed to stop focusing on him and get to know the people who touched his life. In a surprise move – to them both – he grabbed Janelle's hand and gave it an appreciative squeeze. "Thank you, Janelle. You really are a sweet person. I'm glad you're my secretary." He fell short of saying he'd see her at the wedding because he'd actually have to be there to see her. At this point, he wasn't sure that would be the case.

Janelle blushed.

Ty released her hand and a lengthy yawn. "Maybe I will take that nap." *Or indulge in a few glasses of scotch to take the edge off.*

Logically, he couldn't rest or imbibe in alcohol. He had a lot of soul searching to do in a short amount of time and the only way to clean up the muck going on in his brain was to meet it head on.

In the break room, he filled his oversized coffee cup from the pot labeled bold. Strong thoughts needed strong coffee. A sip made him grimace. The coffee wasn't just strong it tasted like tar. He took a few more sips and topped off the cup with more tar.

He wandered back to his office, opened the manila folder again and searched until he found what he was looking for. Since Vincent Oil was an independent oil and gas company they occasionally met with other independents to discuss how to stay competitive and profitable in a tight market while maintaining environmental integrity. In two weeks he'd head to Houston and he needed to do some homework beforehand. He leaned back in his leather chair and studied the first document. He made it halfway down the page and his thoughts drifted to Maggie again. Last night they'd been in the throes of passion. They were so close to making love. So damned closed again. Of course, the gods of interruption interceded again. This time they'd sent his mom. A pattern seemed to be emerging – aroused then doused, turned on then turned off. It was frustrating as hell. This latest disruption was the catalyst for yet another falling out with Maggie. He didn't mean for his temper to get the best of him, but it did. The desire they'd shared was replaced by anger. Blowing up at Maggie because she'd sought comfort from his mom was stupid. It took him awhile to decide he was glad the two got along. He'd almost called Maggie at three in the morning to apologize.

Ty pulled his cell phone from his shirt pocket and laid it on the desk. He drummed his fingers on his desk pad calendar.

Was Maggie picking out flowers with his mom right now or sitting at her dad's kitchen table telling him why she wouldn't be marrying him? Was her engagement ring on her finger or thrown down the garbage disposal?

Ty could not stay sitting. The clock was ticking and he had decisions to make.

* * *

"Short-stemmed red roses with three short-stemmed white roses in the center?" The florists' silver brows knit to the center. "Miss, are you sure? The dark red and vivid white are beautiful but they'll be fighting against each other for attention. The symmetry of the bouquet would be off just a bit."

Maggie wasn't about to cave to his expertise. She also wasn't worried that the flowers would fight or that the symmetry of the arrangement wasn't perfect. "It's what I want."

Ellen offered her two cents. "I would never try to push my opinion on you, Maggie, but I think he's right –the bouquet might look odd. Maybe you could alternate red and white." Maggie's pointed look made Ellen add, "Or not."

"While I respect both of your opinions, I have a reason for wanting those three white flowers in the center."

The florist put his palms up, not in a dramatic way. Maggie understood the gesture. He wouldn't argue further. Good. She wouldn't bend.

With the bridal bouquet out of the way, they moved on to Nancy's bouquet, strictly short-stemmed red roses. For Ellen, a wrist corsage with tiny red roses, no greenery, no baby's breath. The boutonnieres for Quinn, Loy and her dad, a small red rose. Ty's boutonniere – small red roses also with three tiny white roses – received quiet disapproval in the form of uplifted eyebrows. The florist asked about flowers for the church and reception hall. Loy had taken care of most things for the wedding and it dawned on Maggie that he might've taken care of the flowers too, including her bouquet. Didn't matter. She would carry what she'd picked out. But to keep the peace she needed to touch base with him. "I need to call Loy." She fumbled in her purse. "I can't seem to find my phone. I must've left it at home on the charger."

Ellen dug her cell phone from her purse and handed it to Maggie. "You can use mine. Don't get upset if Loy doesn't answer. He tends to ignore my calls. Plus, he's probably still pissed at me."

To their surprise, Loy answered on the first ring. "What can I do for you, Ellen?"

"This is Maggie. Ellen and I were wondering about flowers for the church and reception hall."

There was a moment of dead airspace. "Uhhhhh. I can't believe I forgot about flowers, Maggie. I'm sorry."

"No worries. You've been great with the other stuff and I'm grateful." She actually was filled with appreciation for everything he'd done, with the exception of getting her terminated from her job. "We're at the florist right now. Do you have any preference regarding the flowers?"

"Something elegant but subtle, like you, Maggie."

Maggie's mouth dropped open. "Thank you, Loy." She coughed modestly to clear a sudden clog of emotion. "I have to go. See you tonight."

"What in pray tell did he say that made your eyes glaze over?"

"He said to pick out something elegant but subtle, like me." Maggie shook her head in amazement.

"Oh my God, the man must be dying. He's such a control freak and wouldn't relinquish that job unless he was on his deathbed." Ellen shook her head too. "Just when I want to hate the man he goes and does something nice."

Maggie smiled at the florist. "Can you suggest something?" She owed him that much for being mulish about her bouquet.

The florist grinned like she'd given him a gift. "I didn't mean to eavesdrop but I heard you say elegant but subtle. My suggestion is: tall crystal vases of long-stem deep-red roses for the church but short-stem arrangements for the tables at the hall. Difficult to look around the tall vases to talk to people when you're seated."

Maggie agreed.

Ellen put her hand on her stomach. "My stomach is growling."

"Mine too."

Maggie and Ellen walked from the flower shop and were met by a half-dozen cameras.

"Maggie, how are you feeling? Are you ready to become a Vincent?" Chaz Rosston asked. Before she could answer, he frowned at Ellen. "This lady couldn't handle the pressure, are you sure you can handle it?"

Maggie experienced a moment of alarm. If she said it would be a breeze being a Vincent, she would make Ellen sound like a weakling. If she said it would difficult, it would make the Vincent's sound like tyrants. She pulled in a short breath and went with her gut. "It will be different from my quiet life, that's for sure." She wrapped her hand around Ellen's and brought them up in a show of solidarity. Chaz and the handful of other reporters were looking for an unguarded moment of weakness or anything else they could exploit. All she would give them was the truth. "I love this woman *and* her son. Becoming a permanent part of their lives will be incredible."

Chaz looked skeptical but he moved on. "You work at the soup kitchen. Do you intend to continue? Or will you go into hiding like Ellen did?"

You'd better lay off Ellen or I won't be responsible for my actions. Maggie hoped she projected that thought with her narrowed eyes. Chaz seemed unaffected which meant the buffoon was about as perceptive as shelf paper.

Maggie glanced at his camera and then shifted her attention to his crotch. Break his camera? Or knee him in the groin? Both would land her butt in front of a judge, plus the fines would clean out her bank account. Maggie remembered Loy's words about smiling. He seemed to think a smile could fix everything. She scoffed without making a sound and took a step toward Chaz and smiled. "As a matter of fact, Ellen has decided to help out the soup kitchen." A small intake of air from Ellen widened Maggie's smile. "If you're free on Tuesday's and Thursday's you can roll up your sleeves and help out too, Chaz. What do you say? Are you willing to put down your camera for awhile and help the less fortunate?"

"Umm…"

She'd caught him off guard and it took all she had not to laugh. "Come on, Chaz, say yes." The other reporters clicked away. She could only imagine the headlines they'd compose to go with the pictures.

Chaz recovered in an instant. "We'll see."

Maggie winked. "Deep down, you're a good guy, Chaz Rosston. Now, if you don't mind, Ellen and I have a ton of things to do." She borrowed a move from Rachel Montaigne and used her elbows to clear a path. Chaz and his unruly band of news thugs continued to snap pictures but when Maggie pulled away from the parking lot they didn't follow.

"Maggie Gray, you little vixen. You handled those guys better than I ever could. The look on Chaz's face was priceless."

Maggie shared the diabolical plan to either break Chaz's camera or knee him in the family jewels.

Ellen cracked up laughing but stopped abruptly. "By the way, I love you too, and I'm glad you love my son even though he's put you through hell."

"It hasn't been hell. There have been some hellish

moments, but there's been some that have been pure heaven." Words rolled out of Maggie's mouth that took her by surprise. "Ty's just trying to figure things out. Same with me."

Ellen tendered a smile. "Want to tell me about the white roses in your bouquet and Ty's boutonniere?"

Tears sprang to the corners of Maggie's eyes. She sniffed hard to delay them. "One for my mom and one for his dad. I know they'll be with us in spirit, but I wanted to give them something special. I wanted them to be in the center of our day."

Ellen rested her hand on her heart. "Thank you so much for remembering Toy. That means the world to me, Maggie." She engaged in some sniffing too. "What about the third rose?"

"For Genevieve."

"Ohhh, Maggie," Ellen's voice quivered, "when Loy finds out, he will love you more than he already does." She dabbed at her tears with a tissue.

Maggie had to pull over because she could no longer see to drive.

* * *

Ty called Maggie's phone for the tenth time. Six rings in, it went to voice mail again. "Darn you, woman." He'd driven by her apartment building at least five times. His mom's car was in the parking lot but Maggie's was missing. The two were out gallivanting and they needed to be home. He couldn't clear the air if she wasn't there.

To his surprise, *his* phone rang. "Maggie?" he said breathlessly.

"Nope." Laughter sounded through the air waves.

Damn. He should've checked who'd called before he answered. "What's up?"

Quinn laughed again. "Let's have a few beers. I need to

vent."

"I don't have time."

"Sure you do. I just talked to Loy and he said everything's done. He even picked up our tuxes. Actually, Rosie did, but he took credit. The only thing left for you to do, is have a few beers with me before you lose your mind and say 'I do'."

Maggie wasn't answering her phone. Loy had taken care of all the wedding details. And Quinn needed to vent. *Sweet*, Ty thought sarcastically. "I'll meet you at Sam's for one and then I have to go."

"Atta boy."

Ty gave his phone the evil eye and flung it on the seat beside him.

Fifteen minutes later two bottles of beer sat on the bar.

Quinn opened the door to the bar with a loud racket and let the blinding sunlight override the cool comfort of the dimly lit establishment.

Sam Bright uncapped the bottles of beer and uttered what Ty was thinking. "He's about as subtle as a clan of hyenas."

"I'd put him in a chokehold but I'm sure someone would put it in the paper."

"Ty, my boy." Quinn slapped Ty on the back and took up residence on the vacant stool beside him. "Your last day as a bachelor. What do you have to say for yourself?"

Ty made an obscene gesture, tipped his bottle of beer and almost found the bottom with one long guzzle.

Quinn snickered. "Not a damned thing I see." He sighed. "I may be trying to drown my sorrows too. It's your fault, Vincent. You just had to propose to Maggie and throw together a quickie wedding. Now Tori thinks we have to follow suit."

"You've been engaged for two years, dumbass. Don't you think it's time to at least set a date?"

"Misery loves company, huh?" Quinn drilled Ty with a look that could've easily been poison darts.

"Give it a rest, Casanova. Tori's dropped a boat load of hints about getting the wedding plans underway, so don't blame me. I'm surprised she let you stall this long."

Quinn shrugged. "The ring was to keep her from sleeping with someone else. That's it."

"You're an ass."

"I told you I was and I don't intend to change. Nor do I intend to get married. Ever."

"Yet you can't wait for me to get a ring through my nose." Ty lifted his empty beer bottle so Sam would get him another one.

"Something like that." Quinn snorted a laugh.

Camera or no camera, Quinn was one hyena-laugh away from that chokehold. "Is that what you wanted to vent about, Tori pressuring you?"

"Nah. I wanted to have a few beers with you. I'm your best man and you screwed me out of your bachelor party." He made a face. "You stuck me with Jake and Trigg, ya prick."

Ty laughed for the first time since he woke up. Trigg was Trigg. He was a Casanova too and he complained a lot. Jake, on the other hand, didn't say much. Sometimes you didn't know he was there. "You had it coming."

"For what?"

"You know why."

"For not going gaga over Maggie?" Quinn mocked him with an eye roll and then took a slug of beer. "You're getting as bad as Trigg. Bitch. Bitch. Bitch."

"Sam, I need a new best man. You busy tomorrow?"

"Forget it. You're stuck with me. Right, Sam?" Quinn whined.

"Leave me out of it. I've got problems of my own."

Ty cocked an eyebrow. "How so?"

"There seems to be an epidemic of girlfriends wanting to become wives." Sam hit Ty with a sharp but teasing look.

"Mine has been badgering me since she saw your engagement picture in the paper." He dried a beer mug with a bar towel. "I'm not husband material."

"None of us are," Ty stated matter-of-factly. "Yet we still end up with..." He borrowed his granddad's words. "...an old ball and chain."

Quinn fell into a loud rant about women. "They take away a guy's freedom as soon as they get Mrs. in front of their name. And what's with wanting to know where we are 24/7? Hell, they might as well tape a homing device to our ass and be done with it." He took another long swig of beer, belched and clunked the bottle on the bar. "Six days out of the month you can't say a word without getting into trouble."

"Yet we still chase them," Ty teased.

"Aww hell, you're right. But I'm going to have to ditch Tori." Quinn rolled his beer bottle between his hands.

Sam and Ty exchanged a look of curiosity.

Ty pulled his cell phone from his shirt pocket. "Gotta call the little woman."

"See. Told you." Quinn ordered another round of beers.

Ty wandered to the far side of the bar with his phone glued to his ear, listening to it ring and hearing it go to voice mail yet again. "Maggie, where the hell are you? You'd better answer or..." Or what? He'd withhold marriage? Yeah, well, there was a better than good chance before the night was through both he and Quinn would have their eligible bachelor status back, not by choice.

Chapter Thirteen

Ellen passed out peppermints to calm nervous stomachs and was now perched in a pew reading last week's church bulletin. Loy was busy checking out the Stations of the Cross instead of slicing everyone with mean looks. Richland Gray stood in the middle of the main aisle, alternating glances at his watch and at the heavy wooden double doors at the back of church. Quinn, Trigg and Jake were near the holy water fountain in hushed conversation. And the kind reverend that didn't appear the least bit upset by the delay was at the altar straightening the altar cloth, dusting the intricately carved preaching podium and flipping through pages in the Bible.

Ty was painfully aware of the time and that everyone was giving him space. For once, he didn't want breathing room. He didn't want to be alone with his ragged thoughts. The distraction of Quinn's shallowness and Trigg's constant grumbling would be welcomed. Even his grandfather's penchant for bossing people around would be better than sitting by himself wearing a mask of gloom while everyone tiptoed out of his way.

Where was she?

He was sure everyone in the church, and everyone in Dallas for that matter, expected him to be on the wedding lam, not Maggie.

Five more minutes. That's all. If she didn't show up by then, she was history.

"Ty?"

"Yeah?" He lifted his head to take in the concerned faces of his mom and Richland Gray.

Ellen rubbed the back of her neck like she was working out a bloom of tension. "I wanted to share something with you. I think it was supposed to be a surprise but given the circumstances," she looked around before continuing, "it might be helpful. Today when Maggie and I picked out flowers, she had a tussle with the florist."

"What does that have to do with her not showing up to rehearsal?"

Ellen joined him in the pew. "Maggie isn't afraid to stand her ground. Her bouquet – much to the dismay of the florist – has red roses all around but three white ones in the center." Her voice broke. "One for her mother, one for Toy and one for Gennie." She offered a wobbly smile. "A woman doesn't do something that special unless she cares deeply for the guy she's about to marry. She's in love with you, Ty."

"If she's so in love with me, where is she?" Ty asked gruffly, while his insides splintered. "And do you see Nancy anywhere? I think it says a lot when even the maid of honor doesn't show."

* * *

The creaking of the doors made everyone's heads snap around.

Nancy bustled in, sopping wet and out of breath. "Sorry for being late. I got tied up in a department meeting and there was no easy way to sneak out. When I did manage to leave it was raining so hard I couldn't see to drive so I had to wait a little bit." She fished a handful of tissues from her purse and blotted droplets of rain from her face. "I couldn't find my umbrella." She snickered but stopped when no one else appeared amused. Her eyes zipped around from person to person. "Where's Maggie?"

"That's what we'd like to know," Trigg said.

Quinn elbowed Trigg in the ribs.

"What?" Trigg asked.

"You're not being helpful."

Nancy focused on Ty. "You don't know where she is?" He remained silent. "I tried calling her cell but it went to voice mail right away. I figured she turned it off because she was in church."

Loy had wandered out the side door before Nancy arrived but now he was back and in the thick of things. "It's raining like crazy." He brushed rivulets of water from his suit coat. "I don't want to alarm anyone, but I tried Maggie's phone again and it says her voice mail box is full."

"There may be a reasonable explanation," Ellen said. "Maggie wasn't sure if she lost her phone or left it at home on the charger. That's why she used my phone to call you earlier."

"She called you?" Ty looked at his grandfather with surprise. "Why am I just now hearing this?"

Loy raised his palms. "I can't win for losing."

Ellen looked thoughtful. "By the way, Maggie stood up to Chaz. Funniest damned thing."

The reverend joined the group and cleared his throat at Ellen's curse word.

"Anyway, there's a better than good chance that Chaz Rosston will be helping out at the soup kitchen." She moved her head side to side. "That woman of yours is amazing."

"My woman. Right," Ty said flatly.

"After we had lunch, she dropped me off at my car. She said she had something to take care of and left before I pulled out of the parking lot." Ellen met Richland's worried eyes. "Any idea what that might have been?"

Richland shook his head. "Not a clue."

Ty sifted through the information. He found himself going back to the bit about the bouquet. From out of the blue, he put two and two together and knew where Maggie had gone. At least he was pretty sure that he knew. Where she was now, however, he had no idea. A range of emotion swept over him and he pulled his mom in his arms. He kissed her forehead and took off down the center aisle. He hollered over his shoulder, "If you hear from her call me right away."

Adrenaline pumped heavy in his chest and he opened the heavy oak doors that separated the main church area from the foyer with little effort. He grabbed the even heavier entrance doors and gave them a solid shove. The push was met with resistance. A whimper of distress followed. "Maggie?"

Lying flat out on the concrete apron of the entry – looking like a drowned rat – wasn't Maggie. "What are *you* doing here?"

The second Rachel Montaigne was vertical she threw herself into Ty; the wetness of her clothes soaked his right away. "No apology for knocking me down?"

"Sorry about that." Ty peeled her off of him and scanned her for injury. Satisfied that everything – except her abrasive disposition – was fine, he started to walk away.

Rachel darted in front of him. "We need to talk."

"No. We. Don't." His nerves were raw and stretched to the breaking point. He tried to sidestep the annoying woman.

Rachel grabbed his bicep and blinked up at him with dewy lashes and a sex-kitten smile. "Ty, you deserve someone within your own social class, someone who understands what wealth and privilege are all about. You deserve me, not some bumpkin who wouldn't know Kate Spade from Kate Winslet." She pressed her breasts into his side.

A slow smile spread across Ty's face.

"See," Rachel moved her head up and down, "I knew if I could get you alone you'd come to your senses."

Ty used his forearm to nudge some distance between them. He was ready to rip into Rachel with the truth that he didn't like her, not even a little. Before he could, someone else took the stage.

"Touch my man again and this *bumpkin* is going to give you something *you* deserve, and then some."

Rain pelted him, but relief washed over him. "Maggie," he said.

Maggie pushed past Rachel. Dripping wet and struggling to breathe since she'd ran from the church parking lot and up three sets of steps, she stopped inches from Ty. "I know I'm late, but I can explain."

Ty gathered her in his arms. "I was so worried, Maggie. I thought something happened to you." He kissed the top of her head. "I also thought you'd changed your mind about us."

"Ohhh brother," Rachel said.

Maggie heard the click of heels and knew that Rachel had given up, at least for now. She was pretty sure they'd meet again, but it was good not to have to ruin the moment by having to punch her lights out. "Yeah, you better leave." The taunting comment was just loud enough for Maggie and Ty to hear.

Ty chuckled but the laugh didn't meet his eyes. "Are you okay?"

"I'm fine." She wasn't fine. Not even a little. "No. Really, I'm not. I've been a nervous wreck for the last hour and a half. But I haven't changed my mind about us."

"You still want me?"

"More than ever." Maggie stretched up to peck his mouth with a kiss.

"I've been a wreck all day too. But I'm with you for less than five minutes and everything feels right with the world."

He lifted her hand to his mouth and planted a soft kiss on the top, before turning it over and doing the same to her palm. "You're wearing your ring," he said.

"A girl doesn't need a ring to get married, but it's nice to have one to show the world that I'm in love."

"You love me, Maggie?" Rain ran down his face.

Maggie didn't hesitate or over-think her answer. "Completely in love with you." She backed up the proclamation with a groan and laughed at Ty's look of confusion. "In one short week, I lost my mind and fell in love. That has to be some kind of record."

Ty ran his thumb over her cheek. "I think we both set a new record. Somewhere between 'do you want me to call 9-1-1' and the little white lie you told the clerk at the airport, you hooked me. I haven't been able to think about anyone else."

Maggie gnawed on her bottom lip while she processed the information. "That was day one, Ty."

"Tell me about it." Ty inhaled and exhaled before he grinned.

"So you're saying you love me too?"

"I love you with all my heart, Margaret Gray."

"Then kiss me. Hard. So I know deep in my heart that it's for real."

"Oh it's for real." Ty lowered his head and ravished her mouth with a kiss that made Maggie's toes curl.

When the kiss was finished, she ran her tongue over her lips. "Best. Kiss. Ever."

Ty's eyes sparkled. He lifted her chin so they were eye to eye. "Now that we have our hearts back on track, want to tell me where you've been?"

Maggie pressed her lips together for a few seconds. She would tell him where she'd gone but she'd omit one tiny detail. There was no use getting him worked up over something that didn't matter. "I went to the cemetery to pay my mom a visit."

"I knew it," Ty replied.

"How did you know?"

"Gut instinct. Plus my mom told me about your bouquet and then things clicked."

Maggie lifted an eyebrow. "She told you about the flowers?"

"The woman can't keep a secret to save her soul." Ty held her eyes. "Thank you for remembering my dad and grandmother with those white roses." He clutched her hand and laid it on his chest.

"I looked for your dad's grave. It took me awhile but I found it. I wanted to introduce myself," she said softly.

Ty's reply came out as a hoarse whisper. "I know that he was happy to meet you."

"I stayed too long at the cemetery and tried to make up the time by taking a short cut. I got lost." Her sigh was heavy. "I found myself in an area that looked a little risky. I didn't have my phone and I was afraid to stop and ask for directions. It took me awhile but I managed to find I-635. Of course, I also found myself in stopped traffic due to an accident."

Ty brushed his lips across her forehead. "As soon as we get back from the honeymoon, I'm getting you a new car with a navigation system. Or…" He swept his lashes over his eyes to tease. "…Bostwick can drive you around."

"Yes to the honeymoon. No to the new car and no to bothering Bostwick to drive me around."

"You're going to give me gray hair."

"Bound to happen, my last name is Gray."

"Your name will be Vincent," he corrected.

Maggie wrinkled her nose. "Speaking of Gray, is my father upset?"

"Mmm-hmm. Everyone is. I think even the priest was saying a few prayers."

Maggie puffed out a breath of air. "Time to ease

everyone's nerves then."

"Thanks for easing mine. I love you, Maggie."

"I love you too, Ty."

* * *

Ty took a swig of scotch, leaned against the bar and scanned the crowd that had gathered in the posh country club's dining area. There had been all of ten people at the rehearsal but Loy in his usual pretentious style didn't miss an opportunity to rub elbows with well-to-do friends and had invited them to the extravagant rehearsal dinner. "You've outdone yourself, Granddad."

"Only the best for my family." Loy laid a hand on Ty's shoulder. "Tomorrow will be even better."

"You know, Maggie and I don't need all this hoopla. We'd be just as happy with a small, personal celebration."

"She might as well know upfront that pomp and circumstance is the norm."

Ty turned to order another glass of scotch. His grandfather turned with him. In the large mirror behind the bar, their eyes met. "Don't scare her off like you did mom."

Silver brows bumped into a frown, and in that commanding voice that Ty expected, Loy leveled a warning. "Watch it, Tysen." He swilled a sip of bourbon and sat the glass down with a considerable clunk.

"Weren't you the one who said you can't blindside people or the damage can be staggering? Or was that just a line that served the moment?"

"Maggie has proven on more than one occasion that she can handle whatever circumstance she lands in." Loy tapped the side of his glass of bourbon. "You do underestimate people, don't you?"

"I've never underestimated you."

"Touché." Loy nodded to where Maggie stood in a circle of Dallas's wealthiest. She was laughing and appeared relaxed. "Your bride-to-be is handling herself just as I expected. Beneath those amazing blue eyes and that soft exterior, lurks a woman who has almost as much grit as my Gennie had." Loy squared off in front of Ty. "I put Maggie to the test and she passed with flying colors, so stop worrying."

"Are you referring to getting her fired so you could contract her to marry me?"

Loy's mouth fell open and his eyes nearly bugged out of his head. "She told you I hired her?"

"She doesn't keep anything from me. That's the way it's supposed to be when two people are in love." Ty was deceptively calm but he was a hair away from going off on his grandfather. "You manipulated Maggie and then hired her to manipulate me. Just so you know, I did the same thing. I contracted her too." It was best to get everything out so there'd be no surprises that would come back to haunt them later.

Loy's aged eyes grew large. "You did what?"

"You heard me. I hired her to marry me."

Loy shook his head in disbelief. "I hired her. You hired her. Who the hell else hired her, I wonder?" Anger hissed from his throat and he glared in her direction. "Miss Maggie Gray apparently isn't what she seems. I thought I could trust her."

"Let me tell you about Maggie. She's bright, has a heart the size of Texas and is the most honest person I know. Her only flaw – she's easily coerced. In the end she does the right thing because that's who she is."

"Maggie's playing us both."

Ty made a sound of frustration. "You went after her, not the other way around."

In the bar mirror, Ty caught sight of Tori a few feet away. He was certain she'd heard everything. *Awesome*, he thought sarcastically. Tori didn't like Maggie to begin with, now she had a reason to be even more of a pain.

"I did go after her because she took good care of me in the hospital. I thought she'd take good care of the arrangement too. That was a huge blunder on my part. I took her out of her comfort zone and she soothed herself with the idea of big money. I offered her a million dollars to get you to the altar. How much did you offer?"

"No way is Maggie in this for the money. She loves me."

Maggie unsuspectingly walked into the hornet's nest with a grin. "This is a great party, Loy. Thank you."

Loy poked Maggie's chest just below the hollow of her throat with his index finger. "I know all about your little con."

Maggie looked taken back. "My con?"

"Double money," Loy accused heatedly. "A million from me. Who knows how much from Ty? Not a bad haul for a six-month acting gig."

Maggie's happy stance changed to stick-straight defensive. Her eyes zipped wildly between Ty and Loy.

Ty tried to grab her hand but she tucked it behind her back.

"I don't want your money," Maggie said with undeniable hurt streaming through her voice. "I told my dad early on that I wouldn't take a dime from you. Not now. Not ever. I was wrong to agree to a second arrangement but I didn't think I could get the first one to work without taking part in the second one."

Ty wanted to pull her into his arms, but he knew if he moved a muscle she'd bolt from the room. "Maggie," he said, trying to find the right words that would smother the bonfire he'd inadvertently started.

"All I wanted to do was help."

"Your *special* kind of help, I don't need," Loy replied stiffly.

Maggie placed her attention on Ty. "I don't want *your* money either."

She fell short of saying she didn't want his love, but Ty sensed she was a breath away from saying that as well.

For once in his life, Ty was at a loss for words; to his surprise, Maggie wasn't. Lethal daggers swung back and forth in her eyes. "Tomorrow, precisely at one o'clock, I will walk down the aisle to marry you. I'll fulfill my contract to you and to your grandfather. He asked for six months. You asked for a year. Put your heads together and come up with an exact time frame. I will become Maggie Vincent. I will play the part of a good wife and daughter-in-law. When you no longer need my services, I will walk away and won't look back. No money will exchange hands." She turned and engaged Loy in a stare-down. "Whatever debt my father owed you will be satisfied. You will be able to retire from Vincent Oil knowing that it's in the trusty hands of your grandson. Now if you'll excuse me, I have some high-grade *smiling* to do. Smile, smile, smile."

Chapter Fourteen

Nancy had been unusually quiet since they'd arrived at the bride's room in the church basement. Maggie had been too preoccupied to pay any real attention. Until now. From her peripheral, she watched her best friend shift from side to side on the deacon's bench and repeatedly smooth the front of her dress. Nancy was no slacker when it came to conversation so her silence meant something. Regret for ratting out Loy? It couldn't be that. Besties had an obligation to expose vermin.

Maggie wrestled with the zipper of her wedding dress. "Can you help?"

"Sure." Nancy hopped from the bench and pulled the delicate fabric together so the zipper would go up without a fight.

"I don't remember the dress being this tight." Maggie sucked in her belly and adjusted the waist and bodice.

"Care to enlighten me?" Nancy finally said.

Maggie was tempted to say 'you first'. "Not sure what you mean." She looked in the mirror and touched the diamond and pearl tear-drop earrings that had belonged to her mom.

"You're not acting like Maggie."

You're not acting like Nancy.

"Nerves," Maggie said. The word was self-explanatory. She

was on edge and her nerves were brittle. One wayward look or malicious comment from the Vincent men and she would splinter.

"I get that you're nervous. What bride wouldn't be on her wedding day? What I don't get is the façade that everything's peachy."

"I'm not holding out on you, Nancy. Everything's fine." She puffed out a breath of air. "Mostly fine."

"Riiight. You drove yourself to church."

"I've always been independent, you know that."

"There's a time and place to be a free spirit, Maggie, but not on your wedding day. I overhead Bostwick tell Loy that you refused to ride in the limo."

"He told on me?"

"His allegiance is to Loy, not you."

"Still."

"There is no still. Loy pays his salary."

"True."

"I'm surprised your dad didn't bring you."

"He thought Bostwick was bringing me."

"And the merry-go-round goes round and round. Level with me. What's going on?"

Maggie slumped down on the bench. "Bostwick narked me out today. Ty narked me out last night."

Nancy sat beside Maggie. "Forget Bostwick. He doesn't even play into this equation. Tell me what happened last night."

"Ty decided to spill his guts to Loy and in the process ruined everything. Loy now views me as a money-grubbing scam artist. Kind of the pot calling the kettle black, right?"

"Given this whole soap opera where you did this and he did that, who exactly are you pissed at?"

Maggie closed her eyes and dropped her head back. Heaviness centered in her chest and the knots in her stomach tightened. "Myself."

"So you're not mad at your dad or Loy or Ty?"

"Of course I am."

Nancy made a sound of exasperation.

"Maggie," her father said from the other side of the door. "Come in."

"There's my girl." He smiled like all was right with the world. If he knew about last night's altercation, it didn't show. "Aww, Maggie, those earrings look as lovely on you as they did on your mom."

Maggie's heart clenched. "Thanks, Dad."

Soft organ music filtered into the room, a sign that soon she would take her father's arm and walk down the aisle to meet Ty. A moment of panic joined a dozen other emotions wracking her insides.

"Take a deep breath, Maggie." Nancy squeezed her hand and stood to leave. "Let the love that you and Ty feel for each other be the only thing that fills the church today." She winked and excused herself from the room.

Maggie stared after her friend with her mouth slightly ajar.

Richland Gray perched in the spot vacated by Nancy. "Maggie, I've struggled all week, trying to come to grips with the fact I pushed you into this." He sighed long and hard. "At the time, I was on board with Loy's plan. Now it all seems foolish." He paused like he was searching for the right words. "It's not too late. You have a small window of time to do what's right for Maggie." He lifted her hand and placed a soft kiss on her knuckles. "In fifteen minutes you'll either be married or halfway home. What's it going to be, sweetheart?"

Last night, in the darkness of her room she asked her mom for a sign to tell her what to do. Sometime after three in the morning, she'd fallen asleep on a pillow soaked with tears. No sign. No clear answers.

Rosie popped her head around the door. "It's go-time, Maggie."

"We'll be there in a second."

Maggie and her father sat without speaking until the click of Rosie's heels could no longer be heard. Richland leaned over and kissed Maggie's forehead. "Follow your heart, daughter."

With her arm looped through her dad's, they made their way up the basement steps and to the back of the church.

Maggie stared down at the white roses in her bouquet with one last plea. *Mom, what should I do?* It was then Maggie noticed that the three white roses were arranged with two on top and one underneath. They formed a heart. A burst of joy exploded somewhere close to her soul. The answer she'd cried for, begged for, prayed for, was right there – her father's words and now her mom's – 'Follow your heart'. In that moment, she decided that marrying Ty was the right thing to do. Not to fulfill ridiculous contracts. Not because she was stubborn. She was headed to the altar because it's where she needed to be. She was deeply in love with Ty Vincent. Right or wrong, she would risk her heart. Her soul. Her mental well-being. For him.

Three hundred pairs of eyes carefully watched her every step. Maggie smiled the entire length of the aisle. It wasn't for show. It was for real. She smiled because she wanted Ty to remember this day. Even though their marriage would contractually end in three hundred and sixty five days, she wanted to give him something to hold onto long after she was gone.

Maggie spotted him standing beside Quinn looking damned handsome. He was smiling too. Maybe it was real. Maybe not. She would soon find out.

She must've stiffened the last few steps because her father whispered, "You don't have to walk this plank, Maggie."

"Yes I do, Dad."

He looked worried when he handed her to Ty.

The second Ty had her in his clutches, he said, "I love you, Maggie."

The reverend grinned. "We haven't gotten to that part yet."

Nancy chuckled. So did Quinn.

"Some things can't wait." Ty held her hand tight, his eyes held her tight too.

A feeling of calm swept over Maggie.

The mass went surprisingly quick and the priest motioned for them to join him at the threshold of the altar.

"Are you ready?"

Ty grinned. "I've been ready for this woman forever."

The reverend tried to keep a straight face but the corners of his mouth curved. "The correct answer was yes."

Maggie jiggled with a laugh, but her pulse was racing. "Yes," she said.

"Tysen, take Margaret's hand and repeat after me. I, Tysen, take thee Margaret to be my lawfully wedded wife."

Maggie felt lightheaded and was glad Ty had a firm grip on her hand.

"I, Tysen, take thee Margaret..."

* * *

Ty couldn't believe he was married. To Maggie *Vincent*. It had been an incredible ceremony where they pledged to be good to each other in good times and bad, in sickness and in health. To love and honor each other all the days of their lives. Those words were as disturbing as they were reassuring. In the context of *forever* he'd had a hard time saying them, since he and Maggie were supposed to be temporary. After the heated exchange at the rehearsal dinner he was surprised, but overjoyed, that she showed up today. While she'd promised to be there, she'd had enough time to let his grandfather's hurtful comments sink into her heart and Ty expected her to ditch him, the wedding, the contract, the whole shebang. The fact that she didn't said a lot. Either she was a glutton for punishment, or...she really did love him.

"Maggie." He nudged her with his shoulder while they shook hands with people filing out of church. "We did it. We're man and wife."

Maggie chewed on her bottom lip. "I know. Now what?"

"Now we celebrate with food and champagne." Ty raised his eyebrows up and down without his usual cockiness. "Tonight, we have a room at the Ritz and if anyone knocks on the door, they'll be taking their life in their own hands." He laughed and gave her a quick kiss before greeting his godmother in the receiving line. "Justine," he said. "I've been dying to know what you whispered to Maggie the other day."

"You haven't told him?"

Maggie smacked her lips. "Nope."

Justine cracked up laughing. "She must have a good reason for withholding the information, Ty." She hugged him and added, "Maybe you can persuade her to tell you tonight."

"I'll give it a try." He winked.

Richland Gray slid into the receiving line and shook Ty's hand. "Happy to have you in our family, Tysen." He looked at Maggie with a smile and then placed serious consideration on Ty. "I have a whole list of things I want to say to you, Ty, but I think I'll limit the lecture to one – be good to her."

Ty nodded. He met Maggie's eyes. "I intend to, Richland. Maggie's the best thing that's ever happened to me."

Richland hugged him and then gathered Maggie in his arms. "Ty has a lot of love to give and so do you, Maggie. He's a Vincent, so things won't always be easy." He gave Ty a half-smile. "No offense."

"None taken."

Ellen Peppersmith-Vincent joined the tight circle. Richland Gray acknowledged her with a nod. "What I'm trying to say is that you and Ty will be tested almost every day. Ellen can vouch for that. There may be times you want to call it quits because the pressure is too much. But if you..."

Ellen butted in. "If you put each other first, then you'll be fine. Toy and I learned that the hard way." Her voice broke with emotion but she quickly recovered. "Don't let anyone or anything keep you from loving each other." She lightened things up with an impish smirk. "I'm happy for you, son." She kissed his forehead and then Maggie's. "I finally have a daughter." She looped her arm through Richland's. "Let's give these lovebirds some space." They headed back into church.

"Lovebirds," Ty repeated, grinning at Maggie. "We are, ya know? We're lovebirds."

Maggie scoffed with a smile.

Ty tugged at the collar of his stiff white shirt. Instead of being inside in the air conditioning they were outside in the heat making small talk and accepting congratulations from those who'd attended the ceremony. His grandfather and Rosie were busy handing out helium filled balloons with *Mr. and Mrs. Tysen Loy Vincent, III*, written on them. Ty thought they were cheesy and silly. His grandfather thought they'd make a great picture.

Quinn slapped him on the back. "You did it, old man." He snaked an arm around Maggie. "You lost your mind and got married."

Maggie cocked a teasing brow.

"What I meant to say was that you found the prettiest woman on the planet and took her out of commission."

Tori rolled her eyes. "Don't get excited, he says the same thing at every wedding. You need some new material, Quinn."

Quinn was coming around where Maggie was concerned. Tori, however, was still as pleasant as a stiff neck.

"Time to release the balloons." Loy handed Ty and Maggie a handful of balloons too. "Everybody smile. Ready. Set. Go."

Hundreds of red and white balloons floated up to a

Married to Maggie

cloudless blue sky. It was a breathtaking sight that was followed by squeals of delight.

Loy allowed the guests a few moments of awe and then he shooed them off to the reception hall. "The rest of you, it's time for pictures."

Ty groaned. All he wanted to do was take off the monkey suit, show his face at the reception for a little bit and then whisk Maggie away to the hotel.

"I was wondering..." Maggie hem-hawed.

"What is it, Maggie?" Ty asked.

Loy's impatience was growing. "The photographer is waiting."

"That's what I wanted to discuss." Maggie blinked up at Ty. "Would you allow Chaz to take a few pictures?"

Ty was surprised by the request. "Are you serious?"

Loy threw his two cents into the discussion. "Absolutely not. No paparazzi."

"Not your call, Granddad."

"Sure it is. I protect this family. The paparazzi are buzzards that scavenge through people's lives. They rip the truth apart and print lies."

"Ty?" Maggie said. "Please?"

"I don't understand, Maggie, but if this is important to you, then let's do it."

Loy fumed that people like them didn't cozy up to the press. It was unheard of and if she and Ty did this they would be asking for trouble. They'd be setting a precedent for the other members of the press to shove a camera and microphone in their face anytime they damn well pleased.

"Chaz has been decent to me. If we give him a few pictures, who knows, he just might help you protect the family."

Loy waved off the idea with a grunt. "Is there money in it for you, Maggie?"

Maggie almost choked on a breath of air. She didn't expect Loy to change his opinion of her overnight but it hurt that he still thought she was out to take advantage of him and Ty.

Ty frowned. "Don't speak to Maggie like that again."

Loy didn't apologize. He set hard eyes on Maggie, then on Ty. "Two pictures. That's it." He walked away cussing under his breath.

All Maggie wanted to do was to thank Chaz for his kindness by letting him snap a few pictures. Yesterday he'd followed her to the cemetery and when she broke down crying he turned off his camera and came out from his hiding place to see if she was okay. He even gave her a hug. He might be paparazzi but he'd shown compassion when she needed it the most.

Maggie stood on the church steps and waved to the man standing beside the red SUV parked across the street and then she gestured for him to join them. There were possibly a hundred more paparazzi waiting for her to invite them. Wouldn't happen.

Chaz stayed put.

"Chaz, we need you."

Chaz looked around like he couldn't believe his ears and then rushed to meet Maggie and Ty. "Umm…" He seemed dumbfounded. "Congratulations on your wedding."

"Thank you," Maggie said. She leaned against Ty. "Would you like a couple of pictures?"

Chaz's eyebrows gathered in the center. "Really?"

"Mmm-hmm. Just a couple."

Ty put his palms up. "This is all Maggie's doing."

Chaz posed them with Ty standing behind Maggie with his arms hugging her tight. The second picture was more traditional, Ty down on one knee, smiling up at Maggie with her hand in his. "One last picture? Please?" Chaz handed Ty the big, bulky digital monstrosity and put an arm around

Maggie. "This one isn't for the papers."

Ty squinted hard. "If you use it for personal gain or to hurt my wife in any way, I swear I'll hunt you down and break every camera you own. I might even break your nose. Am I clear?"

"You're clear. Just so you know, I'm not the least bit intimidated by you, Ty. Now Maggie," Chaz gave Maggie a cheesy smile, "I'm afraid of her."

Ty finally chuckled. "Me too."

Maggie laughed like she had the world by the tail. Today was possibly the best day of her life.

* * *

"Just water," Maggie said to the barmaid. She was hot, sweaty and parched from dancing. But she was happy. Happier than she could've ever dreamed. She smiled at the fun still happening on the dance floor. People were bumping and grinding against each other and laughing so much while they were doing it that it wasn't vulgar. Who knew Dallas's elite liked to burn up the dance floor? It might've been the nonstop flow of alcohol or maybe they were just a bunch of folks who weren't as uptight as their reputations would have you believe. Whatever the case, they were having a blast.

From her perch near the bar, she scanned the huge hall for her drop-dead gorgeous, slightly tipsy husband. Maggie put her hand on her chest when she spotted him with his arm around his grandfather. She watched him laugh and her heart swelled with even more affection. Being married to Ty Vincent would be a challenge, but a good one. From across the room, their eyes met. He was the first to smile. Warmth poured over her like thick, rich, melted chocolate. Suddenly she was too hot to be in a silk dress.

The barmaid sat a glass of ice cold water in front of her.

"There you go, Mrs. Vincent."

Mrs. Vincent. Hearing her new name was surreal. "Thanks, Kylee. And thank you for helping out today."

"My pleasure," Kylee said, holding up the bouquet Maggie had thrown earlier. "I'm the hired help and shouldn't have been in the circle of single women you tossed the bouquet to. That privilege should've included only your guests." She bit on her bottom lip. "A certain person, who shall remain nameless, insisted rather strongly that I join the group. Needless to say, I think I upset one of your friends when I caught the flowers."

Instinctively, Maggie said, "Quinn nagged. Tori bellyached."

Kylee confirmed Maggie's guess by wrinkling her nose.

"No worries." Maggie swilled a sip of much needed water. "I'm glad you caught it. And for the record, you're a guest too."

"Thank you," Kylee said, refilling Maggie's glass with more ice water.

Maggie took another refreshing sip. Soon she would head to a private room on the lower level to make a special phone call. She'd borrowed Nancy's phone so she wouldn't draw Ty's attention by fishing her own phone from her purse which was stashed under the heavily decorated head table designated for the bride and groom and attendants. In all the confusion and back and forth of events, she and Ty hadn't planned a honeymoon. They had a room reserved at the Ritz for the night, but that was it. Maggie grinned with wicked satisfaction that she would surprise him with a trip back to Reno and Lake Tahoe. It was only fitting since it was their beginning. She slanted another glance in his direction. Instead of Ty, she caught sight of Terron Wade heading for the bar. He looked directly at her making her wish she hadn't stopped to quench her thirst. Red flags of warning popped up all around. Terron had caused problems at their engagement party and she had a feeling he was about to do it again. Maggie looked away long enough to find a certain phone app and palmed the phone so Terron was none the wiser.

The troublemaker moved into her space. "How does it feel to join one of the wealthiest families in the country?"

The question made something surface that Tori had said at the restaurant – 'Good things happen when you're with the Vincents'. She'd been partly right. Good things happened when she was with Ty. Her husband. The man who had her heart. The one who seemed intent on consummating their marriage even though the initial agreement said no bedroom activities. Thank goodness he was making exceptions to his own rules.

Ty was now on the dance floor laughing it up with his buddies while doing a country line dance. None of the guys knew what they were doing and turned the wrong way. Maggie chuckled and answered Terron. "It feels great."

Terron inclined his head toward her husband. "Not to put a damper on all that greatness but I should warn you that you're in for a world of trouble. Ty Vincent isn't what he seems. You think he loves you? Guess again. Ty is out for Ty. I have it on good authority that he intends to throw you away in six months."

Maggie was jarred. She shouldn't be, but she was. Having the information thrown in her face on her wedding day by this guy, went against the grain. The heat of anger found her cheeks. "Why are you telling me this?"

"I thought you should know so he won't rope you into believing that he loves you. This way when he pulls the rug out from under you, you'll be able to keep your balance and take him for all he's worth." Terron touched her forearm and Maggie drew away like she'd been stung. "You know, we could team up to take him down. It could be sweet, Maggie. You'd get a hefty divorce settlement and I'd finally get my reward for the all time and effort I put into the company."

"I thought your salary was reward for your work."

Terron gave her an odd look. He must've thought she was a pushover who wouldn't dare sass him. *Ha! Guess again, buddy.* She could sass with the best of them. In fact, she wanted to call him *Terror* but that wasn't so much sassing as it was name calling. Funny, but juvenile.

The oaf's bushy brows became an ominous frown, and Maggie almost burst out laughing. *Terror* didn't just have eyebrows he had a forest growing above his eyes.

"It's a pithy amount compared to what I should be making. I'm the brains of the outfit these days."

Yeah? And you need a wax job.

Maggie smiled at Kylee who was just an elbow away. "Can I get a shot of ipecac syrup?"

Kylee's brows drew into a look of confusion. "Ipecac syrup?"

"You know, to induce vomiting."

Still baffled, Kylee explained that she had grenadine syrup but not ipecac.

"Never mind," Maggie said, trying to keep a straight face. She went back to Terron's stupid comment. "You think you're running Vincent Oil?"

"I don't *think* I'm running it, I *know* I am. I have the power but not the title. If you side with me, I'll make sure you have enough money to buy a small country. It's a win-win for both of us."

"What makes you think I want a small country, or to turn my back on Tysen and Loy?" Maggie eyed his forehead. She wasn't qualified to perform lobotomies but if this guy didn't back off, he was getting one.

"All women want a small country. Figuratively, of course. And you should turn your back on those two before they turn theirs on you. They'd do it in an instant, if the situation warranted." He lowered his voice. "Don't forget Loy got you fired."

Married to Maggie

The fine hairs on Maggie's neck stood up. Loy had used her for ill-gotten gain and Terron was trying to do the same thing. She must have a sign on her back that read – See Me For All Your Diabolical Needs. "Ty loves me. I know he does. So does Loy." That was a bit of a stretch, at least the part about Loy. "I'm not sure who's feeding you information, but they got it wrong." From out of the blue, a bit of truth surfaced – Loy wasn't the culprit; he was, but he wasn't. The person at the hospital that accepted the sizable donation from him was actually the bad guy. Maggie frowned at the reality that someone else had sold her down the pike. She shelved the disconcerting thought for now. When the time was right, she'd deal with it. For now, she had to deal with a goon. "I would never do anything to harm the Vincents. You shouldn't either. They're good people. Loy took you under his wing and you're trying to repay his kindness by stabbing him in the back. He taught you a lot about business and now you think you're smart enough to take over…the world?" She wanted to needle him by adding that Loy wouldn't have pushed his grandson to get married and settled if he wanted Terron to run the company, but it was better left unsaid.

Terron snickered sarcastically.

The newspapers carefully planted the seed that Loy had gotten her terminated without coming right out and accusing him, so Maggie wasn't surprised that Terron had that in his bag of tricks. The comment about Ty tossing her out in six months was only known to a select few. She poked Terron in the chest with her finger. "Who's your source?"

Terron brushed her hand away. "That's not important."

"Yeah, it kind of is."

"I'm not one to name names, but I can tell you that it's someone you would never suspect. I plan to inform the Board that you and Ty are trying to scam them."

She would warn Ty of a possible spy, although he already

had his suspicions. "I love Tysen."

"I have to protect the company."

"I think you're trying to protect your hind quarter with a bunch of lies. By making Ty look bad you think you'll look good. You're underestimating the members of the Board. They're smart, Terron. They'll pick the right guy to lead the company."

"They're a bunch of lame brains who don't know shit." Terron's tone was caustic. "If I'm unable to sway their opinions about Ty I can certainly influence what they think about you. All I have to do is tell them that you offered to sneak off with me."

Maggie's mouth dropped open but she quickly snapped it closed. "Bite me."

Instead of going to the lower level to book their trip, Maggie flew across the dance floor to Ty. Breathless from anger, she allowed him to fold her into his embrace. She snuggled into his chest, torn between exposing Terron as a threat to their happiness and keeping their wedding day free from drama.

Ty smiled down at her and brushed his fingers across her cheek. "He asked me why you're giving him the cold shoulder, Maggie."

Maggie almost said, "He just tried to blackmail me". At the last second, she realized they weren't talking about Terron. "Is giving him the stink eye the same as giving him the cold shoulder?"

"It's cold shoulder version 2.0."

"Call it what you will." She wrinkled her nose. "He wasn't very nice last night."

"I know. He was out of line. I'm sure once all the celebrating is over and life gets back to normal, granddad will apologize."

A voice scalding with fury singed the air around them. "I

Married to Maggie

don't think so." Loy stared at Maggie with fire in his eyes. "Tysen, we made a huge mistake." Each word was tipped with self-disgust. "No good deed goes unpunished, I guess."

Ty dropped his arms and a distinct chill of foreboding coated Maggie with goose bumps. He searched her eyes for answers. She had none to give.

"Now what?" Ty's patience was clearly cracked.

Loy pointed at Maggie with a shaky finger. "Your *wife*," he spat, "isn't what she seems. She's been playing us all along. To our face she's sweet. Behind our backs she's been cozying up to Terron."

Maggie's mouth dropped open. "That low down good-for-nothing skunk." How in the world did he get to Loy so fast with his lies? Loy had come from the far side of the room and Terron was still perched at the bar...smiling. A dawning of awareness was as good as a sucker punch. Terron had spilled the poison to Loy before he ever approached her.

"That's right," Loy accused. "He told on you."

Maggie locked gazes with Ty. "If you believe that hogwash for even a second, we're done." She took a step forward so she was nose to nose with Loy. "Terron set us up."

"He said you'd say that."

Maggie considered herself to be one of the most non-violent people on the planet, but she was tempted to whap Loy upside the head to rattle some sense into him. "I'm not a bad person and I won't waste my energy trying to convince you otherwise."

"Maggie," Ty said, trying to pull her away. "We can settle this later."

"We'll settle this now," she said stiffly. "I won't rewind all that happened to this point. You're well aware of what took place." Her eyes zipped between Ty and Loy. The more she thought about this latest indictment, the madder she became. "Let me bring you up to speed. I'm no longer a nurse, Ty is still fighting for his job and you have a granddaughter-in-law that you assume stabbed you both in the back. Sweet deal, huh?" She shook her head with disappointment, mostly with herself. A week ago she'd made a gross error in judgment and now it was coming home to roost.

Loy's face turned beet red. "You played both sides of the fence and you have the audacity to be upset with me? I trusted you, Maggie."

She met his accusing eyes without flinching. "Trust?" The word heated her blood even more. "You got me fired, mister."

"You already said that. A hundred times. Yes. We got you fired. It was for the greater good, okay? The hospital got a sizeable donation for the heart unit and I tried to help my grandson find love. So sue me. That's probably how this will end anyway."

Maggie listened to what he was saying but she'd really only heard one word. "We? Who else was in on the firing?"

Loy widened his eyes from possibly having said too much. He turned to walk away. Maggie would not let him leave, not without giving her a name. She grabbed his forearm and held on for dear life, scaling back the emotion to get him to talk. "Tell me," she said, removing the anger, but using that authoritative nurse voice he knew so well.

Loy's shoulders sagged.

"Tell me who partnered with you."

"No good will come from you knowing."

"Tell me anyway," she demanded.

"Maggie," Ty intervened, "I agree with my grandfather. Knowing will just expand the wound. Let it go."

"Was it you, Ty? Were you in on this from the beginning?"

"No to both questions." He looked hurt. Well she was hurt too.

"I'm going to ask you one last time. Who helped get me terminated?" Her voice increased but she couldn't stop it.

"Lower. Your. Voice," Loy said.

"The whole place is about to know everything if you don't give me a name." It was a form of extortion but necessary.

A weighty sigh discharged from Loy's chest. "She wouldn't hurt you for anything in the world, Maggie."

Ty grasped Maggie's hand and held it tight.

"Let go or you'll need to call 9-1-1."

Ty dropped her hand.

"You have two seconds, Loy. One…" Tears burned the back of her eyes.

"It was Nancy." Loy took a step back as if he expected her to punch him in the nose.

The air seized in Maggie's lungs. "You're…you're…lying."

"I wish I was."

Ty tried to drape an arm around her. She shoved him away.

Guests started to close in.

"This is it." Maggie let out a sigh that served as a barricade. If anyone tried to climb it they were dead meat. "We're done."

"Maggie, please," Ty begged.

The lobster and steak of the wedding meal had started to churn in her stomach the second Terron cornered her, now it was inching up her throat. She no longer needed ipecac syrup. If she didn't get out of there soon she'd throw up without it. She unfurled her hand to reveal Nancy's cell phone and shoved it at Loy. "Hit this button." She'd recorded every word said by Terron. Tears leaked from the corners of her eyes when she faced Ty. "In six months or a year, whatever works for you, file for a divorce. Until then, leave me alone." She turned to leave but stopped short. "The persons leaking your personal information are Victoria and your grandfather."

Loy defended himself right away. "Not true." He said a lot more but Maggie tuned him out.

"It doesn't matter, Maggie. None of it. The only thing I

care about is you," Ty said.

"It matters. It definitely matters." She inhaled and exhaled. "Victoria relishes the limelight. She wants to be in the middle of whatever you have going on regardless of whether it's good or bad. And your grandfather, well, that goes without saying. He lets your whereabouts slip out. Word of mouth is as good as telling the press firsthand. He knows exactly what he's doing."

"Why would I do that?" Loy hissed between clenched teeth so his adoring public didn't hear.

"Because you can't help yourself. You're an expert manipulator." Her voice broke with emotion. "You've been trying to control Ty by using his behavior against him. If he constantly sees pictures of himself engaged in mischief, maybe he'll straighten up. Right?"

"You're one deluded thought away from a straight jacket, lady."

"Sadly, I'm right on the mark."

Maggie flew past the security guard posted at the side door of the reception hall with her heart pounding in her ears and hot tears stinging her cheeks. Her body got ahead of her feet and she fell down two concrete steps, scraping the tender skin of her palms and snagging the front of her dress.

A familiar face crouched beside her.

Maggie swiped at the tears clouding her eyes. Chaz Rosston. Of course he'd been lurking around the perimeter of the hall. Why wouldn't he? There were probably a dozen other reporters waiting for a juicy scoop too. Usually it was Loy or Ty making headlines. This time it would be the newest addition to the family. Maggie wished she could liquefy like her tears and seep into the cracks of the sidewalk.

"Please don't take my picture," she begged.

Chaz studied her for a long moment.

Maggie Gray-Vincent scuffed up with tear stains on her

cheeks, mascara smudges under her eyes and a torn wedding dress – it didn't get much better than that. The bride at her worst. Any second now she'd hear a series of camera clicks.

"C'mon. Let's get you out of here." Chaz balanced his oversized camera in one hand and extended the other to Maggie.

"Chaz?"

"Shh." Chaz led her through a thicket of bushes.

Maggie glanced over her shoulder. The magic. The marriage. The brief taste of love. Gone. Over. Done.

Chapter Fifteen

Ty flattened his hand across his chest and closed his eyes. His heart hurt. Instead of the piercing pain of a knife slashing across his midsection, it was a dull ache that was moving throughout his body at a rapid rate down both arms and heading for his stomach and legs. He assumed the long feared big one was upon him. He didn't have the strength to panic. Pulling his cell phone from the inside pocket of his tux, he punched in the number 9. He took the time to take a deep breath and exhale it before following up with the number 1. Looking around, he hit the last number. Before he sent the call out to emergency services, Quinn crowded next to him.

"Aren't you going after her?"

"No," he said tightly, but without raising his voice. "The insanity stops right here, right now. Maggie can run all the way to San Antonio, for all I care." Ty made a point of tapping the end button on his phone to do away with the call. He wouldn't chase after his wife. He also made a firm decision not to be wheeled out of the hall and shoved in the back of an ambulance. The doctors had given him a clean bill of health this week so there was a better than good chance he wasn't having a heart attack and that it was all in his head. His subconscious gave him a quick poke not to brush off chest pain. Shit.

"I think you're making a mistake, Ty."

"Add it to the list," he said sullenly.

Quinn laid a hand on his shoulder. "I'm the last one you should take advice from, especially since I have no intention of having a ring put through *my* nose, but I think you'll regret not going after her. Since you met Maggie you seem happy. Not right now, but you know what I mean."

Ty pictured Maggie's smile and those amazing blue eyes that seemed to see what no one else could. She saw the man he was and the man he wanted to be. He had a lot of issues but she didn't judge him, just the situation. He could deny it with his anger, but the truth was, Maggie loved him! Margaret Gray Vincent loved him! And…he felt the same about her. The admittance eased the discomfort; well, the physical discomfort. "I am happy, Quinn. A little distracted by her leaving, but we'll work it out." He hoped anyway.

"Damn. For once I'm right. Let's celebrate with a shot of Jagermeister."

"Tempting, but I've had enough alcohol."

"I forgot," Quinn heckled, "you're this really nice guy now." A weird look passed over his expression. "You're a husband." He lifted his eyebrows high. "That's surreal, man. Are you sure you don't need a shot of Jagermeister?"

Ty chuckled but he wasn't feeling the least bit light. Quinn had gotten it partly right. He was a husband. But he wasn't a nice guy. Nice guys didn't rearrange a woman's life, question her loyalty and accuse her of duplicity. Maggie had gotten a raw deal, from everyone, including Quinn and Tori. "I think you're the one who needs the shot of Jager, Quinn. Catching the garter means you're next to tie the knot." He deliberately hardened his expression when he thought of Tori. "By the way, the fiancée you say you're never going to marry seems to have a special affection for reporters."

"Say what?"

Ty shared Maggie's hunch.

"No way. Not Tori." Quinn shook his head repeatedly. "She would never do that."

Ty remained silent so Quinn could fully grasp the allegation.

"Seriously, Ty, Tori wouldn't…" Quinn scanned the room. He used the back of his hand to tap Ty's arm and then he pointed to where Tori stood in conversation with Jake Garrison. "If I find out that she's the one with loose lips…" Lines creased his forehead and his growl was low and feral. "Victoria and I are about to have words."

"Don't rip into her, Quinn. Just make it known that I'm aware of what she's been doing and that I'm not pleased."

"I can't guarantee I'll go easy." Quinn shrugged. "It depends on her. You know how she is."

"Yeah, I know."

"Anyway, buddy, are you going to be okay?"

"I think so."

"I'm here if you need me. As soon as Tori and I clear the air, I'll be back." Quinn took off.

Ty stood there feeling alone in a crowd. His grandfather had left to confront Terron with the evidence of his betrayal that had been keenly recorded with Nancy's phone. Nancy had made a mad dash to the restroom when she overhead Loy drop her name to Maggie and she was now a few yards away talking with Trigg. Quinn was set to knock heads with Tori. And the music and merriment continued in spite of it all.

His mom came from out of nowhere and slid her arm around him. "It's been a day, hasn't it?"

"Understatement."

She hooked him with a firm look. "It doesn't have to end on a sour note."

"Sour note?" Ty's laugh was loaded with self-deprecation.

"You know what I'm talking about. Don't pretend that you don't want to go after your...wife." His mom's emphasis on the word wife twisted the knots in Ty's stomach. "You and I know it's exactly what you want to do, yet you're still here. I know you have your pride, son, but better swimmers than you have drowned in their pride."

Ty pulled her close. "Maggie knew what she was getting herself into and so did I. We entered into this marriage with our eyes wide open. At the first sign of trouble, she takes off."

Ellen Peppersmith-Vincent blinked up at her son. "It's not the first sign. More like the tenth. And she's not made of steel, Tysen. I didn't miss this latest," she cleared her throat, "problem. The only reason I hung back until now is to see how you would handle it." She winced. "Like a typical man, you're blaming her."

"I'm not."

"You can BS everyone else, Tysen, even yourself if you have to, but I won't let you bullshit me. Let me give you a quick recap, dear boy."

"This is not football, Mom. The play is not under review."

"It *is* under review." She pushed away and placed her hands on her hips. "Here are the specifics: hardworking, conscientious nurse, Maggie Gray, was unjustly fired from her job and coerced by you and your grandfather into marrying your sorry behind. Her father played a huge part in this too. A little bit ago she found out that her best friend aided and abetted you. In the mix, is the evil Terron Wade who keeps trying to bring her over to the dark side. What woman wouldn't give in to a meltdown after all of that?"

Ty groaned.

"Now you're getting it," Ellen said victoriously. She stretched up and kissed his cheek.

He'd gotten it long before his mom assessed the disaster. "Thanks, Mom." Ty gave her a swift hug.

Before another beat of his heart, he plowed his way through the crowd, not connecting gazes with anyone for fear they'd break his momentum. He'd already wasted too much time over-thinking things.

* * *

Two blocks from the church in Albertson's Supermarket parking lot, Maggie sat in the passenger side of Chaz's SUV blotting tears and piling used tissues in the cup holder of his console. "I can't thank you enough for coming to my rescue."

"Just repaying your kindness."

"I don't understand," she sniffed.

"That's what makes you genuine, Maggie. Being decent to people isn't an effort for you. You just do it. Instead of flipping me off or cussing me out, you smile or wave. You invited me to help out at the soup kitchen. And," he clicked his tongue, "you let me take pictures of you and Ty. Close up. I've been in this business for fifteen years and I've never met anyone quite like you." He handed her another tissue.

Maggie blew her nose. "I'm just a regular person who got caught up in the whirlwind of the Vincents."

"Don't kid yourself for a second. Ty Vincent would never marry just a regular person. He saw something special in you."

Maggie couldn't explain that Ty proposed because he was desperate and she was convenient. Or that she had an annoying habit of being helpful and the Vincents capitalized on it. The media would eventually get all the particulars, just not from her. "You're good medicine, Chaz. Better yet, you're a good friend."

He grinned and tapped the steering wheel. "We *are* friends, aren't we?"

"We are."

"I'm still paparazzi," he said point blank. "When you least expect it, I'll be there with my camera."

"Sometimes friends have to do what they have to do." Maggie was struck by the power of that thought. She and Nancy were *best* friends. Nancy had done something extreme. The motive was sketchy but Maggie knew in her heart that Nancy wasn't capable of being malicious. Whatever her reason for doing what she did, had to have been done out of friendship. It still wasn't easy to accept, but at least she had some understanding.

"I'll occasionally lurk in the bushes to get a picture of you."

A fresh set of tears coated her bottom eyelids. "The public will go gaga over the first few pictures of Ty's ex-wife and then they'll move on to the new loves in his life." She hadn't offered a reason for running and falling out of the hall and he hadn't asked.

Chaz's brows formed a V. "Are you saying what I think you're saying?"

Maggie's heart squeezed. The thought of permanently ending things with Ty was too much to bear. She lowered her head while tears spilled from her eyes and dripped down her nose.

"Tell me you're not headed to divorce court already."

Maggie remained silent.

Chaz shifted in his seat. "What did Ty do that was so wrong?"

It was a deep question that had Maggie scrambling for answers. "He..." She couldn't pinpoint exactly what she wanted to say. "He..."

"What, Maggie?"

So many things, too numerous to count. Maggie swallowed hard and surrendered to the one thing that bothered her most. "He...doesn't love me."

Chaz made a sound of disbelief. "Let me show you something." He tinkered with his high-powered digital camera, hitting a few buttons, scrolling through pictures, until he found what he was looking for and handed the camera to Maggie. "What do you see?"

* * *

Ty gasped without making a sound at the sight of Maggie marching across the reception hall. She looked distraught and tattered. The heaviness surrounding his soul lightened. After his mom had laid it all out, he went in search of his wife. Her car was still in the church parking lot but she was nowhere around. The news rats had come out from their hiding places, one by one, and snapped pictures of him in his dazed state. He could've cared less that they were there and sure as hell didn't care if they used up their entire memory cards with pictures of him. The only thing he'd cared about was finding Maggie. He'd combed the surrounding area three times and came up empty. And now she was back. He wanted to meet her halfway but fear that he was about to have his ring thrown in his face kept him anchored in place.

He watched Maggie change routes and land in front of a microphone on the band stage. Ty swallowed hard.

"Sorry to disrupt the music, folks, but I wanted to ask my husband, and also Loy, Ellen, Nancy, and my father to meet in the lower level in five minutes." She gracefully stepped from the stage and disappeared into the crowd.

Quinn met Ty before he reached the stairs that led downstairs. "Do you need backup?"

The only thing he needed was Maggie. "No thanks. I've got this."

"Tell her I'm sorry for being..." Quinn shrugged. "...me."

"You can tell her yourself. Later."

Loy and Nancy approached. So did Richland and his mom. Nancy's voice shattered into bits. "She must think I'm the worst friend in the world."

Loy closed his eyes, steepled his hands over his mouth and nose and shook his head as though he was dreading what was to come. He opened his eyes, dropped his hands and faced Ty. "I'm not proud of myself, Tysen. I've caused a lot of problems. But I meant well." He placed a hand on Ty's shoulder. "You are your father's son. You're bullheaded, resilient and in love with a woman who's just like your mother. Together, you and Maggie will be a force to be reckoned with. Apart, you'll make no sense." He pointed to the stairs. "Let's find out what she has to say."

Loy and Ellen walked side by side down the wide staircase. "Somewhere in that little spiel was a compliment," Ellen said, touching her shoulder to Loy's.

Loy slanted a glance at his former daughter-in-law. "Maybe."

Ty's blood pressure had gone sky high when Maggie walked out on him. It went even more spastic when he went after her and she was nowhere to be found. But now, it felt like his system had shut down. No blood seemed to be pumping through his chest. His lungs weren't contracting. And he was having difficulty putting one foot in front of the other. Maggie was going to step away from their marriage. To make her point, she'd probably set fire to their marriage license.

Richland Gray offered no assurance that things would be fine. His mouth was set in a grim line and he barely blinked.

They found Maggie in a far room standing with her arms crossed. "Dad, close the door."

Richland obeyed without comment.

"Everyone please take a seat," she directed.

Ty wanted to apologize and take her in his arms. "Maggie."

Maggie shut him down right away. "Don't speak." The authority in her voice was spectacular and not to be taken lightly.

Ty took note of her puffy eyes and that the tip of her nose was red. She'd obviously had herself a good cry and was now ready to raise hell.

Maggie paced back and forth in front of them, taking the time to glare at each person. "This craziness is only a week old but it's been long enough to skew reality, not just for me, for all of us." Her posture was stick straight and there were severe creases in her forehead. The only indication that she was still under siege by her emotions was the faint tremble in her voice. "Loy thought by tangling Ty and I together that all of his problems would be solved."

Loy started to pipe up and Maggie pointed a strict finger at him to make him hush.

"My father had some kind of huge debt hanging over him..." The faint quiver became not so faint. "...and he wanted to trade even up – a daughter for a clean slate."

"Maggie, that's not...," her father began.

Maggie narrowed her eyes so tight they almost closed and Richland Gray clammed up. "You can pile up on me when I'm finished," she snapped. "The key word here is finished and I'm not even close."

From Ty's peripheral, he watched Nancy drop her head with the knowledge that she was next in the guillotine.

Maggie bore down on Nancy with a boat load of indictment. "You, of all people, should have known better than to get mixed up in this. We were closer than sisters. We shared everything. Our hopes. Our dreams. Our most intimate secrets. We cheered each other on and laughed at one another when we did something stupid. We had each other's backs. You came to my apartment to nark out Loy. What was that about?"

Nancy reared up to answer and Maggie shook her head vehemently.

"It was rhetorical." Tears leaked from the corners of Maggie's eyes. She brusquely pushed them away. Nancy sank lower in her chair.

She moved on to Ellen. "You're the one person in the room who is innocent of wrongdoing. I wanted you here because I feel better with you around. Silly huh?"

To Ty's surprise, Maggie allowed his mom to say a few words.

"It's not silly at all, Maggie. I feel the same about you."

Maggie drew Ellen into a swift hug.

In the time it took Ty to pull in a short breath, Maggie stood in front of him. While words couldn't actually kill, he was afraid that what she had to say would be as good as ripping out his heart with a meat hook and tossing it across the room.

"Tysen Loy Vincent, III." Her emphasis on *the third* was stiff with sarcasm. A river of tears flooded her eyes but Ty stayed put. If he moved a muscle she'd open a can of whoop ass on him or she'd dart up the stairs.

"I'm not without fault in this relationship," Maggie said, her resolve hanging by a thread. She stopped to take a much needed breath. "If I hadn't stalked you in Reno I wouldn't be in this wedding dress and we wouldn't be having this conversation." She messed with the silken string that had once held a strand of pearl beading, filled with regret for ruining the dress with her hasty exit. "I'm going to stop playing the victim. I allowed myself to be manipulated and used, not because I'm weak, but because I have a tendency to care too much. I won't apologize for that. It's who I am." She aimed her sentiments at Ty, but they were for everyone in the room. Ty sat with his eyes wide and his mouth clamped tightly shut. "It's also the reason I'll fit into this family just fine." Ty's eyes widened even farther, yet he remained quiet. She shifted her attention from person to person to gauge their reaction. Everyone except for Ellen seemed surprised by the comment.

Maggie connected gazes with Loy. It was a thirty-second stare-down where neither one blinked. She was the first to give in so she could go back to Ty. "Because you found it necessary to propose to a complete stranger and because I'm too freaking nice, I said yes. Just so you know, all that niceness is finished. The not-so-nice Maggie Gray...erm, Vincent...is about to emerge."

Maggie began to stroll again, beaming a look of irritation at anyone who would meet her eyes.

Loy squirmed when she specifically hit him with mean eyes.

"Tysen, did you have Maggie sign that pre-nup?"

"No."

"You forgot to have her sign it?" Loy threw his hands in the air.

"I didn't forget," Ty stated matter-of-factly.

"Are you deliberately trying to sabotage all my hard work?" The vein that bulged in Loy's forehead when he was angry looked like it was about to pop.

"Calm down, Loy," Maggie instructed in her bossy nurse's voice. "You are my grandfather-in-law and I want you around for a long time."

Her remark rendered Loy speechless. Good. He needed to stop talking and listen.

She shifted her attention back to Ty with a scowl. "You wanted me to sign a pre-nup?"

Ty nodded and used her words against her. "I wanted to protect my grandfather's company. It's who I am. I won't apologize."

A series of light snickers bounced around the room. Maggie almost snickered too.

"I've caused you so much stress over the last week that I couldn't put the document in front of you, Maggie."

Maggie twisted her mouth to the side trying to decide how to handle the issue since she hadn't seen it coming. "Good thing I didn't have to sign the darn thing because I have a list of demands." She deliberately made it sound like she was going to take a chunk of their wealth.

"See. I told you, Tysen." Loy's face was a shade darker than maroon. "You never listen."

"I told you to calm down, Loy. If you continue to rant like a lunatic we'll have to call 9-1-1 and you will have to deal with me all over again because one of things on my demand-list is that I want my job restored. You can bet your sweet ass that I'll boss you around so much when you're in Cardiac Care that you'll wish you'd calmed down when I told you to. Got it?"

"Got it." Loy lowered his head.

"Excellent. Now where was I? Oh yeah, my long list of demands." Maggie hadn't intended to say *long* list, but she couldn't help herself. "Contrary to current opinion, I'm not out to steal your net worth. Tempting, but no. I will need a small loan though since my bank account is in sad shape."

"Money won't be a problem," Ty said.

"Great. I'm going to buy a few things right off the bat. A mini-van. The cutest little Bassett hound that I saw at the pet store. And a new belly dancing outfit for private performances." She raised and lowered her eyebrows at Ty.

The look on Ty's face was priceless. It was a mix of happiness and surprise. "I love you, Maggie."

Maggie put a finger to his lips to make him stop talking. "I love you too, Ty, but if we get all sappy with sentiment I'll never get through my list."

"Proceed," he said.

"Here's the deal. In our original agreement we said no kids, no sex, no telling each other what to do." Maggie shrugged. "I can't live with those stipulations. If you want me in your life you're going to have to declare that stupid thing null and void. I want kids. My dad would never forgive me if I didn't give him grandchildren. Ellen would probably enjoy having a few little ones around too. And Loy needs them to fill the hole in his heart." She smiled warmly at her grandfather-in-law. "They can't replace your son but he can live on through them."

In a shocking turn of events, Loy started to cry. Not muffled whimpers, all out sobbing. His slight frame labored with grief. "I haven't been the same without him."

Ty was at his side in a flash, drawing his grandfather into his arms. Tears flowed freely between the two men while everyone else ensconced themselves in a cocoon of silence, with tears rolling from their eyes as well.

Maggie wanted to hug them both but she was fairly certain this was a private healing that was long overdue.

She met her father's eyes and he gave her a slight nod.

Loy and Ty separated and both exhaled. Loy pulled the red silk decorative handkerchief from the breast pocket of his tux and blew his nose. "The tux rental place is going to love me." He wadded the handkerchief and stuffed it back in the pocket.

Ty returned to his seat and slowly slid his eyes up to meet Maggie's. In those magnificent watery orbs Maggie saw a vulnerable moment where he seemed to be telling her that like it or not, this is what she married into. She responded with a huge smile.

"I love you guys," she said softly, still keeping her distance and taking control again. "I have a few more things on my list. I hope your building association allows pets because I need that Bassett hound. It's not just for me. It's for you too, Ty. After a hard day at the office you will need the unconditional love of your wife and that adorable dog. Our kids will love him too. They'll most likely become business sharks like their dad and great-grandfather, but along the way they'll have a soft spot for their furry friends."

Her father made a noise by scooting his chair.

Maggie smiled at his clever hint to wrap things up. "I promise that I'm almost finished." She knelt in front of Ty.

"Regarding the less fortunate…"

Ty brushed a lock of hair across her forehead. "We're on the same page, sweetheart."

"I don't think I could be married to someone who wasn't. What I wanted to say is that I want to continue helping at the soup kitchen and the animal shelters."

"I wouldn't dream of stopping you."

"You couldn't if you tried. I just wanted to go on record." She moved in so close their lips almost touched. "I have two more demands. If you can't fulfill them then…" She shrugged.

Ty's blue eyes shimmered like he knew exactly where she was headed. "Speak your mind, woman."

"I want a wedding night to remember."

Ty smiled like he'd heard the best news a guy could receive.

"And I want a honeymoon. In Reno."

Ty searched her eyes and then dove to her mouth with a heat-seeking kiss that melted Maggie's heart. His hands caressed her shoulders and he whispered how much he loved her.

Richland interrupted again, this time with a not-so-subtle cough. "Can the rest of us speak?"

Maggie giggled. "Yes."

Her father urged Nancy to go first.

Nancy blotted her eyes with a tissue and stuffed it back in her purse. She vaulted off her chair.

Maggie stood so they were eye to eye.

"I've always had your back, Mags. I know that's difficult to comprehend in light of recent information, but it's the truth. I'm not proud that I had a hand in getting you let go from the hospital, but I did it with a pure heart." She blanched at Maggie's wince, but continued. "You and I spent many a night sharing a bottle of wine and talking about guys. We both thought that love would never come our way. When Loy approached me with his offer, I jumped at it. Not because of the money for the heart unit, although that was incredible. I teamed up with him because he was so stressed. We spent a good hour talking about love and loss. He thought you and Ty would match because he'd lost his dad and you lost your mom. You had something in common and could help each other. There was something else that made Loy think you were perfect for his grandson – you were a lot like Loy."

"I'm not..."

Nancy stole Maggie's tactic. "Shh. Don't speak."

"After being in the middle of this madness, I see that he's right. You and Loy have similar traits. You're both intelligent. Unafraid to do what you have to do. Bossy when you have to be. And you love with all your heart."

Maggie was choked up, but she fought the reasoning. "Fancy words to justify what you did."

"Sometimes a friend has to make tough choices for the greater good. I went out on a limb, but I did it for you, Maggie. I wanted you to find your Mr. Wonderful. I did what I thought was a good thing. I won't apologize. It's who I am." Nancy borrowed Maggie's words too, but instead of a smile her mouth quivered like any second she would break down crying.

Maggie was also overwhelmed with emotion. She wrapped an arm around Nancy. "As soon as I get back from Reno, we'll get together for sushi." She turned to Ellen. "Are you in?"

"I'm in," Ellen grinned.

Maggie shoved the weight of her hip against her best friend to ease the tension. "I'm still trying to process all of this, but I know you weren't out to mess up my life. Bottom line: I know you love me. And I love you too. Always and forever. Thank you for going out on that limb. I hope I can do the same for you."

Richland Gray took his turn. "I'm glad this whole thing has worked itself out, but I need to clear the air. I should've leveled with you from the start, daughter." He looked at Loy and received a nod. "Regarding that debt settlement…" He exhaled heavily. "It wasn't about me owing Loy. It was Loy thinking he owed me."

Maggie bumped her brows together. Loy Vincent was a billionaire who couldn't possibly owe anyone anything. "I don't understand."

Her father looked to Loy again.

"Tell her everything, Richland." Loy sounded like he was emotionally spent. "When this is over, I need a stiff drink."

Her father motioned for Ty to join them. "This may be difficult to hear but it's the foundation for what you've both labeled as madness." He put a hand on Ty's shoulder and the other on Maggie's. "The day your father was in the accident, I witnessed the whole thing. I saw the limousine careen out of control and hit the overpass. As soon as I could get my car stopped I ran to help. I recognized your father right away. There was nothing I could do for him or the driver." His voice fell away and he closed his eyes.

Ellen, Loy and Nancy crowded around them.

"You never told me this stuff, Dad," Maggie said in a voice so low it could've been a whisper. Ty remained silent and his eyes were pools of tears.

"I should've shared, Maggie. I don't know why I've kept it inside for so long." He puffed out a breath of air. "There's more."

Maggie wasn't sure she could handle more.

"I called for help and then assumed the task of keeping people away, more specifically, the press." His voice shook with emotion. "There were two vultures hell bent on getting up close to take pictures. How they got there so soon is still a mystery. Maybe they were following the limo to begin with. Who knows?"

"How did you manage to stop them?" Ty asked.

"I posed as a lawyer and threatened to sue if they took even one picture. The police and ambulances arrived shortly thereafter. When Loy got there those news hounds went wild. I had to up my game. I caught them off guard by snatching their cameras and took off running. I didn't get far before they tackled me. Thank goodness another squad car showed up or they might've broken my nose. The cops wrestled the thugs off me and took our statements. No charges were filed but we were ordered to get out of there. I thought that was the end of it." He kissed Maggie's temple. "The next day, the damndest thing happened – Loy showed up at my house. He came to thank me not only for safeguarding his son from the press but also from him. He'd said those were the saddest, darkest moments of his life and he didn't want them captured for all eternity." His voice cracked. "Over a cup of coffee, we cried together. I have to say, when two grown men bawl their eyes out, it ain't pretty." He shook his head. "No one in the world would believe it. I still don't believe it. But it happened. From that point on, Loy thought he owed me. He said someday he would find a way to repay me. When he thought he was losing Ty to his grief, he contacted me with a plan to make things right between us – he wanted to give me what he loved most in life, his grandson…as a son-in-law. He said he owed you too for taking such good care of him in rehab."

Maggie's emotions were at full tilt. In the last few minutes, she'd experienced anger, joy and sadness. But there was one thing that remained even and steady – her heart.

* * *

Ty slid the chain lock in place and clicked the deadbolt without taking his eyes off of his wife. "I gave the front desk orders that we're not to be disturbed for any reason."

Maggie latched onto his hand and led him into the

luxurious master bedroom of the hotel suite. "What if the building catches fire?"

"We're sure to generate enough heat to set off the smoke alarms and sprinkler system, but I doubt we'll burn the place down. Besides, there's a fire extinguisher anchored to the wall outside the bedroom." He grinned.

"Handy," Maggie teased. She traipsed to the window to draw the drapes.

It was a beautiful night. The moon was unobstructed by clouds and surrounded by stars. A perfect backdrop for their wedding night. "Leave them open," Ty said. His heart thundered in his chest and his body was desperate with arousal. He'd waited all week – which felt like a lifetime – to make love to Maggie. Soon he would. Slowly and thoroughly. He moved across the room and closed his arms around her. "Tonight, you're mine."

"Hopefully more than just tonight." Maggie's voice was sensuous; raspy and rich. Her eyes shimmered with expectation when she blinked up at him.

He pecked the tip of her nose with a kiss. "We've been through a lot, Margaret." He chuckled when she made a face at her full name. "Everything is out in the open and we're free to start our life together. Just one question." He laid his forehead against hers. "What made you come back? I know it was because you love me, but what convinced you?"

Maggie lifted her chin with a sheepish smile. "Chaz."

Ty snorted a laugh. Of all the answers he could've heard, he wasn't expecting that one. "I don't understand."

"I know he's annoyed you for a long time, but he's really not a bad guy. He showed me some pretty great pictures earlier."

"Meaning?"

"When I left the hall, I bumped into Chaz. Tripped into him is more like it. When I thought all hope was lost, he comforted me with pictures of you in your recent carefree days, which didn't appear as carefree as you put on. You looked tired and sad."

"Sometimes he was as thick as an oak door. Like now. "And?"

Maggie giggled. "The pictures he took this past week are much better. You look like you've gotten some sleep."

Ty playfully rolled his eyes. "I need a better answer."

"You look content, Ty."

Ty swept his lips across Maggie's with a brief kiss. "I am content, Maggie. Thanks to you." He snickered without making a sound. Only he would marry for convenience and fall head first in love. And the woman he'd fallen for was no ordinary woman. She was a belly dancing nurse who was chummy with paparazzi. Who wouldn't be content? "Remind me to thank Chaz, too, the next time he pops out of the bushes." He nuzzled Maggie's neck and caressed her shoulders, savoring the feel of her warmth at his lips and fingertips. She'd changed into a short leopard print dress with spaghetti straps before they left the hall. It was a sexy little number that emphasized her hour glass figure and he couldn't wait to get her out of it. He slipped the straps from her shoulders and tugged the dress to her breasts. "My woman. My wife," he said sucking the tender flesh at her collarbone.

Maggie quietly called his name and the blood rushing through his veins became liquid heat. Every muscle throbbed with want. He was so turned on he could barely restrain himself. But he had to go slow to fulfill one of the things on Maggie's list of demands – a wedding night to remember. He carefully moved toward the hollow of her throat with tiny nips at her skin. Again, Maggie cried his name.

God he loved this woman! He'd fought the idea, now he couldn't imagine not loving her.

Ty ran his hands up and down her back, giving a flick to

the hooks of the black lacy bra that held her creamy treasures.

Moving slightly away he encouraged the dress and bra off her shoulders and down her arms, so the garments could pool at their feet.

Maggie smiled with approval and pushed her firm nipples into his chest. All of Ty's nerve endings came alive at once. He hugged her to him with a solid embrace and seized her mouth with a hot kiss, sucking her lips before prompting them to open with his tongue. Maggie reacted to the delicate intrusion by curling her hands into his hair, holding him fast. Their tongues tangled and teased against each other. French kissing took intimacy to a whole other level. It escalated the need to epic proportions and right now, Ty was so aroused he hurt. He lowered them to the bed and stretched out over his wife, kissing her deeply, hungrily, until they were both breathless. He smiled with love oozing from every pore. What he felt for Maggie was pure and powerful. Whatever she wanted from him, not just tonight but forever, he would give. Willingly. Freely. With no regrets.

He kissed her chin, the soft under flesh of her neck and trailed his tongue to her breasts. Like a man possessed he cupped her fullness, drawing velvety moans from Maggie. Circling her nipples with his lips, he suckled and then drew the distended buds out, morphing those delicious moans into full cries of delight.

Ty rose up and locked eyes with Maggie. Wonderment and expectation shone brightly in those magnificent blue orbs. "I love you," she said, urging him on. "I love you too, Maggie. With everything I have inside, I love you." He caressed her thighs with his hands, while her chest heaved upward.

Maggie ran her tongue provocatively over her lips and in a heartbeat he aligned them perfectly. The cherished moment of anticipation had finally come. He brushed her hair from her face, kissed her with everything he had and intimately connected their bodies. Ty gave Maggie a few moments to adjust to this new circumstance before he began to move. Slowly. Carefully. His body begged for fast but his mind said to go slow. To make this good for Maggie. To make this good for him too. When Maggie moved with him, it seemed to trigger a wildfire in them both. They thrashed and bucked against one another, drinking in the pleasure, moaning with joy. Every blissful movement was loud and magnificent.

Hot, sweet sensations became a high-speed euphoria. Maggie held onto Ty, arching into him with wide eyes and jagged breaths. She was on the cliff of ecstasy and seemed to be waiting for the okay to jump off. Ty whispered, "Go, Maggie. Take me with you."

He could tell the moment she reached the bright, brilliant point of no return. Her long lashes fluttered across her eyes, her body tightened around him and she called his name with exquisite gasps.

Ty held off, waiting for Maggie to fully enjoy the magic before he allowed his own body to reach that heavenly pinnacle. One incredible smile from his wife took him there. He burst into a downpour of fiery explosions that rocked him from head to toe. He shuddered against the soft body beneath him, enjoying the exclusive paradise that only she could bring.

They clutched and held onto each other for the longest time, waves of passion continuing to roll over them after the dazzling success of their lovemaking.

"Oh Maggie," he said, moving to his back with his fingers laced through hers.

"That was incredible, husband," Maggie replied, her breaths still coming in broken gulps.

Bathed in moonlight and the fine sheen of giving it their all, they laid silent for a few minutes.

Ty rolled to his side and Maggie rolled toward him.

"Maggie," he said, bringing her hand to his mouth. "I just

Married to Maggie

wanted to say thank you."

"Thank you? That's an odd thing to say," she said with a cheeky grin.

Ty chuckled. "Yes, thank you. Not for the lovemaking exactly, but for everything. I was a mess until I met you. I had a tear in my heart big enough to drive a dump truck through. As corny as this sounds, you mended it. And as wrong as it is to talk about my grandfather while we're naked," he raised and lowered his eyebrows, "the old goat knew exactly what he was doing. He knew you were the right person for me."

Maggie smiled. "Gotta love him." She brushed a lock of hair across Ty's forehead. "The mending wasn't one-sided. After my mom passed away I felt like I would never be truly happy again. I can tell you without reservation that I'm happy. Deliriously happy."

Ty kissed her gently. "Now that we're man and wife, no secrets. What did Justine whisper to you?"

Maggie's breasts shook when she chuckled. Ty cupped them like it was his job. "It's been eating at you, hasn't it?" she said.

"No." At her pointed look, he lifted his shoulders in a shrug. "Yes. It's been eating at me. What did she say?"

Maggie cocked an upper-hand eyebrow.

"If I have to kiss your sweet body inch by inch to extract the information, I will," he threatened with a wicked smile. "I'm going to do that anyway, but I need to know what she said."

Pursing her kiss-swollen lips, Maggie sent an air kiss across the small space between them. "She gave me her take on things."

Ty brought her palm to his mouth and dragged his tongue across it. "Tell me."

The erotic kiss made Maggie squirm, but she didn't cave until he teased the dusky tip of her breast with his thumbnail.

"She said she was happy that you were finally giving love a chance. Of course, I thought she was loony. It was the most amazing thing. Later at the engagement party she said you would never propose unless you saw potential for us." Maggie propped up on her elbow. "I balked at the idea but she explained that the Ty Vincent she knew wouldn't consider taking a wife until he was ready, no matter what."

"Justine is a wise woman."

"She certainly gave me a lot to think about."

"This is going to sound far-fetched, but it's the truth as I know it." Ty put a hand on his heart and raised the other like he was swearing an oath. "The moment you touched my neck in the airport I knew my life would be different. How exactly, I had no idea. All I knew for sure was that I was intrigued. You tried to help when you thought I was having a heart attack. Then you fibbed to the gift shop clerk. When Chaz was on the hunt for me, you instinctively blocked his view. I know you were sent to deal with me, but I have a feeling you weren't just there to satisfy a contract. I think you were looking to fill a void." He tapped her chest and then affectionately brushed a kiss across her lips. "We're good together and I know without a doubt that being married to Maggie Gray-Vincent is where I'm supposed to be. For the record, I'm amending the contract again. I want 365 years, not days. If you'll have me."

~ The End ~

~ About the author ~

Jan Romes is a hopeless romantic who grew up in northwest Ohio with eight zany siblings. Married to her high school sweetheart for more years than seems possible, she is also a proud mom, mother-in-law, and grandmother. She likes to read all genres, writes contemporary romance with sharp, witty characters who give as good as they get, works as a part-time fitness trainer, and enjoys growing pumpkins and sunflowers.

Other books by Jan

One Small Fib
Lucky Ducks
The Gift of Gray
Stay Close, Novac!
Three Wise Men
Stella in Stilettos
The Christmas Contract
Mr. August

You can follow Jan here:
www.authorjanromes.com
www.jantheromancewriter.blogspot.com
https://twitter.com/JanRomes
https://www.facebook.com/jan.romes.5

Made in the USA
San Bernardino, CA
05 June 2016